QUIET MAN

QUIET MAN

ANGELA KAUFMAN

trash panda
press

Published by Trash Panda Press

ISBN 978-0-578-78834-0

Typesetting services by BOOKOW.COM

For the Voiceless.

Acknowledgments

Just as no critique of animal exploitation or human oppression is complete without acknowledgment of the part we all play in greasing the wheels of the machine of predatory capitalism, so too is it unfair to pretend that I singlehandedly wrote this book.

There are more people who helped inspire, critique and guide the process of writing Quiet Man than I can possibly fit into one page, but I'll try. I owe a debt of gratitude to so many whose work, research and tireless efforts to organize and fight for social justice helped to inform this book, including but not limited to, all of the investigators and authors mentioned in the Resources section, especially Gail A. Eisnitz and Mark DeVries.

Without the help and instruction of Linda Lowen, and developmental editing and guidance of Ginnah Howard. Quiet Man would not exist. I am also grateful for the nurturing community of writers facilitated by Ann Voorhees-Baker, founder of Women at Woodstock, and Yvonne Daley, founder of The Green Mountain Writer's Conference. Thank you for the feedback and chance to workshop sections of the book at the risk of ruining dinner.

I'm grateful for the editing staff at My Two Cents Editing and Sun Literary as well as the feedback from Robin Demers, Colleen Geraghty and Lawrence Wittner. Credit for the beautiful cover art is owed to James from Go on Write. Thank you to Steve at Bookow.com for assistance with formatting. I would also like to acknowledge Carol J. Adams, whose activism and writing is an inspiration and who recommended Quiet Man for Runner Up in the 2020 Siskiyou Award for Environmental Literature. Finally, thank you to my dad, Jim Kaufman, for the introduction to activism and labor issues and to my partner, Michael Dahlquist, for the continued support and for being the first one to read Quiet Man. And the first to suggest court scenes, which I did not want to write.

"While there is a lower class, I am in it, while there is a criminal element, I am of it, while there is a soul in prison, I am not free."
Eugene V. Debs

Advance Praise for Quiet Man

In the vein of Upton Sinclair's "The Jungle" and Daniel Quinn's "Ishmael," "Quiet Man" is an intentional tale crafted to unsettle the intellect. It sneaks in through the back door of storytelling, a thief that that takes nothing but seeds its reader with doubt. Covid exposed the human toll of meat-processing plants on its lowest-rung workers, and Kaufman probes their pain and mental distress to anguishing effect. Not for the weak-stomached, "Quiet Man" insists on our witnessing the cost of eating meat while maintaining the horror of slaughter at arm's length, and the terrible price somebody somewhere eventually has to pay.

–Linda Lowen, New York Times essayist, writing instructor, Publishers Weekly nonfiction book reviewer

Angela Kaufman's moving novel, *Quiet Man*, provides a devastating exposé of the meatpacking industry. The book, set in small-town North Carolina, centers on the work of a giant corporation, Monarch Industries, that not only slaughters vast numbers of pigs with the utmost brutality, but routinely injures and dehumanizes its workers. Kaufman tells this story with great sensitivity, peppering it with believable characters and imaginative vignettes. Overall, *Quiet Man* provides an exceptionally well-written, powerful indictment of corporate greed and its devastating consequences.

–Lawrence Wittner, author of *Confronting the Bomb*

Quiet Man by Angela Kaufman is a book that grabs you by the throat and doesn't let go. A well-told story that explores the life and tragic death of the men and women whose lives have been destroyed by factory farming and the subsequent dehumanization of workers and mistreatment of animals. The story pulls at our heart strings and awakens us to the tragic conditions for animals and workers subjected to the toxic and dehumanizing work conditions of the meat packing industry. *Quiet Man* slams us awake and asks us to take hard look at the tragic impact that deregulation and the consolidation of the industry has had on the health and well-being of slaughterhouse workers, their families, and our communities. A good read.

–Colleen Geraghty

Quiet Man is set in a small town in Mosier, North Carolina in 2016, the location of Monarch Industries: a place where 1000 pigs per hour are killed each day. As a veterinarian working for the Fairness in Farming Project says, "If you write a story about the slaughter industry, you would have a best seller, but you would have to put it on the shelf labeled Fiction." Or as Ricardo, a man who worked on the chain doing the killing tells it: "electrocuting, slicing, cutting, taking the guts out of squealing pigs… you get fucking crazy."

And "crazy" is what happens to Collin Griffin, a young father who needs employment so badly., he works on that chain for almost a year until in a psychotic, delusional break, he accidently kills his infant son. Collin Griffin, the quiet man, is at the center of this compelling novel and his story is given to us through multiple points of view: his father, mother, and wife; his legal aid lawyer, Cam; his social worker; a vet with his own Traumatic Brain injury who becomes a therapy dog handler who brings his pit bull, Dodger, to visit Collin in jail to finally bring him back to reality.

The page-turning is increased by gripping trial scenes as we sit with the jury and many in the town to hear the witnesses, and then Cam and the prosecuting attorney's arguments to learn the verdict: Will Collin Griffin be sent on to rehabilitation care or will he be found guilty and be executed?

–Ginnah Howard, author of *Night Navigation*, a *New York Times* Book Review Editors' Choice

PART I

Quiet Man

CHAPTER 1

March 9, 2016 7:15 p.m.

Collin

The last thing Collin Griffen wanted to hear as he pulled into the badly crumbling driveway, was the grinding coming from his aging car. The sound reminded him of mechanical destruction. The backdrop of his twelve-hour shift at Monarch Industries meatpacking plant. A harbinger of expensive breakdowns to come.

Sounds of metal and yelling vibrated in his brain. These, and the screaming of pigs, had left him with another migraine by the time his shift ended. The third this week. He stumbled out of the car, winced at the front porch light, left on for his arrival. A piercing glow against the evening darkness. The light refused to be still. It pulsed and he swore it even danced from place to place. He found his way up the steps, fumbled with his keys. His not-fully-healed right thumb seared with pain, reminding him of his latest work-related injury. He opened the door.

The light and sound from the television in the living room blasted his throbbing head and sent a surge of nausea through him. He felt something at his feet. Another pig? How did this one get loose?

Pull yourself together, you just drove home.

Testing this theory, he opened one eye, squinting, trying to shield himself from the blinding light with one hand. He smelled blood. He felt something tugging at him. He yelled out. "Get back! Get back in there now! Don't make me do it! I don't want to do it so just get back in there!"

He kicked at the lump, and for a moment he thought he heard a dog yelp in pain. Not a dog. It was a pig. Another damn pig had gotten loose. Going to make a mess. Going to hold up the chain. And we can't have that. He tried to wade through the blood on the floor, scraping his feet back and forth to clean the layers of filth so he wouldn't track it with him.

"Make those fuckers stop. Make them shut up, somebody just make it stop."

Had he said that out loud? Where was everyone? He couldn't chase them back in the holding pen now. If it didn't hurt so bad. If only he could see clearly. He put both hands to his head covering his eyes and tried to ignore the pain. He thought he could hear his son, somewhere in the distance.

* * *

Quinn

"Daddy coming home now?"

"Almost baby. You be good and play while mommy gets ready for work."

Quinn sat on the floor and ran his hands over the red plastic farmhouse. His plastic piggy gripped tightly in one hand, occasionally he lifted it to his mouth and sucked on the pig's snout.

He heard the jangling of keys and at last, his daddy appeared in the doorway.

Daddy wanted to play hide and seek. Quinn knew because his daddy had covered his eyes with both hands.

Both hands. He wanted to hide.

"I found you! I found you, Daddy!" Quinn jump up and hugged his father's legs. They were dirty and had slimy stuff, but Quinn didn't care. He wanted to play.

"Play pig farm!" Quinn reached up to show his father the plastic piggy.

"Get those damn pigs back! How did they get out?" His daddy yelled.

His father was still covering both eyes, Quinn didn't know which piggy he was talking about.

He didn't like to hear his father yell, but his daddy had used a bad word. His daddy used a bad word at the pigs and Quinn laughed because you're not supposed to use bad words.

But then his Daddy yelled and kicked Suzie. Like last time. But last time Daddy had gotten on the ground and hugged Suzie, said he loved her and was stressed out and would never do it again. This time his father still stood in that strange pose, holding his head in both hands now like he was afraid it would fall off.

This time he didn't apologize and try to calm everyone down. This time he started mumbling about pigs.

"Make them stop it, someone just shut them up, someone shut them up."

Quinn began to shake. He didn't know what pigs, his toy pig? He didn't see any real pigs. He tried to shut up. If that was what his Daddy wanted. Was his Daddy calling him a pig?

"Why you doing that? You step in poop?" Quinn asked, hesitant. He had seen his father scrape his feet back and forth before like that. It was when Suzie had pooped in the driveway and Daddy had stepped in it. He had scraped it off his shoe. Quinn remembered how back then Daddy had laughed. He hadn't yelled or called names or kicked Suzie. He had laughed. Mommy had laughed, Quinn laughed and covered his nose back then. But he didn't smell poop now. And he knew this was not a time to laugh. He felt more like crying.

He didn't want to cry. Didn't want to upset his Daddy. He brought his favorite toy, a peace offering, to calm his father. He held up the plastic pig, but his Daddy didn't seem to see it. He held it up higher as if to say "Look, Daddy, this is a good pig, not one of those bad-curse-word-pigs." But his father didn't take his hands from his eyes.

Quinn thought of how every time he got scared, his daddy would make him feel better. He would sing Twinkle Twinkle, or his favorite, so Quinn started singing to his father.

"Old McDonald's had a farm...Eeeeyyyiii eeeeeyyyiii oh!"

But his daddy wouldn't stop hiding. He kept his hands up. Quinn tried not to cry. He tried not, He tried not, He tried not and then he cried loud.

Then daddy stepped on the farm. Quinn dropped the piggy and tried to run. Daddy broke the table. Then everything crashed.

* * *

Jolene

"My God! Collin! What have you done?"

Jolene thought she had heard Suzie yelp but brushed it off. Maybe Quinn had stepped on her tail by accident? But when she heard the yelling, the smash, and her two-year-old son scream, she bolted from the upstairs bathroom where she had been getting ready for her overtime night shift at the hospital. She didn't recall her feet touching the stairs on the way down.

When she turned on the light, she first saw Collin. His expression confused and eyes vacant look. She lowered her eyes. His shirt was streaked with blood. The coffee table leg in his hand, the broken furniture on the floor. Quinn's toy farm now a mass of red plastic splintered shapes. The accompanying little plastic animals scattered through the rubble.

She heard a whimper and followed Suzie's voice. The elderly beagle sat hunched in a corner with her head low. A puddle of urine flowing across the floor, swirling through the plastic carnage.

Her panic turned to terror as she adjusted her eyes to the scene and recognized a fleshy mound on the floor amidst the wreckage. Their son, only moments ago singing his favorite song, then crying in fear, now forever silenced.

CHAPTER 2

March 9, 2016 8:30 p.m.

Ronnie

Ronnie lifted his head as the sound of James McGuinn backed by the Byrds came through the speakers, filling the bar. He hated this song. "The damn hippies," he grumbled. They thought they were funny, he ruminated. Singing a fake country song about a hard-working man who drove truck for a drugstore. He wished he could give those liberals a taste of hard-working country. He took another drink and bellowed.

"Jimmy!"

It came out sounding like "Jeemaaay!" but that was to be expected this late in the afternoon. Jimmy appeared from the kitchen, wiping barbecue sauce and pork grease off his hands on a dish towel. He clapped Ronnie on the back.

"Whatcha need, buddy?" he asked one of his most frequent flyers. Ronnie pointed to the speakers.

"What is this hippie bullshit they got playin' here? How's a man supposed to get mellow around all this tree-hugging bullshit on the radio?"

Jimmy kept his smile neutral and nodded toward the young man behind the bar. The man with his hair in what the young and hip in Mosier North Carolina called a "Man-Bun."

"Aiden was just about to change the station, weren't you Aiden?" Jimmy asked, winking at the young bartender in training. Aiden nodded and waited to turn his back before rolling his eyes. He fussed with the radio momentarily. A fresh sound filled the PigPen Tavern. This time, the voice belonged to Merle Haggard, who was inquiring as to whether the good times were really over for good.

"That's more like it," Ronnie continued, as if there was no one else in the room but he and Jimmy. "What're ya hiring these hippies for now? Don't you know some of us were fighting, dying, in Vietnam, and these long-haired hippies, what were they doing?"

Jimmy brushed it off.

"A man needs a job, don't he Ronnie?" and with that he retreated into the kitchen. Ronnie returned to his beer. Staring deep into the glass. Were the good times really over? He sat thinking of the good times. In high school. Before the recession, before the war, before the immigrants had taken all the jobs. Before his wife turned into a nag everytime he had a beer. When he could still get a hard on just by looking at her. He shook his head.

"I'll tell you about the good times," Ronnie began speaking, to no one in particular. "The good times, before all this..." he waved his hand vaguely. "See," he turned now, grabbing the elbow of the man seated next to him. The man indulged him. "See, my son, he's one of these soft men," Ronnie snorted in disappointment. "Collin is a good boy, but he's also good for nothing. Not military, not football, not anything a man ought to do. You know what I mean?"

The man nodded, waiting for the chance to return to peacefully sipping his beer in quiet. That moment would not come.

"He may as well have had a daughter!" Ronnie continued.

A shadow appeared over his beer and a voice broke into his diatribe. It was Man-Bun. Another pussy. Just like Collin. Worthless, Ronnie supposed.

"Sir," Man-Bun began, "phone call for you." Ronnie reached for his cell on drunken instinct then remembered he turned it off so Maggie, his wife, couldn't disrupt his mellow time. He snatched the phone away from the kid.

Maggie's hysterical sobs reached his ears before the phone did. He cringed in annoyance. When she finally could speak, what she had to say sobered him.

Chapter 3

March 9, 2016

Collin

Collin's wife's cries grew hysterical, but Collin didn't hear her. Nor did he see her grab her cell phone and run through the back door, into the yard. He didn't hear her frantic call to the police. Although the description she gave was appropriate…

"He's lost his mind! My God, he's gone crazy! I think he killed our son!"

Collin was oblivious to this.

Instead of the sound of sirens, his ears were filled with the humming of machinery. His head throbbed still. The screams of pigs filled his ears, still. He raised both hands to his head once more, dropped to his knees and groaned.

When the police arrived, they found Collin curled into a fetal position on the floor. Blood on his hands, ground into his blond hair.

He didn't see them. He saw grey. Steel. Blood.

He heard screaming somewhere in the distance now, interwoven with words about remaining silent.

I have remained silent. He thought.

All his life he had remained silent. It was his right. To remain silent. Anything could be used against him, a distant voice intoned.

When they gripped his arms, he reacted by thrashing his body from side to side, screaming in pain. They tranquilized him like a wild animal. Restrained. Transported to Mosier County Correctional Facility. But in his mind, he was still in the grey place. Until the pain in his head finally stopped and he slipped from violent hallucination to restless sleep.

* * *

Mosier Tribune
March 10th, 2016
Town Shocked, in Mourning, after "Quiet" Man Beats Baby to Death
An investigation is underway in the beating death of baby Quinn Griffen, who turned two last month. Quinn's father, Collin Griffen, has been arrested for allegedly beating the child to death on the evening of March 9th, 2016, in the home he shares with his wife, Jolene.

Family and friends report Collin to be a quiet, kind man and are shocked and saddened by this tragedy. Close family report Griffen had been acting increasingly troubled in recent weeks and appeared to be under financial stress. No word yet on whether alcohol or drugs played a role in the incident.

CHAPTER 4

March 10, 2016

Cam

"Well, if it isn't the Patron Saint of Lost Cases," The DA joked when they were finally back in the Chambers of Judge LeClair.

"Really, Steuben, you aren't over me sticking it to you with the Donovan case?" Cam pushed back.

"Well, I guess if anyone in town will be assigned to a psycho Baby-Killer it would be a bleeding-heart anti-police rabble rouser," Steuben retorted.

"Representing a young man who was harassed by local PD is not anti-police, Mr. Steuben. And while you're at it, why don't you just come right out and call me 'uppity'?"

"Now, now, you're both pretty," Judge LeClair interjected with a laugh. "Cam, I know you're always champing at the bit for some of these overflow cases and you were top of mind. I know how you like these people."

Cam grit his teeth. He didn't want to get on the bad side of the Judge or the DA but was tired of being considered the go-to defense for the mentally ill. People who needed therapists, not incarceration. First Jack Donovan, then Darnell Jones. Now Collin Griffen. Patron Saint of Lost Cases, he would remain.

"Much appreciated, Judge LeClair. I'm going to order a psych eval. It appears he's still psychotic and not able to supply much information. Not guilty by reason of insanity plea may be in order."

"Oughta be an open and shut case, there's no question he killed his kid," Steuben commented.

"There are plenty of questions. Starting with why," and before either had a chance to respond, Cam gathered his paperwork and walked out the door.

* * *

This case was already a headache, and the files hadn't been in his hand a full day yet. Cam considered himself a rational man. But throughout his career, he had developed a sixth sense about cases. It was subtle. This time, he wondered if it was the case he was feeling, or the anxiety from this morning's events.

He thought back to his trip to the county jail earlier that morning. He had stopped by to make his rounds and meet with Collin Griffen, his new assignment from the Legal Aid overflow cases.

"And who exactly are you? It's too early for visitors," an officer had stopped him at the front desk when he tried to sign in. Cam didn't recognize this guard. Being a fixture at the jail, like every other attorney in Mosier, Cam was used to coming and going with few problems. This morning, however, the young man, a fresh recruit maybe? Eyed him suspiciously.

Cam knew he was being profiled. He was introduced to life in a Jim Crow society. Laws change, but decades of experience had shown him how little people's attitudes evolved. He knew all too well that attitudes couldn't be legislated.

"My name's Cameron Burton, I am working on behalf of the Legal Aid Society. I'm here to visit Collin Griffen, inmate number …"

"Baby Killer?" the guard interrupted him. The man looked Cam up and down again. "Man's a dangerous criminal. I can't take a chance on letting the likes of you back there without showing proper ID first."

"I assure you," Cam rubbed a thumb over his steno pad, gripping it tight to keep his tone from betraying mounting anger before continuing. "I assure you, if you talk to Marv, Nan or the new young lady, Dierdre back in the Mental Health Unit. They all know me. Your staff knows me. I am working as an attorney for Legal Aid. I am here to meet with a client. Your refusal of granting my client a visit is unconstitutional."

"Oh, so you're threatening me now?" The guard became more hostile.

Cam didn't want to make a scene. He took a breath and set down his steno pad so he could rifle through a folder with his paperwork from Judge LeClair. He held it up for the guard to see. He then reached into his wallet and produced his driver's license.

"Sign in here and a CO will walk you to your client's tier," the guard replied, as if nothing out of the ordinary had just happened.

Cam was escorted to a meeting room. He sat at the table and eyed part of the ceiling where stains suggested a recent leak. The jail was in disrepair, but Cam thought this stain was new. The door opened and two guards led a young man, in shackles, into the room. Collin looked sedated. This didn't surprise Cam. He was no medical expert but had been assigned so many clients with significant mental illness that he had learned to recognize common patterns.

"Mr. Griffen, may I ask you some questions?"

Collin's expression remained blank. He had the familiar unkempt appearance of those who break with reality and find themselves in a cell.

"Mr. Griffen, I am the attorney who will represent you. My name is Cam Burton."

Silence.

Cam watched as the young man, disheveled, bruised, one thumb wrapped in a bandage, stared at something he himself could not see. Collin could, by his estimation, see it though. His eyes moved in time with whatever imaginary scene played out in his mind.

Cam tried again.

"Mr. Griffen, can we talk now? Can you hear me?"

Nothing.

Cam sighed. He had represented clients with psychosis before. It was his least favorite type of assignment. He would waste his time filing papers for someone who was off in another world. Maybe the client would become lucid and be able to speak for themselves, maybe not. Either way, there was little he could do. In a perfect world, clients like this would be diverted into treatment. But that was seldom the case, especially in Mosier.

The young man didn't respond to Cam's appearance or to his question. This was a waste of his time. All of this, Cam thought, would go nowhere. Insane or not, this man was as good as dead.

CHAPTER 5

March 10, 2016

Dierdre

Dierdre Scott hadn't even put her coffee and purse down on her desk when she was confronted by Nan. Her senior colleague stood staring down her nose, two-page printout in hand, Eyeing Dierdre like a teacher suspicious of a cheating student.

"I took the liberty of printing your census," Nan informed her.

"Thank you, but I could have done it," Diedre then turned to review her caseload. "Ugh, Mackenzie DeMartina was picked up again. I thought she was going to complete the halfway house. I pulled strings to get her in there."

"Why are you so disappointed? You know the kind of people we are dealing with. That girl has been prostituting herself for years, you think she's going to stop because you get her into a halfway house?"

"Sex work, and it's a result of her addiction," Dierdre corrected.

"Listen to you! Yankee liberal talk if I ever heard it. *Sex work*. No honey, that girl is a prostitute." There was a moment of silence and she continued. "I see that Jones boy was picked up again too. Trying to rob a bank. I know that boy is dangerous."

"He wasn't robbing a bank. He was off meds, probably psychotic. Just because he's acting strangely outside of a bank, doesn't mean he was trying to rob it," Dierdre stopped short of reminding her colleague that calling a Black man 'boy' is racist. Instead, she turned her attention back to her census. Second on the list was fresh meat, inmate 16-2763, a man by the name of Collin Griffen. His name sounded vaguely familiar, Dierdre thought. Heavier footsteps echoed down the hall. It was her supervisor, Marv Bellinger. Nan perked up. Something Dierdre had learned was the sign of a predator about to strike.

"So, who gets the Baby Killer, Marv?" Nan asked. Dierdre thought the older woman sounded gleeful.

Baby Killer. Collin Griffen, the name clicked as Dierdre recalled the story she had heard driving in to work this morning. Some guy had snapped, gone completely ape-shit and killed his kid. Like so many other cases, no one seemed to have seen this one coming.

"I've got it all under control," Marv replied coolly.

Dierdre glanced at Marv, who looked away. She felt nauseous.

"I will need supervision," She said.

"Yep, I'll email you, we'll set something up for that," Marv mumbled, eyes on his own clipboard stacked with forms as he headed for what Nan referred to as his *man cave,* the office to which he retreated and spent as much time as possible when something serious was brewing.

As he made a beeline for the door Nan began her loud protests.

"You're going to let her manage a killer? She isn't even from around here! How…" He was already out the door. Nan turned on Dierdre.

"I don't think you're cut out for this case. You know you can't post about this on Facebook. I'm just saying, because I know how you people like to put your entire lives on the internet."

Silence

"That's all I'm going to say about it."

Dierdre knew that Nan had a long way to go before she had said all she would say about anything. I guess the best person equipped to deal with a murderer would be you. You arrogant, ignorant, Confederate Flag waving hick. She wanted to say. So, she said nothing.

CHAPTER 6

March 10, 2016

Collin

Collin's hand ached from the recent stab wound that nearly severed his right thumb. That special digit sacred to all of humanity, which in combination with the prefrontal cortex had given man access to his throne atop the food chain.

"My Flumb!" as his mother tells the story, two-year-old Collin would exclaim when this stray digit would get caught in a door or in his shirt.

He had almost lost his flumb.

He felt the pain of it. Damn pigs. Almost had him out of a job. Luckily, the doctor had been able to keep the flumb attached.

He can feel the pain now.

Men's voices argue, loud yet distant as if through a tunnel. Machines roar and clash, bang and squeal. Collin hears it like a train coming down railroad tracks, getting closer but in slow motion.

His head, not his hand, now throbbing with pain. But that bickering won't let up. Nor will the shouting- name calling, barking demands he hears it like a constant stream of elevator music in a grocery store. Like that fucking mellow 1960s bullshit *Girl from Ipanema* his mom used to listen to on her old records.

He squints. Trying to figure out where he is. It's grey, everywhere. And metal. But he doesn't see blood on the floor. He hears the gears. Hears the grinding of metal, the shouting. But he isn't on the chain. He hears the squealing. But can't see the pigs.

The grey becomes his living room, but there weren't bars on the windows.

The sounds of the machinery, the yelling and squealing, are in his living room. Then grey place. He can't keep the scenery from changing. It's nauseating.

Back to work.

He tells himself he has to just get back to work so the shift could be over. The sooner it was over, the sooner he would be home.

But, aren't you home?

The question raises from a hidden part of his mind. The part that has tried, and failed, to keep score. He feels a surge of panic. Maybe he was just home, but how did he get back here? To Monarch?

Just work, he tells himself.

He just had to hurry and finish working. Just finish...

The squealing gets louder. His headache now blasting, streaking the grey place with flashing lights.

And there are other sounds. Sounds that are here. Now. Sounds of squeaking. What is that squeaking? Running. Pounding. Squeaking. Squealing. Now squealing becomes screaming. It's a brawl. It's like a brawl going on in his house.

Like people he can't see are running their fingernails down a chalkboard and throwing the coffee table.

And a fucking squeak.

Now a squeal, loud and piercing.

The obnoxious voice of a dinosaur from some B-grade movie. The noise penetrates through his mind, disorienting him. His temples throbbed; he could feel the sounds now. Feel the squealing, the squeaking, the desperate cries of....

Who?

Collin is up and running toward the banging and squeaking and squealing. It fills his ears, flooding his head. He stumbles, hands outstretched, he reaches something. A wall he can't completely see keeps him from falling.

There is no escaping the sound. He needed it to stop. No way to drown out the squealing. In frustration, he grabs at the vague outline of objects he can't fully see. Something heavy fills his hands, and his grip pulls. Pulling down this heavy thing to stop the screaming. Stop the squealing.

"It's what we do around here! If you don't like it tough shit!" A disembodied voice reminds him.

His head throbs harder, ready to burst. It will explode. It will pop and run around the room and the only thing you can do is smash it. Smash that motherfucker, kill it! Kill it, don't just stand there! Get it back in line before they come for you because if you don't kill it, if you stop the line you are fucked pussy boy! You are fucked! They will kill you!

"You are no better than those goddamn Mexican sombitches," the sound of his supervisor's voice taunts him, "so you just go ahead and stomp the mother fucking shit and don't listen to nothin' else. Beat that motherfucker's head in! Stubborn sombitches run all over the place. Hold everyone up all day unless you just kill! That! Screaming! Motherfucker!"

Collin tries to will this voice to go away, he just wants to be left alone to finish the shift. He sees the explosion as his head pounds harder. The squealing has stopped. The running has stopped. He reaches out to grab that stubborn sombitch and get him on the line.

As he lifts the bloody mess from the floor, he hears another scream. This time not a squeal or a squeak.

"Collin!" his wife screams through a distant tunnel, "What have you done?" And this, and the smell of his own piss stained bed, wake him.

CHAPTER 7

March 11, 2016

Jolene

Nothing she had seen in her budding career as a nurse at St. Joseph's General Hospital could have prepared her for that night. How could it? The patients she treated, a name, an ID badge, a paper bracelet with demographics, they were cases. Quinn was her son.

The scene replayed in her mind as she returned home for the first time after Quinn's murder and Collin's arrest. The yellow caution tape, a reminder that her home was a crime scene, was no longer needed. She pulled at it and cleared it from the front sidewalk. Taking a deep breath, she opened the door. The smells and sights returned. She turned and wretched over the side of the front steps into the bushes that grew along the front of the house.

Then she walked in. Someone would have to help her clean the mess that remained of her living room. What wasn't confiscated as evidence. She walked through the living room into the kitchen as if walking through a dream. Surveying the remnants of normalcy, now preserved in mundane artifacts. Like the archeologists who unearthed Vesuvius. On the table, unpaid bills. On the counter, unwashed dishes from dinner. Mac and Cheese. Quinn's favorite. She cried. Jolene walked to the counter as if entranced, held the plate in her hand and breathed in any remaining scent, to feel or absorb whatever was left of Quinn. Memories, senses, anything. The plate had Paw Patrol characters, from his favorite show. She ran a hand over the chunky mess of day-old macaroni. The last thing she would ever make for him. The last meal he would ever eat. The last time she would ever see a dish left from him.

She set it back on the counter and turned, tears streaming faster. Now to his bedroom. She turned on the light, breathing deeper. She walked to his crib and picked up the blanket that had warmed his body just the day before. When he had woken up. Here. Alive. She held the yellow blanket edged in ribbon and brought it to her face. First crying into it, then trying to breathe any last scent of her son. Any last part of his life, trying to preserve it in her mind.

She squeezed the blanket harder and heard herself scream inside her head while tears soaked her face and Quinn's blanket. She saw him in her mind as an infant, a corner of the blanket in his mouth, his father's smiling eyes taking in the world around him. She turned away, not wanting to lose the image in her mind but also not fully able to face it yet.

On the other side of the room, the blue crayon scribble still marked the wall from several months ago. Quinn had created his first mural, or so he thought. Jolene was upset. Collin reassured her.

"It's no big deal. Kids draw on things. I'll repaint that room anyway when he gets his big boy bed," he had said this last part while eyeing Quinn, who had been hiding from the sound of his mother's scolding.

Quinn had come out from behind the chair then, smiling.

"Paint it with a farmhouse?"

"Sure!" Collin had agreed.

She had been reassured then. So had Quinn.

How had it gone from that to this? How had the same man who could always laugh things off, find the bright side, remind her it was no big deal, that they could make anything better…?

Where had that man gone?

"It's going to get better. I just need some more time," he had tried to reassure her. She remembered his words as they sat at the table eating dinner just a few weeks ago. He had become more distant, distracted. For the first time since she had known him, since high school, he had begun to lose his temper.

He had finally confided in her that night that his new job, no longer brand new but new enough, was harder than he thought it would be. That he didn't know how much longer he could do it. That he was having nightmares.

"Quit. It's not worth it. I'll pick up extra shifts at the hospital. You'll find something else," she had reassured him. Uncertain that any of that would be true, but wanting to see him return to his normal self.

"I can't do that," Collin had insisted. "We're still trying to catch up from the last time I was out of work. I'm almost there."

"But if it's that bad. It's not worth it. Maybe you could work with your dad?" His mind had been made up. He would stay at Monarch until the last of the credit cards were paid off. Then he would find something new.

"You could at least look. Keep an eye open. You might be surprised."

He had agreed to, but she was sure he wouldn't have the time or heart to change his plan. Looking back now, she wondered if she should have insisted. But why? Lots of jobs are stressful. Her job is stressful. That doesn't turn a person into a....

She couldn't say it. Not even in her mind. No. Collin is not a murderer.

* * *

Collin Griffen Case File
  Inmate Number:16-2763
  DOB: 09/06/1988
  Date of Service: March 12, 2016

Psychiatric Evaluation: Met with Mr. Griffen at 1500 hours. He is a married Caucasian male appearing younger than stated age. At the time of this assessment he is noncommunicative. Hygiene is poor. Vital signs stable. Does appear to be responding to internal stimuli. He is refusing to take part in his assessment. When asked questions, Mr. Griffen is largely nonresponsive although he does occasionally make brief eye contact. Mr. Griffen appears disheveled.

Staff report Mr. Griffen sleeps excessively and frequently not eating. Will begin course of Haldol and monitor response. Will continue to monitor for progress.

Dr. Holland, Chief Psychiatrist

Mosier County Correctional Facility

CHAPTER 8

March 12, 2016

Dierdre

Dierdre had heard so much about Collin in the time before she got to meet him. Between the news, the radio, gossip around town, she had already built up an image of the monster described for the past few days, in surround sound.

What she found when it was finally time to assess Collin Griffen, inmate number 16-2763, was a sickly looking, gaunt man. His facial expression fearful. He looked like a child. Dark circles framed his eyes and she could see bruises on his arms, likely the results of rough handling by the police, since she didn't recall hearing that there had been a fight leading up to the murder.

His blond hair was slick and oily, grime covered his fingers, and she imagined he had not done anything remotely resembling bathing since his arrest.

Still, she was afraid of him.

What kind of man kills his own child? The randomness was as frightening as the act itself. She had requested extra security when meeting with him and was accompanied by Corrections Officers. Because of his ongoing psychosis, she had been given permission to meet him on the tier where she could stand outside of his cell.

Had she been overreacting? She wondered, looking at this young man in such a sorry state. She tried to stand in his line of vision and waved a hand lightly to get his attention. He continued to look through, not at her.

"Mr. Griffen?" she tried. Then, "Collin?"

Silence.

"Collin, my name is Dierdre Scott. I'm the social worker who will work with you."

No response.

"Collin, can you verify your name and date of birth? Collin…"

Silence.

"Collin? How are you feeling? Are you hungry?" She asked.

She had found that food was a common language even when someone was lost in psychosis. With this in mind, she asked if she could bring some food from breakfast to build a connection. She offered a plate with toast, sausage and something that looked like Styrofoam and was likely intended to be eggs.

Collin's expression changed when the paper plate of food was passed into his cell. He sniffed at the air curiously, then his face contorted in dread. He raised his hands to cover his eyes. He sank to the floor and began screaming.

"I can't go back! Not one more day! No! Get the pigs!"

The sudden change startled Dierdre. The guards escorted her away from Collin's cell. Instinctually, she knew it was not right to leave him in hysterics, but she also knew there was nothing she could say that he would respond to. Tranquilizing him would be someone else's job, but she also had a job to do. Returning to the office, she flipped through his file until she came to an emergency contact family release of information form and reached for the phone.

* * *

Dierdre Scott Case Note
  March 14th, 2016
  0800

Met with client for attempt at evaluation. This is the second attempt. Client appears alert, slightly disoriented. He does not respond to his name, not able to respond to questions about location or date, answering only "I don't know." Client has poor ADLs and appears in a low mood. Client becomes unresponsive to questioning, appears confused. Client denies suicidal and homicidal ideation, denies Audio/visual hallucinations.

Urinalysis comes back negative for any intoxicating substances. Writer arranged for medical transfer for MRI and CT scan of brain to rule out cognitive impairments. Client has several lacerations to right hand and thumb of unclear origin do not appear to be recent. Client denies they are self-induced. When writer questions him about these injuries, he says "work". Will continue to monitor.

Dierdre Scott, LCSW
Mosier County Correctional Facility

CHAPTER 9

March 14, 2016

Cam

Snapshot! Cam Burton thought to himself.

It was an old joke between him and his friend Gerald, who once mused that he wished he could carry around a camera to take a snapshot of that look white folks get when they first heard him speak. The clear disconnect between the slang they expected and his articulation causing a momentary stunned look to appear on their faces. Cam had replied that he wished he had a nickel for every time someone inferred he was "A credit to his race." A nickel for every time he'd seen eyebrows raise and he'd hear "You're so nice," or "you're so articulate." He knew they meant to finish the compliment with, "for a Black." This was not a nickel moment, but a snapshot moment.

Cam was getting the look from the tear streaked white woman who now sat across from him. He tried not to hold it against her. She seemed to be a nice woman. She probably didn't realize that her eyebrows had shot up in astonishment. Cam could tell she was adjusting the gears in her mind as it dawned on her that he wasn't the assistant or a well-dressed custodian, but the attorney representing her son.

But he didn't yell "Snapshot!"

Nor did he take a photo, and the fleeting moment of surprise gave way. He listened and observed, recording questions, answers, and strategies in his trusty Steno notebook. His wife and col-leagues teased him, he should have been at ease with a tablet or some such electronic device. Nevertheless, Cam was a stickler for his pad and pen. He imagined himself like his favorite TV show in his youth, *Columbo*.

"You've got to help me. That… that was not my boy, there is… my boy couldn't do a thing like that!" Maggie Griffen pleaded.

"I understand your concern, Mrs. Griffen, but I hope you un-derstand that to a Jury, you're a mom, saying what every mother in your shoes would say. You say he didn't do it. Do you have a suspicion who did?"

"No!" she said in an exasperated tone. "No, he… yes… he… He, yes, he killed the baby, but… that isn't the real him. Something came over him. The past few weeks before it happened," She began to cry and persisted in telling the story. Cam tried to follow with some difficulty through her jumbled recollection.

"His daddy tried to take him hunting. Even bought him his first hunting dog, Suzie. Collin wouldn't do it. When he told his daddy 'No, I don't want to take Suzie hunting' everyone in the whole town could have heard Ronnie yelling at him."

She cried into a handkerchief and Cam waited in silence for her to continue.

"Do you realize…" she began much more clearly now that the tears had subsided. "His daddy, my husband. He was in Vietnam, and he's proud of it. He wanted Collin to go into the army after High School, went on and on about it from the time the boy was in Middle School, what with the nine-eleven attack. Was furious when Collin refused. They fought and fought." She sobbed heav-ily, blew her nose in the handkerchief, and took several steadying breaths before continuing.

"My husband even offered to take a second mortgage on the house to buy him a car and help get him settled when Collin came home if he would just enlist. He wasn't never going to pay for college any other way and his daddy wanted him to get a good start in life. Always told him his way into college and a good job would have to be the military. Collin never wanted to listen," Maggie stopped to dab her eyes with a handkerchief and steady her breath. She was on the verge of sobs again.

After a moment, she continued. "Ronnie, that's my husband. He also thought sometime in the service would be good to help the boy grow up and, you know, be a man," her face tightened as she added, "especially with them terrorists attacking this country and whatnot."

"So, was Collin stressed about repaying college loans? Or being indebted to his father?" Cam interjected, trying to follow her point.

"He never enlisted. There was no college. They didn't even speak to each other for almost a year. Collin didn't have it in him, never got in no fights, never raised his voice to nobody. It was Collin who got beat up by the other kids and he never raised a hand in self-defense even," her voice cracked, and the tears returned. Cam waited patiently. The woman continued. "There was something wrong with him, like they talk about on the TV. Some depression or something made him act that way and yes, he deserves to be punished, he will be punished every single day that he wakes up in the morning and remembers what he did. He doesn't deserve the needle. They all out here calling him a killer, but that ain't him!"

"What changed in the months prior to this incident? Anything that may have been a trigger for him to act this way?"

CHAPTER 10

March 15, 2016

Jolene

Jolene woke with a start. The sound of metal scraping on metal had invaded her dream. The last thing she saw before returning from sleep was Collin, drenched in blood, sharpening a knife. Now, as the room took shape around her, she was certain. It wasn't just the dream. She could hear dragging and scraping. Someone else was in the house. She gripped the rails of Quinn's crib and lifted herself from the pile of blankets, Quinn's blankets, in a heap on the floor. This had become her new bed. Early morning sun came in through the blinds and forced her to squint.

Emerging from the bedroom, she followed the noise into the kitchen. Turning to enter the doorway, she saw an elbow, then an arm, and with a deep exhale of relief, the form of her mother, bent over the kitchen sink cleaning.

"I didn't know you were coming today," Jolene tried to hide her irritation. Her mother had cleaned up the mess in the living room, sparing her the sight of it again. She had avoided that room since Collin had been arrested. She had begun entering and exiting the house through the back door just to avoid walking through the scene.

"I figured you needed to sleep late, and I wanted to help you finish cleaning this mess."

Jolene didn't hear her mother label her home a mess. As soon as she realized what her mother was scrubbing, she had already lunged into the kitchen and grabbed at the plate.

"No! What are you doing?" Jolene was hysterical, gripping the plastic red and yellow kid's plate. Marshall, the Dalmatian with a firefighter's hat, smiled up at her. Suds ran down his face. The traces of Quinn's last supper, proof that she had once made his favorite meal, and he had been alive, that he had eaten, grown, was alive and thriving, all had been erased.

She fell to the floor, white knuckling the plate with both hands, staring at the smiling cartoon Paw Patrol dog in his flat, plastic face.

"No! What did you do? What did you do?"

She hadn't realized the food had been caked on for a week now. She hadn't noticed the maggots that had found their way to the uncleaned counter. She didn't realize how much time had been spent avoiding contact with anyone and staying in Quinn's room, alone.

And she now didn't know whether she was screaming at her mother or her husband.

* * *

Going back to work would be good for her, the doctor had decided. Her mother agreed. Jolene no longer had opinions on most things. She clutched the amber bottle and sat in the hospital parking lot. One bitter pill down, how many more to go?

She pulled herself from the car. Slamming the door behind her, she turned to examine her expression. She practiced pushing her lips into a flat line. This look would have to do.

CHAPTER 11

March 17, 2016

Dierdre

Marv Bellinger tossed the newspaper onto the table in the staff lounge and set about opening his sizable lunch bag. "You got any plans for St. Patrick's Day weekend? A bunch of us are going to the PigPen for the Sham-rock fundraiser. It's to help the Police Benevolent Association. Green beer, barbecue. What d'ya say?" He grinned. Dierdre didn't return his smile.

"I don't think so, going to be putting in some extra hours catching up."

"Suit yourself, I'll have an extra beer for you."

"I'm sure you will," she replied. As he took a massive bite out of his lunch, she continued. "You never got back to me about dates for supervision."

"Well, no time like the present. Whatcha got?" he asked, thick red barbecue sauce dripping from his fingers. She thought for a moment that the sauce looked like blood. Thought again of her recent case and cringed slightly.

"The Griffen case. He's still psychotic, no history of other hospitalizations, no criminal record. His UDS was negative for substances."

"Family collaterals?" he asked, words muffled as he chewed his lunch. Southern manners were just about all they were cracked up to be, but Marv was the exception to almost every rule. He was less concerned with having a polished image than many of his colleagues. Sometimes he would come to work with mismatched shoes or coffee stains on his shirt. He chewed his food with a blend of vigor and carelessness.

Reckless Abandon, Dierdre thought, recalling the words she often read in her romance novels. She shook her head then, trying to break free from the image of her boss having a love affair with his food.

"I only have his mother as an emergency contact. Would like to speak to his wife. Ask about any history of violence at home."

"Mothers!" Marv interjected, shreds of pork dripping onto the table as if for emphasis. He wiped the pieces up with his napkin. "What's her take on this?"

"She's shocked, says her son was more likely to be bullied than to be the bully. Quiet, kept to himself, loved his son. I encouraged her to get counseling for herself. She didn't seem too interested in that, worried about her son though.

She describes her husband as a heavy drinker, says he doesn't have the best relationship with Collin. Still, not every child of an alcoholic goes on to kill his own kid."

"A grieving family member is likely to be in denial. It may be helpful to have her in for a meeting after a little time has gone by."

"Have you seen all the memorials?"

"Seen 'em? Can't miss 'em, can we?"

"I've never seen anything like it."

"That's because you're a Yankee," Marv teased. "See now," he leaned back in his chair and stretched, "in this town, we live, work, worship, celebrate and mourn together. Doesn't matter if any of these folks would have known baby Quinn if they had tripped over him walking down the street. This baby becomes a symbol. The town's baby."

He took another bite of his sandwich and put what was left of it down, pausing to wipe his hands and face. He followed this with a swig from his thermos. Who uses a thermos? Dierdre wondered. It had become a joke in the office, everyone taking a guess as to what Marv carried in the opaque container to quench his thirst.

He turned solemn then, looked at her, and asked, "How are you doing with all of this?" His sincere concern caught her off guard.

"It's hard to process. I can't imagine what would make someone do this. In the news they're calling him 'baby killer' they've already pegged him as a monster, and then I go back there and see a kid sitting in that cell. Out there, though, they're ready to come after him with pitchforks. In the name of baby Quinn, they've already judged him. I don't know what to think. On my way here this morning I drove through a neighborhood where every house had a sign out 'God Bless Baby Quinn' or 'We'll pray for you Baby Quinn.' Little stuffed animals and candles on the street corners, and then you see the other houses where they're already putting signs up that say 'Fry the baby killer!' and 'Revenge for Baby Quinn!' it's like…." Dierdre smirked.

"What?"

"It's like the presidential campaign, but instead of signs for Trump or Clinton the choices are 'Pray for Baby Quinn' or 'Rot in Hell Baby Killer.' I don't know, gallows humor, I guess." She thought for a moment, then continued.

"It's just different, seeing him in there, Collin, he's totally out of it. Oblivious to his hygiene, he has this vacant stare and says things that don't make sense. It's like watching a person in a cage like an animal, or worse. Do you think he will snap out of it?"

"Hard to say. It will be a whole other shock to him to realize where he is and what has happened."

"Yes, and thank you for putting me in charge of that!" Dierdre replied.

"Don't get so full of yourself now," Marv began, wiping the corners of his mouth with his napkin. "We don't know what's going to take place, or how. Something I've learned, and you will too.

People, even those who are severely disturbed, have a way of adjusting to things that us 'normal' folks could take a cue from. You'd be surprised."

He paused, looked off into space in recollection. "One time we had a young lady, schizoaffective, homeless. She was pregnant. Well, she ended up in our clinic. This was before I worked for corrections. In the middle of a session gets up, puts her hand on her belly, says 'I'm not feeling so good.' So, we get an ambulance, take her to the ER, yours truly escorting her, thinking what the hell have I gotten myself into. She lost the baby. Born dead."

He stopped to sip from his coffee before continuing. "I hear the news and of course I'm sitting there all thinking 'What the hell am I going to do when this lady finds out her baby is dead?' She could be violent at times, you know. So, we get all us professionals, doctor, nurses, even security guards crowded into this room to tell this woman the bad news. Here we are walking on eggshells like there is going to be an explosion. You know what she did?"

Dierdre waited.

"Nothing. She nodded her head, cried, spoke to the Pastor in the hospital. Was discharged to a group home. Talked to staff, cried some more and went on with life. What we didn't realize. She might have the deck stacked against her in many ways, but every person has the capacity to heal. Everyone. Sometimes we pros need to just step aside and witness rather than trying to manage. You understand?"

She nodded.

"Then there is the other issue," Dierdre began.

"And what is that?"

"They're talking about death penalty if they find him guilty."

Chapter 12

Maggie

Maggie Griffen washed flour and chicken fat off her hands, lathering under the faucet's stream as she contemplated her uneven fingernails. The kitchen was her sanctuary. Today as Maggie prepared not one but three different pies, for what occasion she didn't know, it was escape. Something to do. To not have to think about her son. Collin. Her grandson. Quinn.

The images flashed in her mind and like a swimmer breaking through deep water; she found that uncomfortable feeling of not being able to breathe. Time to come up for air. She did this by retreating in her mind.

The caution tape marking off the entry to her son's home faded, then became yellow streamers at the party for her grandson on his birthday. She saw Quinn beneath the balloons and decorations, with his little cardboard party hat from Walmart. The one with the cartoon dogs dressed as firemen and policemen. She heard him calling her Gramma.

"Gramma, cake!" he had marveled. It had seemed like more of the cake was on his face than in his mouth.

"Gramma, sing Little Star!" he would crawl up on her lap and they would sing *Twinkle, Little Star*.

She saw Quinn smiling, playing with his plastic pig and singing *Old MacDonald*. Except as a child of his generation, he would sing it 'Old McDonald's' The memory made her smile as tears formed in her eyes. Her memory trailed and the image of Quinn gave way to a vision of her son. She saw Collin, at Quinn's age, looking up at her, his innocent face, just a hint of a smile reaching out to her.

Heavy thudding startled Maggie, then. The steady rapping pierced her fantasy and at first she clutched her heart, not recognizing the sound of her front door knocker. Trisha Murphy was at the door, Tupperware container in hand, smiling nervously.

"Are you ok?" Trisha asked tentatively, "I saw you were home, but I've been out here knocking to wake the d- uh, I've been knocking a few times is all…"

"I am so sorry Trish. I was in the kitchen making some pies. I didn't even hear you 'til just now, how y'all doin'? Why don't you come in?" Maggie stepped aside, guiding her neighbor into the hallway.

"Here," Trish offered entering the home. Like every other home in working class Mosier, it had had no upgrades in several decades. Family photos covered the yellowing walls. They walked past the hall, setting off the Billy Bass fish hanging on the wall.

Trish jumped as the plastic fish sprang to life, singing a request to be taken to the river and dropped in the water. In shock, Trish staggered and caught her balance just in time to avoid dropping her Tupperware dish. She handed the dish to Maggie. "This is for you and Ronnie. I never expected you'd be baking, what with… with everything gone on, so I made some casserole."

The women settled down in the living room. Trish looked around in awkward silence. She was surrounded by smiling photos of Collin and his grinning baby. His wedding pictures. His first-grade photo yellowed with age. She noticed he didn't grin to show a gap-toothed mouth, but instead looked into space, a faint Mona Lisa smile. Pictures of family barbeques with Ron off in the distance, manning the grill, beer in hand, while others posed at the picnic table.

Surrounded by memories preserved in photo paper, she felt entombed. Finally, Trisha broke the silence. "Maggie. I just want to let you know I am here for you. That's all. I want you to know I don't think no differently of Collin. He did nothing but good for me and everyone else. This... this... tragic, just tragic, but I want you to know if there is anything you need, if there is anything Collin needs, I want you to know Fred and I are here for you."

Tears escaped Maggie's stoic exterior. Trish moved to sit closer to her friend, putting an arm around her and giving her a chance to cry tears long overdue.

"I'm sorry," Maggie said, blinking.

"Now you stop that 'sorry' nonsense. If anyone could use a good cry it's you, and no shame in that, you understand?"

Maggie shook her head.

"I just don't understand. Trisha, you know every moment that I don't keep myself busy, and then pray, and cry, you know what I'm doing? I'm going over and over in my head asking myself, what did I not see? What did I miss? What could I have done different? I been wanting to go talk to Pastor Billy, but I'm too embarrassed to leave the house. I can't even think of trying to be out in public.

People look at me and they're all thinking about it and wondering what we all must be hiding here or something! I don't know. I guess I shouldn't care what anyone thinks, but I can't deal with them all looking at me and wondering. Wondering the same things, I'm wondering. What in God's name came over that boy?"

She nodded sympathetically, then leaned in toward Maggie.

"You know I don't like to be a gossip," Trish began, "But you remember the Johnson girl down the other side of town, Missie Johnson? How she was so polite. She even babysat our Michael a time or two? Well, you remember last spring they held the Rite Aid on Main Street up at gunpoint?"

"I guess I recall somewhat."

"Oh, of course. Well anyway, the Rite Aid was held up at gunpoint, Fred heard it on his police scanner. It's his favorite toy, he's been retired from the force two years, but I swear he wishes he could go back to work if it wasn't for his heart condition."

Trish gave Maggie a look conveying how much of a burden it is to have to look after a grown man, as if they shared this secret knowledge. Then she continued.

"Anyways, he heard from a friend on the force that the three that were involved in the holdup, two kids from out of town, rough sorts, might have been gangs, I don't recall, and Missie Johnson." Trish mouthed the word "gangs" barely above a whisper, as if saying the word too loud would summon them.

"I was shocked, of course," she went on, "but he said that this wasn't the first time Missie'd been in trouble. Apparently, that poor girl is caught up in pain killers. They say it started when she fell and hit her elbow at work one day. And a nice girl from a nice church going family."

"I had no idea." Maggie admitted.

"No, nobody knew. The robbery was in the paper, but nothing with Missie's name on it. She was lucky. I heard she went out of state to a Rehab, her parents re-mortgaged their house to afford it. So anyway, I bring it up just to say that what that girl did wasn't a part of who she is. She comes from a good God-fearing family and all. Sometimes people don't show what is troubling them, you know that."

Maggie nodded. "But what trouble could have been so bad for him to...."

"How was he doing prior? Any changes?"

"Well, you know times are tough for us all but that didn't change how he loved his family. He had just gotten a job at Monarch, been there for several months already."

"The meatpacking plant?" Trish asked, her surprise giving way to more chatter. "Fred's nephew works there. Got four fingers of one hand cut clear off. Boy was so happy to get the job and the pay, though. He would get a ton of overtime, could buy himself and his girlfriend one of those foreclosed homes on Magnolia St. and was doing all right for himself with no overpriced degree."

"How's he doing now?" Maggie asked.

Trish considered this before answering. "Well, he is on worker's comp. Even after losing the fingers. He's now got some kind of nerve problem, they say. He says it's common. Everyone goes through a spell of it, what with the repetitive motions and all. He should be back to work soon. He doesn't talk about it much. Last I saw him a few weeks back he was in a rotten mood, I think it's the girlfriend, she can be a real Diva, you know? He didn't have much to say at the barbecue, just kept to himself, kind of quiet you know?"

CHAPTER 13

March 25, 2016

Cam

"Thank you for taking the time to meet with me, I know you must have your hands full," Cam sat across the table from Dierdre in Mosier County Jail's Mental Health Unit meeting room. Far from a fancy conference room, the space was multipurpose and low budget.

"I appreciate you calling me. I had intended to get in touch but was waiting, hoping I would have more information for you," Deirdre replied, flipping through Collin Griffen's chart to review her notes.

"We're probably both in the same boat at this point. I have worked with mentally ill clients before, but this is a high-profile case with a lot at stake and to be blunt, I don't know if there is much that I will be able to do." Cam flipped his steno notebook open and prepared to take notes.

"Well, can't he be considered not guilty by reason of insanity? Maybe sent to a locked psychiatric facility instead of prison?"

"In an ideal world, but there's no denying this case will be politicized."

Dierdre scowled. "I'm so tired of politics, it's so messy and negative. I can't wait for the election to be over!"

Cam kept a professional demeanor. He had long grown tired of pointing out to white people that their ability to distance themselves from politics, save for a vote every four years, was a luxury not everyone could afford.

But he understood the sentiment. Even before his work brought him into contact with the dirty deals and quid pro quo mentality of local politics, the tone of his skin had forced him to contend with the ugliness of American politics.

Cam thought that Dierdre seemed reasonable and well-intentioned, but like so many other white folks, had no idea how little good intentions mattered when her indifference could threaten his survival. His mind began to wander to the upcoming election. He wondered if she knew how much was at stake.

Dierdre began to speak again and Cam pushed his distractions off to the side. He had to focus.

"So, for the tentative diagnosis, I mean, there's definitely a psychotic disorder here. But I am also seeing some signs of extreme fear. He will be catatonic and then responding to internal stimuli, hearing voices, or acting like he's having hallucinations as well. But something is triggering him to flip out."

"Flip out?" Cam asked.

"Well, yes, not the most technical term. I mean, not aggressive toward others, but fearful, cowering in the corner of his cell, crying. He's urinated on himself as well on a couple of occasions. It's like he's terrified of something."

"I'd be terrified too if I was facing the reality of what he did," Cam mentioned.

"But he doesn't know what he did yet, at least I don't think. He has given no indication that he knows where he is or what has happened. He has talked to himself about his family or talking as if he is talking to his family, but to himself. So, I don't think he has even the slightest grasp on what is happening and what he did."

"It will be a whole other can of worms when he comes out of this fugue."

"If he comes out," Dierdre added.

"What do you mean, if?"

"Well, some people remain in psychotic states for a long time, some don't. The fact that he's young, that this doesn't appear to be drug related and that he's never had a past episode of psychosis all work in his favor for a decent prognosis. In other words, he is likely to regain his senses. But damage to the brain may have been done. We don't know."

Cam hurriedly jotted down notes. Dierdre paused for him to catch up, then continued.

"Usually, schizophrenia has an earlier age of onset. Usually early twenties, but not unheard of later in life. Interestingly, it is usually a younger onset for young men and later onset for women. But It may not be schizophrenia specifically."

"You think maybe bipolar?" Cam guessed.

"No, not necessarily. I don't see the pattern of mania followed by depression, although some people can develop bipolar disorder with psychosis, it doesn't sound like he had been manic. His mom called me. She said he hadn't been acting like himself, but nothing extreme that she could put her finger on. Certainly not a period of depression or mania, that she could tell."

"What do you think it could be?"

"Hard to say this early. Though some of the reactions, the vigilance and such, make me think of a patient I once had who had severe PTSD. That's something I want to look into more."

"Do you know of an incident that would have triggered it?" Cam asked.

"He isn't a veteran. It's possible that there could have been something, abuse, an accident, something, but I don't know."

Cam handed Dierdre a business card.

"I'm going to dig a little deeper. I know you have my number in your files, but in case you need it, here's another card. I'll keep you posted."

"Thanks, and same here. I feel so bad for this poor guy."

Cam was taken aback by this.

"Really? Why?"

"It just seems like this is all so out of character for him. As if this really was an action he had no control over. Reminds me of a patient from a few years ago, before I moved to North Carolina. This young man had been abusing hallucinogenic drugs. He was, like, one of those people who followed the grateful dead and that kind of thing, you know?"

Cam nodded.

"He went into a full psychotic break for days. He murdered his best friend. When he came out of it, he was mortified. This was nothing he would ever have done. Kid was practically a hippie. None of it made sense, except for the drugs. He has to live with this for the rest of his life."

"But Collin doesn't do drugs."

"Not that we can tell, no. But it's the same dynamic. Like something came over him that suddenly completely changed his personality. This seems totally out of character for him. It's like he suddenly became the opposite of himself, did something horrible, and if or when he comes out of this, he will have to live with the guilt for the rest of his life."

CHAPTER 14

March 30, 2016

Jolene

Jolene stopped the car just short of the parking lot. She sat staring at the jail. The razor wire fencing. The stone walls. Collin was in there. Her husband. The man who killed her son. She knew she was supposed to visit. She wanted to see for herself. Was he lucid? Did he know what he had done?

She remembered the day they met. Back in high school. She had gone bowling with friends at Rocket Lanes. When they'd gotten hungry, they had stepped away from the game to grab some pizza at the bowling alley snack bar. Collin had been working. He served them pizza.

Her friend joined the bowling league. Jolene couldn't afford such luxuries, but she stopped by to visit her friend after games and would make small talk with Collin during her visits. They liked the same books. Kafka, Camus, and Douglas Adams. She liked the *Game of Thrones* series. He hadn't been able to read the copy of *Song of Ice and Fire* she had lent him.

"It's too violent," he had told her, returning it to her the next week.

"Really? You're a guy, you're supposed to be into all that stuff!" she had teased back. But her comment had struck a nerve, she could tell. His face fell, and he distracted himself with work. A few weeks later they were back to talking and sharing books. Then dating. Then married. She had intended to propose, thinking him too shy. He had surprised her, presenting the ring at a Fourth of July family barbecue.

How could this have happened?

Only then did she realize there were tears running down her cheeks. She had known something bad was coming, and she had done nothing. Said nothing. Which was why, now, like the other times she had pulled up to this same spot and stared at the jail, she would once again put the key back in the ignition. She would once again put the car in reverse. She would once again pull away and do nothing.

CHAPTER 15

One Year Earlier

Jose

Jose's muscles ached. His hands were going numb again. Another byproduct of his latest dead-end job. How had it come to this? He wondered. He recalled a childhood spent avoiding the spotlight. Now an adult, his work kept him invisible. No thought given to the men and women behind the scenes who made sure the stores were stocked with bacon, sausage, ham. He didn't like the work. Often, he wondered at the life that had led him here.

His mind wandered as he drove to work. He remembered being a child, hiding under the blankets in bed, reading. Trying to tune out his parents' fights. His dad, exhausted after his shift at Monarch Industries, reeking of beer, taking out a day's worth of agony on his mother.

"Why are you hiding under the blankets reading another book? Trying to be smart like a geek or something?" his sister, Rosa, would tease. Jose was smart, geeky or not, but it had been Rosa who had gotten the scholarship, while he had become invisible. His sister could get away with being smart. She was a girl.

He recalled the allure of disappearing. Like the character in his favorite series, in which a boy had a cloak that made him invisible. He often wished he had such a cloak to hide him from the bullies, and later the police, but this wasn't Hogwarts. A scholarship might protect you from winding up in a mill somewhere for the rest of your life. Or in jail. But it wouldn't protect you from the big kids. The kids who were so much a part of the machine they couldn't hear it grinding away devouring their souls and spitting them back out on street corners.

When he was ten, he wrote a science fiction story about a futuristic society. His story won a prize in a statewide contest. His papa couldn't get the night off to go to the award ceremony; his mother was there. His heart sank when he saw the sneers from many of the white faces in the crowd. He never forgot what happened during the dinner that followed.

"Excuse me, may we join you?" his mother asked, eyeing the tables with empty place settings.

"We reserve these spots," Came the cautious reply from the white woman who eyed them warily. Part fear, part resentment showed in her face.

This scene repeated table after table until finally Mr. Baker, his teacher, called the family over and motioned to the empty chairs beside him. Jose's excitement returned. Invited to sit with the teacher, in a fancy award dinner with so many pieces of silverware on the table, not just a fork and knife that didn't match. Mr. Baker had looked him in the eyes, smiling with encouragement, and said, "Jose, congratulations. Bring your medal tomorrow to show the class."

But the next day at school, some big kids followed him home. They taunted him and called him names.

"Don't you know your place?" they called after him.

"Why are you trying to be white?"

"Getting prizes for writing stories, what are you, some kind of faggot?" called another.

"You think you're hot shit, don't you?" said one.

"I heard the prize came with some money, let's see if this little wetback has some prize money on him!" another shouted.

The gang of kids jumped him. They tore open his bookbag; they ripped his coat apart. Tore pages out of his notebook. One kid pissed all over his schoolbooks. They bruised his face, chipped a tooth, and bloodied his lip. They called him a no good four eyed fucking pig.

They didn't find any money but succeeded in stealing his reward. Not the medal, but the feeling of accomplishment. The feeling of being in the spotlight just once.

His face was ground into the dirt and he thought the torment would never end. But it did. A voice in the distance broke through the shouts and laughter. Suddenly, the kids split, running in different directions.

Jose pulled his face out of the dirt, retrieved his broken glasses and pulled his silver award medal, now scratched and chipped and broken, out of the gravel. His body ached as he turned. He saw Mr. Liden, the man who owned the gas station nearby. Walking back to his work. Another figure stood in the distance. A boy he knew from around town. An older white kid who never said much, but who stood now watching, his face looked sad. The boy approached. What was his name? Something weird like Colby or ... Collin?

The white kid looked concerned. Not like the other kids. The bullies.

"Are you ok?" he asked.

"Yeah," Jose said, biting his lip to keep back tears.

"What did I tell you about boys who cry?" he heard his father's voice in his mind, reminding him to put on a stoic face.

To stop himself from breaking down in tears, Jose pivoted and gathered his belongings. When he passed the river, he grabbed his prize medal and threw it into the water. That was the day Jose learned the merits of invisibility.

Jose would see Collin from time to time, in passing. Neither spoke about the incident. To his knowledge, Collin told no one. Jose would cross paths with Collin again, as both men came to work at Monarch Industries.

Only this time, Collin wouldn't be there when the bullies were done.

* * *

The day Jose was cornered by his boss outside the kill floor at Monarch Industries.

"I had a fifty-dollar bill in my wallet. It's gone. You took it."

"No, sir. I didn't do that. I don't steal."

"You stole my money and now you're lying," the boss persisted. He called the other supervisors in. Jose felt trouble coming. He eyed Ricardo, the only possible ally among the white people circling him. He didn't know him personally. Ricardo tried to be like the bosses, Jose thought. He never made it a point to be friendly to Jose. For a moment, Jose realized how much Monarch was like being in school. There were a lot of people, mostly guys, on the chain who were from other places. Who didn't speak English, and who were treated the worst. Then, there were the bosses, most of them white. A few of his peers were locals, like him, who were desperate and needed a job. But to the bosses, it made no difference if he was born here or not. To them, like to the bullies at school, he was other. They assumed he couldn't speak English at first. There was a caste system at Monarch that was all too familiar to him. Deep inside, Jose knew there would be no sympathy from the older guy with the tattoos who only joked with the bosses. No one else.

Still, Jose hoped he was wrong. He hoped for some solidarity, some compassion. Ricardo made eye contact for a moment. A look that seemed to say, '*Shut the fuck up and don't make this into a scene.*'

They roughed him up and dragged him out to where pigs were corralled, waiting to be brought into the slaughter chute. The squeals of pigs awaiting their fate was a background Jose had learned to tune out by necessity, but this was not the only time he thought he and the pigs had a sense of common ground.

"I know you stole my money!" the boss demanded.

Again, Jose looked to Ricardo. Wordlessly pleading. Ricardo ignored him still.

"And you know what?" The boss went on, "All I have to do is call the police on you and your ass is in jail and your family is deported because everyone knows they aren't supposed to be here. What d'ya say, boys? Should I help make America great again?" The group laughed. Jose glanced up at Ricardo whose poker face revealed a hint of fear before returning to stoicism, then he joined the others in laughter. He, too, had learned to become invisible, Jose thought.

The boss clapped Ricardo on the back and cracked jokes with the others before turning back to Jose.

"But because I'm such a nice guy, I'm gonna let you go," the boss picked up a lead pipe and threw it at Jose, whose reflexes sprang into action. He caught the pipe and almost lost his balance. The pipes used for porcine crowd control.

"I'll forgive you," his boss sneered, "if you take this pipe and fuck that pig." Jose felt sick. He stared at the ground, unmoving. The crowd circled in on him, shoving and making lewd jokes. Jose had seen his coworkers lash out at the pigs in all kinds of grotesque ways, punching, kicking and even using the pipes to beat and sodomize the animals.

He was guilty of beating the pigs. They all were. But he had never done anything like what was being demanded of him now.

Jose froze, willing himself to become invisible. Praying. Pleading that the laws of physics could make an exception just in this moment. Just for now, he could be like a character from one of his favorite science novels. That he could somehow channel a divine rescue. Wishing, straining himself with the intensity of his thoughts, his need in this moment as if it could allow a tear in the fabric of reality through which he could dive and escape and become invisible.

Like *Harry Potter*, with that fucking cloak, if he could just mutter some hybrid Latin phrase and melt into the floor, be beamed up someplace else. If he could just...

"Come on, you dumb fuck! You deaf and stupid? I said fuck that pig!"

Jose felt time slowing he could hear his heartbeat in his chest, not in his throat, was he even tasting the circulation of his own blood, feeling sweat prickle onto his brow, feel his throat go dry, no saliva, how could there be? No room to swallow with a heartbeat filling your throat.

He didn't bother to look up at Ricardo, afraid to move at all now. And besides, Ricardo wasn't going to bail him out. He thought back again to the time Mr. Liden had come out of the gas station to holler at the big kids. To break up the fight. There would be no one to break up this mess. He was on his own. He could barely keep the pipe in his grip, his hands were going numb again.

He heard the squealing of frightened pigs corralled into makeshift pens by movable metal gates. Maybe, Jose thought in a last moment of desperation, maybe if he locked eyes with the pig, he could somehow trade places. He would have given anything in that moment to be the pig, not the man, be the pig, the pig the pig he began to chant internally as if to conjure some juju that would let his soul leap into the pink body once squealing now frozen before him in terror, or amused, he didn't know, he wouldn't know until he could catapult his awareness into the pig, yes then he would know if it was fear or entertainment that lived in those eyes. Be the pig. Be the one with no choice, no reason, no sense, no ability to choose only to be slaughtered and have it done with.

"See, you pretend to be all quiet you little pussy. Like that other one, Colleen or whatever his name is." Everyone laughed except Jose.

The boss went on, "But I know better. I know there's a bad hombre in there and with just the right training he's gonna come out and then, guess what? You'll be a fuckin' man!"

Jose's mind raced with an array of illogical fluttering scenes....Dorothy clicking her heels chanting *"there's no place like home there's no place like home"* the Cowardly Lion *"I do believe in spooks I do I do I do"* and it almost made him laugh. This newsfeed of irreverence floating by like a fucking parade... like the Thanksgiving Day mother-fucking parade...

He stared at the pig. *Please, buddy, take my place you be me, I'll be you, it's a dirty job but somebody has to do it, pleeeeease, you'll get to live…*

He could swear the pig smirked back saying *'If your life was so great why are you willing to give it to me? Thanks, but no thanks buddy I've got the good deal here, but as the old song says, I'll be seeing you…. in your grocer's freezer…'*

The pig snorted like a laugh. The fucking pig was laughing at him, or was it squealing? Or screaming? Or was it all the same?

"Quite right," the pig continued, in Jose's mind, *"I will be fucked one way or another old chap. I'm fucked, you're fucked, we're all fucked, wouldn't you say? Tallyho!"*

"Ok then," the boss said, "You don't want to play. I get it. Well guess what, that is how we do things around here and if you can't play our games, you don't belong in our playground. So, I tell you what, Bob here will do it," the boss threw the lead pipe to a man with arms all scraped to shit from a career on a slaughter chain.

"He's gonna fuck the pig for you and then guess what? He's gonna fuck you!"

And that night after Jose had been left on the ground, sodomized, bleeding, crying. When he was once again able to walk, he went to the bridge that joins the town of Mosier to the nearby town of Greenfield, the bridge over a river of water carrying the decay belched out by the machine that is Monarch Industries, and he jumped.

CHAPTER 16

2015

Suzie

When her man was around, Suzie's droopy beagley face would seem less depressed. She would lift her head, her eyes would widen, and her face would lift. One could almost believe she was smiling. Suzie's tail would wag, and she would lift both front paws as she circled around herself in a goofy droopy beagle dance until she had his full attention.

She was sensitive to the man and the woman, and she knew well in advance when a pup was coming, long before the woman's belly grew round. Before the party to welcome the pup, the party she remembered fondly because of the amount of pork chops, coleslaw, and pie that found its way to the floor and therefore, her stomach.

She could smell, sense, feel it in the air. She also knew Man to be an ignorant sort, and so she did not ruin the surprise by letting on. She let them find out on their own that they would have a pup.

One had to humor Man. He didn't have the nose for things like she did. She knew one day late that winter. Could smell it in the crisp air.

When her man came home to his wife and new pup, something was wrong. He acted much the same in every regard but sadness, fear, anguish, these things she knew not by words but by a scent and she smelled them wafting from him.

It was the day he lost his job at the car dealer. Suzie didn't understand this or its implications from an economic or psychological standpoint. But she smelled the fear that had now taken up residence in their home, that would stay with them, an unwelcomed guest for the month to follow.

The month when her man was home a lot, and the woman less than ever. And a day came when her man returned home, his excitement renewed, and Suzie leapt to her feet with joy to see her man returned to his smells of happiness and pride.

She wouldn't know the source of these feelings, these smells. She didn't know that her Man had gone for a job interview at Monarch Industries Inc. But the first day he came home from his new job, she smelled something foul. It reminded her of the days living with her Man's pack. When the other dogs would come home with blood on their mouths. She had never been allowed to join them and was both thrilled and for some reason she couldn't explain, repulsed by the smell. It was not a smell she associated with her Man, though. It made her worried for him.

Not my man! She thought to herself. Feeling something corrupt and foul, something she could smell on her Man. Not just the blood. Something else. From that day on she still greeted her man and followed her man and obeyed her man but she did so with her eyes cast down and head held low, haunted by the stench, a vile specter that would invade their home, in place of the fear and worry, and in place of the joy that had once been there.

CHAPTER 17

February 2016

Maggie

"Blasted deer!" Maggie exclaimed, more from fear than anger. She had almost hit the deer and the last thing she could afford was damage to her already beat-up car. She immediately felt remorse at having almost hurt the animal. So caught up in her thoughts as she drove home from an evening of babysitting little Quinn while Jolene worked late and Collin covered his mandatory overtime shift that she almost didn't even see the deer emerge from the side of the road and flit across the dark street.

She was troubled by what she saw when Collin came home from work. Jolene had hinted that Collin seemed to change since beginning his new job, but she also knew a fair number of young ladies who got to be possessive of a man at a certain point in the marriage. Got to be dominant, especially with these young ladies today who want to be both the man and the woman in the family.

But what she saw tonight made her realize perhaps Jolene wasn't just being insecure. Collin had come home a little later than the later than expected. The dark circles under his eyes gave him the appearance of a prisoner long deprived of sleep, or someone who had been punched in both eyes, or both.

Maybe it was her fault, Maggie wondered. It's no good to crowd a man when he first comes home from work, hadn't she seen that with Ron all these years? She had gone to Collin carrying the baby, who had been asking for his daddy non-stop for the last hour.

"Daddy!" Quinn had cried out in joy.

"Daddy! Play Farm! Play Piggy!" Quinn had held up his plastic toy pig.

"Stop!" Collin had cut in. Not loud. Not a scream but certainly not like him, especially to his boy whom he loved and adored. He had brought his hands to his head and rubbed his temples, complaining of a headache. Looking weary and run down. Quinn had begun to cry, and Collin shut his eyes, wincing in pain.

In all the commotion Collin's dog, Suzie, had appeared, cautiously lumbering out to greet him, but he ignored her. She stood in his way, the way stubborn Beagles like to do. And that's when Collin Griffen hauled off and kicked his beloved dog square in the ribs.

Maggie froze in horror at this sight. Collin, seeming to snap out of a fog, had dropped to his knees and hugged his dog. He had cried like a little boy. Wailing and comforting the dog and saying, "I'm sorry girl, it wasn't you, I'm sorry girl, I love you! Who's my good girl? Who's my good dog? I'm so sorry!"

Even recalling the scene now gave Maggie chills and an uneasy feeling. Something was wrong with her boy.

CHAPTER 18

February 2016

Collin

"*Ooooold McDooonaald's haaaaada faaaarm….eeeeyiii eeeeyiii-iooooh!*" Quinn squealed happily up at his father as he bounced his pink toy pig up and down on the plastic farmhouse, its pieces scattered across the living room floor.

"Look! Look, Daddy! Piggy want cheeburga!"

"No, Quinn, pigs don't eat cheeseburgers," Collin corrected.

"Yes! Yes, Daddy! I like cheeburga, piggy like cheeburga… cheeburga from Old McDonald's!"

"Yes, buddy. Old McDonald's."

Collin smiled at his son. Quinn was playing with his plastic farmhouse, a herd of pudgy plastic animals surrounded him. Collin sat down on the floor beside him, and Quinn snuggled into his father's lap. Again, he began to sing, and this time Collin joined in. "*Old McDonald's had a faaarm…*"

Collin's head hurt.

"*eeeeyyyiiii ooooh!*"

Collin looked again. The pig in Quinn's hand was smiling. And then it wasn't. It was screaming. And then it was covered in bloody red streaks. And then Quinn's hand was covered in blood. Quinn turned to smile at his dad. On his face, a bloody, gap-toothed, chubby baby grin.

Collin jumped to his feet. He looked down again. This time Quinn was nowhere to be seen. He was standing shin deep in blood. In his living room. Then on the kill floor. Then in the grey place. With the noise. And the slamming.

"Make it stop!" he screamed. He clutched his head and tried to pry his eyes open in case this was a dream. It had to be a dream. Why couldn't he wake up? He felt hands grab his arms. A sharp jab. Everything grew blurry.

CHAPTER 19

April 2, 2016

Cam

When Cam had made the appointment to meet with Jolene, she had agreed to let him come to the house. Cam liked meeting with people in their home whenever possible. He believed you could tell a lot about a person based on their environment. He was used to all kinds of arrangements. Clients asking 'please use the side door' or 'don't bother ringing the bell, just walk in' so when Jolene had asked on the phone that he walk around to the back of the house and use the back door, it didn't stand out at first.

Cam pulled up to the house and sized it up from the curbside. He didn't like to use people's driveways. Besides, this driveway didn't look reliable, it needed repair. The small lawn was knee-high and scraggly. He thought it odd that so much time had passed and there was still yellow caution tape draped around the front door of the house. The house itself was a small bungalow, he guessed, built in the early 1940s, and as he walked around to the back, he noticed that not much had been done to update it, at least from the outside. A small, unfenced yard was even more overgrown than the front.

Cam thought he spied a yellow plastic wheel peeking out from under a tangle of shrubs. He presumed the rest of a child's beginner's trike was buried in the greenery. Now held hostage by weeds, no one would ride this contraption any time soon.

A clothesline caught his attention. Weren't too many people Collin's age still making use of the old solar powered clothes dryer, but he felt camaraderie with them for their frugality. To his wife's dismay, he preferred this to conventional dryers. He reached up without thinking and touched the clothesline, then lifted it over his head, ducking under and coming up to face the back entry of the house. The steps needed repair as well but bore his weight. He gave a sharp rap on the backdoor. Moments later, a young woman appeared.

If Cam didn't assume that she was Collin's age, twenty-nine, thirty perhaps? He would have thought she was in her late forties. She looked burdened, unrested, and though not unhygienic, her hair seemed to have been neglected. Tangles stuck to her in the heat. The house also did not appear to be air-conditioned. She gestured for him to enter.

"Thank you for agreeing to meet with me, Mrs. Griffen. I am sorry for your loss," he hoped the precursory sympathies were enough. Sentimentality was not his forte. He reached for his steno pad as if it was a talisman against the emotional intensity of what may come from their conversation.

"You can call me Jolene. And thank you. I don't know how much help I can be. I really don't know how this happened," her voice cracked, but she sealed her facial expression back to neutral. Cam felt guiltily reassured by this. They stood a moment in the kitchen and Cam waited for her to offer him a chair or a drink of water. She didn't. Perhaps, he thought, social graces aren't her forte, or perhaps it is the circumstances.

Cam broke the silence.

"I can't imagine how hard this must be for you. Speaking frankly, it will be difficult trying to convince a jury that Collin is innocent and should walk free. That leaves the option of insanity, or hope for imprisonment, hospitalization and…"

She cut him off. "North Carolina has the death penalty."

"For first degree murder, yes. But that is where I need to make a very convincing case that Collin did not intend, plan or consciously decide to commit this crime," Cam explained.

"They're already calling for his blood. They're going to send him to the chair."

"Not exactly. At least, not by those means. Electrocution has not been used in North Carolina since 1938. If, and this is if Collin faces execution it will probably be by lethal injection. Still, not the result we want."

"What do you need to prove, what exactly are you going to try to prove? That he was crazy? That it was an accident?" Jolene was turning pale.

"This may take a little time, Mrs. Gri- I mean, Jolene. May we sit?"

"Oh, of course. Yes," Jolene gestured to the kitchen table. A pile of unopened mail was overflowing onto the floor. He glanced at several bills marked *past due*.

Cam took in the room for the first time since arriving. It was like the exterior of the house, quaint. The appliances appeared to be at least ten years old. It had been painted but not renovated in at least thirty years; he guessed. The walls were neatly painted sage green. Small, cluttered, but not dirty. Something was missing.

"Have you been to visit Collin?" Cam asked.

"No. I tried. But I can't. I just keep trying to work and get through the day."

"That is understandable." Though as he spoke the words Cam couldn't imagine trying to do his job under the circumstances.

Liar. A voice in the back of his mind taunted him. He ignored it and pressed on.

"Well, Collin is still in a psychotic state. He is not what we term an accurate historian at this point. Whatever you can tell me about Collin, about what happened, the events leading up to…"

"I don't know. There wasn't, I mean there was, but there wasn't," she began. Cam thought she appeared to be wrestling with something. He had interviewed abused spouses and children of domestic violence and alcoholic households and was attuned to whether

65

a family member may be hiding something. Was this her reason for hesitation? He wondered.

"Well." Cam responded "I can imagine that the last thing someone ever expects is such a horrible event to take place. All families have their struggles. Young couples, these are tough times. But no one ever imagines it will end in tragedy. What was Collin's drinking like?"

Jolene laughed, then covered her mouth.

"I'm sorry. I forget you don't know him. It's just, the very idea of Collin drinking is funny. If you knew him, you'd understand."

"Why is it funny?" Cam asked.

"Well, his dad's a raging drunk. Everyone knows it. Collin hated alcohol from the time he was a kid. When we got married, he wanted it to be a dry event, but I told him there was no way people would come, so he caved, eventually. But he hates the stuff. Doesn't drink, never has. Maybe tried pot once in high school, but no, Collin didn't drink."

Cam marked some notes in his steno pad. "Don't mind me, I find it easier to collect notes and then I don't have to trust my memory later," Cam said as he consulted a list of other questions with a brief glance.

"How was his mood, relationship with family, with you and Quinn in the months prior?"

Jolene inhaled deep and sighed before responding.

"Collin… things were getting better. He was trying. He was trying, but it was hard. He was stressed out every night after work."

"Why don't we go a little further back in time. When you say things were getting 'better,' what had gone on that they were improving from?"

"The past few years were rough. First, Collin had a hard time finding work when his plant closed. He was in manufacturing since High School. It took a while for him to find something, and when he did, it was a favor from a family friend."

"What was he doing?"

"The new job then, that was working at Dom's Autobody and Sales down on Broad Street."

Cam nodded. He knew of the place. It wasn't far from his favorite restaurant, the PigPen.

"So, the new job was stressful?" Cam asked.

"Not exactly. That job was easy. Or should've been. Look, Collin is no salesperson, and that's what they had him doing first. It's almost as laughable as imagining him drinking."

"Why is that?" Cam already had a guess. Antisocial, maybe difficulties with authority. Maybe introverted.

"Well, Collin's really shy number one. And two, he is the opposite of a used car salesman. The man is like incapable of lying. He tried his best to follow the rules and expectations, but he knew about cars and would inadvertently end up talking people out of sales because he would not bullshit them into buying lemons. Excuse my French."

One out of three, Cam thought to himself. He scrawled a few more notes before continuing.

"So, did he end up getting fired?"

"Not exactly. They tried shuffling him around. Detailing, clerical stuff. Finally, when the recession caught up with them, they ended up cutting people and Collin never really was a good fit. You'd laugh though if you saw the car he drives, that alone would be bad PR for anyone working at a car dealership. It took months for him to find a new job. He ran out of unemployment and still nothing. It took so much for him to find the job at Monarch, that's where he ended up next. After the car dealership and before … before the incident happened."

Cam diverted his eyes and took notes, more to give her a pause and break the tension than from a need to document every word. It worked, and she continued.

"They were always advertising. It was his last choice. He interviewed for the kinds of jobs he wanted. At least the ones that came close. The ones you didn't need degrees for. Do you know you need a degree to work at freaking Starbucks even? It's ridiculous."

"Is that so?" Cam hadn't heard this. "Did Collin have any dreams, aspirations of what he wanted to do?" Cam wasn't sure why this factored in, but he felt the urge to pursue this. He trusted his instincts even when they didn't make sense.

Again, Jolene laughed. She rolled her eyes, which were now tearing up. Taking a deep breath, she continued. "He loved books. He wanted to be a librarian or something having to do with books, like working in a bookstore or something. Something quiet and with books. But he never even tried to take it seriously."

"Why not? That's a reasonable profession for a smart young guy."

"Come on, first of all, have you met his dad?"

"I haven't yet had the pleasure," Cam responded.

Now Jolene laughed even louder. "I'm sorry." She said trying to control her tears and laughter at the same time. "It's just if you knew his dad, you'd never use the term pleasure to describe him. He's like a cranky old man. Drinking isn't an improvement for him. But he's one of these old school guys who thinks women should be bare-foot and pregnant and men should be ex-football-players who do 'manly jobs' the idea of Collin investing in an academic or intellectual career, even if he had the money for school, which he didn't, is just…. It would never happen. It was like too far-fetched for Collin to even take seriously. Maybe a little throwback from his dad's way of thinking."

"Is he like his dad in any other way?"

Jolene didn't have to think before answering, "No. Not at all. He is the opposite of his dad. He made it a point to be. No drinking, not a loudmouth. His dad is a veteran, Collin wouldn't even enlist to get help with college, not even to have an income in all that time that he needed work. No way."

Cam took notes, and there was a pause before Jolene continued.

"But Collin would apply for anything. Then he got desperate. He was walking dogs and mowing lawns and shopping for old ladies in the neighborhood for money, but then he would feel bad for them and wouldn't let them pay him. Does any of this sound like a murderer to you?"

"So, Monarch was the only gig he could get. A slaughterhouse must've been a rough change for a pacifist," Cam speculated out loud.

"Initially he was hired for the cleaning crew. He never thought he would be part of the killing. But then they needed someone on the kill chain. Even then, he didn't want to do it. It was a 'promotion' of sorts and he swore it would just be temporary. Just until we paid off the last of the credit cards," she gestured to the pile of papers stacked on the table.

"We had four cards maxed out and one that we were managing. The maxed-out cards totaled about twelve thousand dollars."

"Ouch. That's quite a burden," Cam commented.

"It's not hard to do with a family. Not hard to do when you've been out of work for months. Not hard to do at all. Nope, there were no luxuries. No meals out, vacations, no. Just basics. Back-logged."

"Did the financial stress make him change his behavior? Was he aggressive or impatient with you or Quinn?"

"Not really. I mean it was stressful, but I think I did most of the complaining and he would always try to stay positive." She choked up and tears fell freely now. After a moment, she continued through sobs. "I mean, maybe that's where I went wrong? Maybe I put too much pressure on him? But I told him he could quit, I told him I could just work extra hours until he found something else."

She heaved a few more sobs and then, wiping tears away and clearing her throat, regained composure.

"I told him after some time. It was changing him. I thought maybe he was having an affair or something because he got so distant, even though I knew that wasn't like him. It was just making me stressed because he turned into…. Into like a ghost of himself.

Like when he was here, he really wasn't here. He wasn't fighting with us, no. He wasn't even talking to us."

"Can you describe his behavior around this time? So, he would go to work, come home and then what?"

"Usually just come home, sometimes eat dinner with us, sometimes not. Just sit in the chair. Not even watch tv. Just stare sometimes. Quinn worshipped his daddy and would try to play with him or sing or talk to him and he would humor him at first, but then he would kind of ignore him. After a while it was almost like Collin would turn away from Quinn, and it was almost like he was afraid to touch him. I didn't think of it until now, but I wonder if he had some kind of… urges or something and was avoiding us to avoid hurting us? It just sounds so crazy though."

"Had Collin ever been depressed, had any mental health issues prior to this?"

"No. He was quiet but not like mentally ill. Not sad, specifically. He had some nervous habits from being an introvert or something, but not anything bad. He, closer to the end, I mean to the incident, he had begun having nightmares, but they were all related to work. I work in a hospital and I've had nightmares too when things are graphic or intense for a while, but not so much that… not so much that I would do something like that. Could stress really make someone go that crazy? His dad is nuts from Vietnam, but that was a war. That was different."

"I don't know. That will be for the medical professionals to figure out, perhaps," Cam dismissed this train of thought. For now.

"What he wanted more than anything was to be a better dad than his dad. What he was afraid of was poverty. He blamed his dad's drinking on the war and on lack of options. He didn't see options for himself, but he wanted Quinn to have choices. Later in life, you know? So much for any of that."

CHAPTER 20

April 5, 2016

Cam

"Collin, son, do you know what day it is?" Cam was hopeful that in almost a month, his client would be in better shape. His hopes were dashed when he saw the dazed young man. Escorted with some effort through the door of the small meeting room. Cam noted the ceiling was still stained. Collin also hadn't cleaned up much.

Both hands and feet in shackles, the young man didn't appear to resist the efforts of the guards who sat him heavily into a chair across the table from Cam. Then again, he also didn't exactly show initiative to walk with them. It was more like Collin was sleep walking. The guards there to direct him and move him into place. Cam gave him a few moments to see if Collin would make eye contact. He didn't. As far as Cam could tell the young man didn't know where he was. Collin sat turned at an angle, almost dismissing Cam, staring instead at a window in the far corner, past Cam's shoulder. The only natural light he's seen in some time, Cam thought. If he is even really seeing it.

Collin finally turned to face him. Instead of looking at Cam, he looked through him. He looked heavily sedated still. Suddenly, Collin jumped back, trying to raise his hands to cover his face, cowering as if avoiding a blow no one else could see. Cam instinctively jumped back in his own seat, though he was never in harm's way. The guards grabbed Collin by the shoulders and held him down in the chair. He didn't fight them but began yelling.

"Get the pigs back!" Collin yelled. He started kicking his feet as if trying to back himself up against the wall. He looked from side to side. Cam thought he looked terrified of something. Then he went silent again.

"You're not getting anything else out of him, I can guarantee you that," A hefty guard standing beside Collin warned him. Cam had seen this routine before. Jails were no place for the mentally ill. Left to the discretion of COs and others trained to be punitive, not therapeutic, his client was likely to be dead meat.

"Collin? You're ok. Collin, my name's Cam Burton. I would like to talk to you."

But Collin had already cut him off, yelling again. "No! Not the pigs! No!"

"I'll come back tomorrow," Cam replied. Collin was hoisted up onto his feet. He shuffled begrudgingly, a guard gripping his elbow as he pulled the young man down the hall back to his cell. Cam walked toward the exit. As he turned to leave, another CO, Chuck, according to his name badge, spoke up.

"I thought it was only you people who called the cops 'pigs', funny, ain't it?"

"You people?" Cam inquired, though he knew full well what Chuck meant.

"Oh, you know, you people, 'Black Power' and 'Fuck the Police' and all."

Cam restrained himself, as he often needed to, from making any number of retorts. It took a few blocks of driving home to shake the feeling he was so often left with, the ignorance he heard on a daily basis from white colleagues and even from those below him on the professional ladder.

Only when he brought the car to a stop outside his home did he move on to wonder about the significance of his client yelling about 'pigs.'

CHAPTER 21

April 5, 2016

Jolene

Jolene hated coming home from work. Her home haunted by regret. She tried to eat the rest of last night's dinner and after two fork-fulls of pork fried rice, a takeout dish left over from yesterday's work dinner order, she had had enough. Everything she ate tasted like sand. Her stomach gnawed and simultaneously threatened to reject anything she tried to eat.

She shuffled in exhaustion back into Quinn's room and settled into the mattress on the floor beside his crib. Now her retreat. Evening sun through the window reminded her that she could still take a walk. It wasn't too late to get some fresh air. Go to the park.

Except it was too late. She told herself.

She tried to stop replaying the film reel in her head, but like clockwork, it was cued up again. When had it begun? When had she first noticed the difference? She thought of last December. Her stupid insecurity. Petty jealousy. The memory brought tears to her eyes. In self-loathing, she balled both hands into fists and pounded at her head as if to knock the memory out of existence.

But you can't knock it out of reality. You can't undo it. You stupid, selfish, bitch. She reminded herself. She saw herself, less than five months ago. Pacing the floors, questioning why Collin had begun acting strange. She remembered the day she and Quinn had come home from Christmas shopping.

"Daddy come home?" Quinn had asked her as they pulled into the driveway. Walmart bags filled with Christmas gifts had been piled in the back seat of their beat-up sedan, and a greasy bag of MacDonald's was wedged between gift boxes in the seat. Quinn had already mashed cheeseburger into his mouth. She remembered trying to wipe at the smear of ketchup and bun around his face.

"Daddy come home?" Quinn had asked again. Jolene had temporarily spaced out and had not answered him the first time.

"Yes, baby, Daddy's coming home in about an hour." She had reassured him. She remembered hoping it would be true. Remembered how angry she had been that he was taking longer and longer to come home back then.

"Daddy play McDonald's Farm?"

"Daddy will be tired. Why don't you play by yourself?" She had told him.

"No, baby, why don't we play? I'll play with you. I'll play any game you want," she told herself now, sitting on the floor beside his crib as evening sun subsided.

She his voice, gleeful, belly filled with junk food. She sang along with the memory now.

"Ooold McDoooonald's Haaada faaaarm Eeeeyi Ooooooh!"

She remembered how mad she had been when Collin hadn't come home in time. Again.

He had insisted it was his job that was making him stay late to meet quotas, and that overtime was mandatory. She remembered now, her suspicions that maybe he was having an affair. Knowing now what she didn't know then, she laughed and cried and clutched at her hair. If only. If only. If only. She told herself. Why couldn't it have just been that? She bargained in her mind with God to erase and replot the past. I'll take an affair. She said. And you give me my son back.

Jolene had known even then it was highly unlikely. Collin was a devoted father, and good to her. He wasn't outgoing, so the idea of him chasing another woman behind the scenes would never have occurred to her. She had been at work at the hospital when she couldn't reach Collin by cell during lunch or later in the afternoon. At his old job at the car dealership, they could hit each other up with quick cutesy text messages. Touching base throughout the day just to show they were thinking of each other and on each other's minds. It had not been so since he got his new job. *How hard is it to send a fucking text?* She would wonder to herself. That was when her coworker had gotten her all worked up.

"If that man can't send you a message or pick up his phone, you know he's up to something and he can't be trusted." Her friend at work had insisted. She then scrolled through her own phone and pinpoint blog after blog of relationship "experts," and their rules and opinions on why he does this or that. *'3 Ways to Know You Got Him,'* or *'5 Things No Man Will Do (If He REALLY Loves You).'*

Jolene hadn't taken it all seriously, at first. She remembered that December day when her suspicions and anger had gotten the better of her.

She had settled on trying to distract herself with a little TV, curled up on the couch with Quinn, who was always an eager source of love and attention, and their beagle Suzie. A commercial had come on for *Psychic Line*, a hotline of professional psychics who could tell you whatever you needed to know about your love life, career, and life purpose.

She remembered thinking it was hokey bullshit. But Collin had been acting different. He just seemed to want to come home, watch his phone and then go to bed eventually. She had reasoned to herself. If a psychic can tell me for sure that he is not having an affair, then I won't have anything to worry about. She had given in and grabbed her phone.

"Play Farmville! Farmville Mommy!" Quinn shrieked with delight to see his mother's phone light up.

"No, baby, not now. Mommy has to make a call," she had dismissed him. After a brief detour through an automated menu, Jolene had been connected.

"Thank you for calling *Psychic Line*, this is Tasha speaking, how can I help you?"

"I need to know if my husband is having an affair."

Tasha had a voice like a professional counselor. Not some fake fortune teller routine and a lot of mystical mumbo jumbo. Jolene could only remember part of the message. She wished she had written it down.

"Listen, this man you're with, he loves you. But he is not himself lately. Spirit is telling me that your husband is troubled deeply and it's not his intention to leave your marriage… but he is fighting with a deep darkness. If he does not make some changes, there is a grave sorrow for him and for you. He carries a heavy burden that is entirely unnatural. If nothing changes, he will bring sorrow and heartbreak to you, though he does not mean to do it…. Do you understand?"

There was more, but Jolene had barely taken it seriously beyond the reassurance that Collin wasn't seeing someone else. How could you be so fucking selfish? She thought to herself now.

That night when Collin finally had come home, Jolene stared at him, hard. He didn't notice. She remembered how she had watched him as if trying to figure out what she had to do to crack the code, break into his mind, shake him to his senses, make him act normal.

She remembered how it had progressed from there. Week after week. He had grown more distant. Like a shell of himself.

It had seemed like the more Jolene tried to be inviting, accommodating or even seductive, it was no use. Her husband kept a distance, kept a wall up. Went from the door to the shower, to the couch. He would remain there, staring at the wall or sometimes his phone. He'd sit like that all night. If she hadn't brought dinner to him, he probably wouldn't have eaten, and even then, he ate minimally. He used to love Baby Back Ribs, but now he had barely touched them at all.

She grabbed Quinn's stuffed dalmatian and held it to her face, breathing in for the smell of him, knowing even this last hint of his existence would soon disappear. She felt for the amber bottle the doctor had given her. If she didn't slow down, her medication would disappear sooner than expected.

CHAPTER 22

April 20, 2016

Cam

Cam wasn't big on conventions, but the National Bar Association's Annual Conference was originally supposed to be a chance for him and his wife Donna to get away. Maybe, he told himself, he would learn a thing or two or make some good connections, and if he was lucky, the food would be decent. This year, the conference was held in Baltimore. Donna could do some sightseeing while he was attending talks and networking, and they could enjoy catching up with each other in the down time. Enjoy the hot tub, go to a restaurant outside the hotel together, maybe sleep in one morning if there was time. Or at least, this was what he had hoped.

After the first day it became obvious that all things that he and Donna did to annoy each other weren't restricted to their home in North Carolina but were transportable. And, if he was being honest, he carried his workalohism with him on the road as well.

Their relationship had been strained since the incident. Neither liked to talk about it. Cam knew his wife resented him. She had dropped out of law school when the baby that would have been their first son was stillborn. She never went back to school. She had fallen apart, taken time off from work and then lost one job after another in a dark, long bout of depression. He had just gone about business as usual. It was his specialty.

* * *

"What, did they forget to bring your steak?" Cam asked the young lawyer seated to his left.

The man's plate was overflowing with greens, where the rest of the men at the table had large servings of meat bleeding to varying degrees according to request.

"I'm vegan," he replied. "They substituted grilled root vegetables and kale salad for the steak. It's delicious. Would you like to try some?"

"Delicious? Sure. If you're a rabbit," Cam laughed at his own joke, as was his habit.

"I'm Matt. Matt Davenport," The man replied, unfazed by Cam's teasing.

"Cam Burton. Don't take my joking personally, it's just that I can't imagine having to sit through one of these tedious conferences without at least having a steak as the carrot on the stick"

"Well, for me a carrot as the carrot on the stick is just fine," Matt replied.

"So, where do you hail from?" Cam asked.

"San Francisco," Matt replied.

I should have guessed. That or New York. Cam thought to himself.

"How about you?" Matt asked.

"A small town called Mosier, in North Carolina. I specialize in criminal defense, especially in marginalized communities."

"You must have your hands full. I'm heading back to North Carolina in a few weeks, as a matter of fact. Working on a project. Planning to take some drone footage."

"Well, don't leave me in suspense. What is this project about? What kind of law are you practicing that involves drone footage?"

"I'm an Animal Rights Lawyer," Matt replied.

Cam's eyes shot open. It was his turn to give the snapshot look. This was a specialty he had never heard of and he had been around the block a few times.

"You represent dogs and cats who are petitioning the court for more treats and better pooping conditions?" Cam joked. Matt couldn't help laughing.

"I am part of a growing but still new branch of law. We address injustices in a variety of practices, from factory farms to animal cruelty in breeding and pet stores. My project focuses on educating the public about factory farms and modern agribusiness and the violations of basic rights of animals. And the human rights and environmental injustices in these industries. The drone footage is for a documentary I'm working on."

Cam took his card. It would be a few weeks before the slight nudge in the back of his mind would develop into a coherent thought. Until the dots would be connected. Until he would call on this man again. For now, the scent of steak filled his nostrils. And the last thing on his mind was Monarch Industries and Collin Griffen.

CHAPTER 23

May 1, 2016

Collin

A crash startled Collin awake. He reached for the bedside lamp, but his hands only hit a wall. More crashing in the darkness as if metal is being dragged against metal and a loud slam.

He heard the yelling.

"Come on! Hurry the fuck up!"

Then, a crash. And the shrieking, squealing, terrified screams, or is it the metal crashing? He can't tell the difference.

Crash.

"Wake up! Wake up, you fuckin' low life, yeah you! Wake the fuck up!"

Collin wished he could wake up, but he doesn't know where he is, what day it is, if it is day, all he knows is-

Crash!

That Jolene will be worried, and he has to get home to his baby and-

Crash.

Shrieking punctuated his heartbeat.

If only someone would shut them fuckin' pigs up! He didn't want to do it, but it's just how things go around here... around where? Where the fuck am I? When he saw those other guys, just easy as cake, you just pick up a pipe and easy as anything, just pick up a pipe and Crash!

"Fucking pigs! Get those fucking pigs! Shut them the fuck up!"
The voice kept yelling. Or was it his own voice?

The stench of ammonia, blood and shit stung his nose, all the way up to his brain. His head throbbed with pain, he couldn't believe his eyes, all around him- they just picked up the pipes and the knives and it never ended.

"That is what we do around here boy, even these here Spics can figure that one out, no won't you go on ahead and…"

He heard a loud thud. Then a crash.

He didn't want to do it.

He didn't want to do it.

He didn't want to…

Now he was yelling it. He heard his own voice, but it sounded distant.

"I didn't want to do it!"

CHAPTER 24

May 1, 2016

Cam

"I didn't want to do it!" Collin suddenly began yelling and swinging his arms violently. Cam took a step back from the cell. He had come once again to talk with his client, this lost cause, who would likely get the death sentence.

Would it really be all that bad?

A voice in the back of Cam's head inquired. This man had killed a baby. His own baby. He's out of his mind. He may never reason again and even if he can, a dangerous person like him.

But Cam pushed the thought aside. Tempting as it was, he knew this logic to be dangerous. In his mind, he scolded himself for even thinking it. Cam had three more inmates to visit before leaving the jail for the day. Easier cases. People who were lucid and who he had a chance of being able to successfully defend. When it was time to leave, he ran into a man he recognized as Chuck, the CO who had walked with him on his first visit to meet with Collin. Like a flash, the fragment of memory returned to him.

"*You people,*" Chuck had said.

"*Pigs.*"

This time it was like a new circuit had connected in Cam's mind. He took out his steno pad and made a note to call Matt Davenport as soon as possible.

CHAPTER 25

May 8, 2016

Maggie

Maggie tried to reassure herself as two guards led her to the meeting room at Mosier County Jail. Her son was still alive. She had lost her grandbaby, and her daughter-in-law had lost her only child. Something no mother should have to experience. Her son was still alive. She stared out the window of the visiting room, waiting for the guards to bring Collin in to meet with her.

It's not so bad. She reminded herself. He's still alive. There's still a chance. Not so bad. It had become more of a prayer than an affirmation. This was her third attempt to visit with Collin. Each time prior, his condition had upset her to the point of nausea. They had escorted her out, but not soon enough. She had witnessed her son collapse to the floor on one occasion, yelling in terror about something she couldn't understand. It sickened her to see him that way. But it's been a few months. She reassured herself. This time it will be different. She dabbed sweat off her face with her handkerchief and turned as the door to the meeting room opened.

It's not so bad. He's still alive. You still have your son.

A thin, haggard man she barely recognized was led to a chair on the other side of a glass screen. He stared at her vacantly. He's still alive. She tried to tell herself. Not a convincing argument.

She lifted a hand to the glass as if to try to touch him through it. He barely even blinked. He doesn't recognize me. She thought.

Tears welled in her eyes. The sight of this person who barely passed for Collin horrified her. There was no light in his eyes. No smile. No recognition.

"Collin. Collin, it's me. Collin?"

The stranger in her son's skin gave no acknowledgement. She flashed back to his first birthday. To Collin riding his first trike up and down the driveway. To him taking her by the hand and pointing out the neighbor's dog, how he had smiled up at her. His first gift to her, a craft jewelry box made of popsicle sticks. Always smiling, thoughtful, gentle. His first day of school. A worried look in his eyes for her, she had realized.

Where was he?

She looked into the vacant eyes of the skeleton of a man across from her. No trace of the same brightness or curiosity. A sleep-walker.

Her head fell into her hands and she cried.

Her son was gone.

CHAPTER 26

May 10, 2016

Jolene

Maybe going back to work so soon was a mistake. Jolene told herself.

Mothers' Day was approaching. She tried to not think about it. Seeing the flowers, cards and balloons, hearing talk from the mothers and children visiting her patients in commemoration didn't help. She had only been out on the floor for two hours, had ten more to go. Keeping busy was supposed to make things better. Working twelve-hour shifts at the hospital was supposed to give her a sense of purpose and distract from the pain. It didn't.

Soon she would have to go back onto the floor. Deal with the people. Their needs. Their pain. She shouldn't take the next pill this soon. It was too much. She would run out. She heard the bathroom door open and froze inside the stall. Her heart was pounding. She didn't want to hear it, so she dropped a few squares of toilet paper into the toilet and flushed. Have to get back out there. She thought about breaking the pill in half and before fully deciding whether to take all, half, none. It was already down her throat.

She went through the day like a robot. She was relieved the onslaught of questions had dropped to a minimum. She knew people meant well, but the constant inquiries, the constant questions about whether she was ok, did she ever see this coming, was

Collin abusive and more, all felt like an interrogation, not a real concern. For weeks she had felt like a circus animal on display, to be examined by others.

That had given way to feeling an enormous sense of loneliness, pain, worry and confusion. She was tired of explaining herself and tired of questioning the past. Tired of dreaming about the son she used to hold and the husband she loved only to wake up to remember that both were gone.

Her doctor prescribed the pills at first, but they weren't doing enough. A coworker had suggested a stronger prescription. Just to get through the day. Just for a little while. Until things got better.

But they never got better.

CHAPTER 27

May 18, 2016

Cam

Sam Cooke's voice carried through the PigPen, serenading a minimal lunch crowd today, with the sounds of men who worked on the Chain Gang.

The table moved, and Cam realized he had been tapping his pen on his steno pad, cover stained with a fingerprint, a souvenir of one of many lunch meetings with clients at the PigPen.

The table shifted again as Matt Davenport settled in to join him. The Animal Rights Lawyer eyed the scenery with a look that reminded Cam of the face one would make had they stepped in dog shit on the street and were hoping no one would notice. He shrugged the expression off as a reaction to the atmosphere in Mosier's most popular low-end greasy spoon.

He noticed his guest eyeing the black and white photos lining the walls. More than the menu. A perfect introduction for the guided tour so many Moserians loved to give of this establishment.

"Why, that picture there, that was Elmer Esterhaus. He and his wife Annie opened the PigPen back in 1836. He came from a family of hog farmers, one of the originals in these parts. Passed down the farm from generation to generation, eventually they distributed all the way to Florida, Texas, even up to New Jersey. Family lost the Hog Farms a few generations back but were able to hang on to this fine establishment." His words took on unintended irony as Cam compulsively wiped a smudge stain from a corner of the table. It puzzled anyone who knew him well, that for all of his orderliness and obsessive-compulsive cleanliness, his favorite place to eat was this greasy spoon. The restaurant was a favorite of the blue-collar folks in Mosier, but a professional like him was a rarity. The PigPen had come to live up to its name in more ways than one. Cam placed his steno pad on the newly de-smudged table.

"Did the farmers lose business during the 1980s financial slow down?" Matt inquired.

"No, they survived Reagan, but not Monarch Industries. They are like the Wal-Mart of Pork industry. They took over the feed lots, then the hog operations then, there's a name for it..."

Matt finished his train of thought.

"They used the Perdue Model- vertical integration- to monopolize the industry and drive the smaller farmers out of business, or into their debt."

Cam blinked in surprise before continuing.

"Well, yes, there you go. Yes, that is it exactly. Matter of fact, Monarch Industries is part of what I was hoping to talk to you about. If you don't mind."

A loud snapping of gum signaled their waitress had arrived to take their orders. Cam requested his usual BBQ Pork special; Matt ordered a salad.

"Salad? You sure? Are you on a diet?" the server asked.

"I'm vegan," Matt explained.

"Ok, I can fix you a Caesar salad with eggs and..."

"No, thank you," Matt cut in, "please, only vegetables are just fine."

The server eyed him suspiciously, as if he had just asked for the ear of a cat to gnaw on. She took Cam's order and strolled off.

"I'm sorry, do you mind that I am eating ribs?" Cam asked.

"I agreed to meet you at a place called PigPen, I knew what it would involve. I'm here to educate."

"How are you enjoying your visit to this neck of the woods?" Cam wasn't great at small talk, but he wanted to give his colleague a buffer before getting into the heavier topic at hand. He still thought Matt was a lightweight. Cam thought to himself, the man eats nothing but salads.

"It's been a nice change of scenery, but unfortunately I have been spending a lot of time in less savory parts of the area. I'm in town with a small crew shooting some scenes in a nearby town of Greenfield for my documentary."

"Really? Why would anyone in the world care about what's going on in Greenfield?" Cam asked. He knew of the small village, or was it a hamlet? But thought nothing impressive went on there.

"They've been the latest victim of Monarch Industry's innovation," Matt began. Cam had lifted his glass to his lips but set it down abruptly at the mention of Monarch Industries. Matt continued. "Industrial farming is like nothing you can imagine when you see those pretty billboards of big green pastures. Just as an example, they had the idea to gather all the pig manure in a giant lake. A big pond of feces and runoff from waste."

For emphasis, Matt stretched out his arms. "Then," Matt went on, "they use the cesspool, cess-lake is more like it, to irrigate their crops to then feed to the animals."

"Circle of life?" Cam tried to quip.

"More like raining shit. It literally rains feces, and not just over the crops."

Cam had heard rumor of this.

"People all around who have the misfortune of living downwind. Their houses get rained on. They have to leave the windows closed even in the heat because the fumes and filth have caused serious illness."

"Wow, that's bad," Cam admitted.

"Yes, the locals have a nickname for the town now, they've taken to calling it 'Shitstorm'"

"I can imagine it becomes a shitstorm when they try to sell their homes," Cam added.

"One of many problems, indeed. So, I'm making this documentary to educate the public of this practice, one of many that is destroying communities thanks to animal agriculture."

"Well, I have been getting quite an education," Cam figured this would be a good time to bring up his newest client.

"It's funny you should mention Monarch, as a matter of fact. That's the reason I wanted to catch up with you. A recent client, a young man, seems to have a clean past, clean record, no mental health history. Father's a hard ass, but that's nothing unusual in these parts. Supportive wife, beautiful two-year-old son. Struggling financially but, that's, take a number, right? Works for Monarch. This one day recently, guy comes home, breaks his coffee table and beats his kid to death with one leg of the table."

Seeing the look on his colleague's face, Cam stops, "Am I being too graphic?"

"I just spent a week interviewing rural Americans who are getting pig shit rained on them, so no, you're fine."

"True, true. So, the state wants to execute this kid, and I know there is something missing here," Cam waited. Matt took a deep breath of air, a deep pull on his beer, and sat back.

"What do you know about the job your client used to do?" Matt asked.

"Slaughter? What is there to know- they get a dead animal, they cut it up, put it into a package, ship it off somewhere, my wife buys it, cooks it, I eat it, all is good…"

But Cam's attempt at humor is met with silence.

"I really know little about it, I can't get anything from my client, he seems to be in some fugue state…."

"Did your client abuse substances after working for Monarch… or before?"

"No, clean, no history, dad's a drunk, perhaps that is part of the reason for his avoidance of alcohol and drugs."

"Unusual but may make an even stronger case in some ways…."

"A stronger case for what?" Cam asked.

"What do you guess the most dangerous job in America would be?" Matt asked.

"Well, were it not for the context of our conversation I would guess. Coal mining, or taxi driver, or police officer, firefighter… but since we're talking about Monarch, do you mean to tell me that …"

"Yes. Slaughterhouse employees are at high risk for on the job injuries. Studies are increasingly correlating work in this field, in any capacity, for any amount of time with high levels of substance abuse, domestic violence, rape and other crimes."

"I don't follow you. I cut up meat on my kitchen counter all the time, as does my wife, my parents before me and their parents before them, how in the world." Cam said.

"Yes, you cut up meat. A slaughterhouse employee cuts an animal. A living, breathing animal, and doing so traumatizes the shit out of them. But that is only one aspect of it. Do you know how many animals Monarch chain—that's what they call the line- chain workers kill, cut, gut, slice and package per hour?"

Cam's deer in the head lights expression suggests he hadn't a clue.

"Between one hundred and one thousand per hour. That's one fellow on the chain slicing an animal's throat every ten seconds. Companies have increased chain dramatically since the 1970s and to increase profits, big operations like Monarch staff under-trained, underprivileged folks with few other options. There are many sources I can give you verifying accounts of worker injury, of animals being sent down the chain still conscious, sometimes kicking and screaming. Workers are injured all the time. Repetitive motion, close quarters, sharp objects, but nothing can touch the psychological impact."

Cam started to recall his conversations with Dierdre now.

Matt continued. "It's like the PTSD soldiers face coming home from war. Just like war, these plants are hidden from view, obscured off in the shadows. We get meat on the table, but we don't ask where it comes from or who really pays the price. Your client is one of many, unfortunately, although the link between occupational stress and criminal behavior seldom comes up in court."

Cam digested this with a heavy sigh.

"Your client's lack of substance abuse could work in his favor. No one can attribute his outburst to drugs or alcohol. His mental health is questionable, yes, but if you can establish that prior to working for Monarch he had no aggressive behavior, no violent tendencies and no mood or emotional disturbance then odds are you can do something unprecedented and long overdue. You can get a judge to rule that your client's exposure to cruel, inhumane acts daily led him to progressively break down the connection between his behavior and his conscience."

"Has this ever been done before?"

"Not that I know of, but it may be your only shot at keeping your client out of the chair. Or you can make the case for insanity, hope for pity from the jury, and maybe he will spend the rest of his days in some forensic psych ward doing the Thorazine Shuffle. But something tells me you really want to sort this out, and if that is true, if you really want to see justice done, set a new precedent that could rock this entire industry and redeem your client as a good guy in a God awful situation, then go after Monarch. But be careful. Behind the business suits these don't play around. They work hard to protect their interests, if you know what I mean."

CHAPTER 28

June 1, 2016

Jolene

Jolene didn't have to guess why her supervisor called her in for a private meeting. What she had to do was figure out, quickly, how to pretend nothing was wrong. She should have been good at it after all this time. But if she screwed this up, she would be in big trouble.

She realized then that her hand had been reaching deep into her pockets. It was an automatic reaction. The spare pill that she usually kept there, wrapped in a yellow post-it note, had been disposed of earlier. The rest of her stash was hidden throughout her purse and car. Maybe there was more at home. She tried to think back to what was hidden where, taking inventory. How much did she have left? Just in case.

Her supervisor finished her phone call and stared across the desk at Jolene. Jolene tried to avert her gaze. Were her pupils still dilated? She wondered.

"Do you know why I called you in here?" her supervisor, Susan, began. Yes. Jolene thought, but I'll be dipped in shit if I will tell you why. She tried to calmly recite the lines she had scripted for herself instead.

"Was it Trudy? Did she complain about me again? That woman has already been threatening to go after my license. She's delusional!"

"No. It's not about that," Susan cut her off. She appeared to be losing patience. "This isn't about a complaint from the patients. I am trying to save your job here, if not your life. I will be blunt with you."

Jolene tried not to squirm in her seat. Here it comes, she thought.

"There have been several staff who have come to me, anonymously, and complained. They suspect you are on something. Jolene, I am trying my best to give you a fair chance here. Maybe it was a mistake to come back to work so soon after losing Quinn."

Jolene fought against it, but finally a tear escaped and steadily slid down her cheek. She looked at the ground and willed herself not to break down. *Don't tell her.* She repeated in her mind. *Just keep your mouth shut and let her babble and then get out of here and home where you can...*

"Jolene," Susan cut into her thoughts.

"Yes," she mumbled, wiping tears away. Her other hand reaching again for the empty pocket. Knowing it was useless to do so, but not able to stop the habit.

"Jolene, we are all real worried about you. I don't want to fire you. But after what happened with Kashira, everyone is watching like a hawk now."

Kashira, she knew, had lost her job. Possibly her license. Jolene felt nauseous. What more could she lose?

"I have had reports about you nodding. In front of patients and family members. Mrs. Robertson's med count was off. I don't need to tell you what this all looks like, do I?"

Jolene thought it was odd that her boss danced around the subject but wouldn't say it directly. What the fuck was wrong with her?

"I am going to go against my better judgment one more time, Jolene. Do you understand that I am putting my license on the line as a supervisor? I don't think you are ready to be back here yet. I recommend that you take a few days off with pay. From your sick leave. Ok?" Susan reached across the desk and handed Jolene a list of phone numbers.

"I will trust you, because I'm giving you a last chance. I trust you to do the right thing. This is the number for EAP and the number for substance abuse counseling and another number specifically for a program for healthcare professionals, ok? This is your last chance."

Jolene took the paper and tried to keep her hands from shaking. She still couldn't look at Susan. If she told her the truth, she was done. Probably jail, maybe lose her license, definitely lose her job. Worst of all, they would make her stop. And then the pain would return. And that was unbearable.

Chapter 29

June 8, 2016

Kashira

Mosier North Carolina doesn't ask that you have a college degree to gain entry. Those in the professional class settle on the outskirts. For Moserians, there are two types of people. Good, hard-working, honest Americans and everybody else. It is known that wealthy folk exist, but they remain like the Loch Ness monster or Sasquatch, the stuff of mystery. The people of Mosier work to the bone, work to death in fact.

They knew, like their ancestors who believed that, if unguarded, the fairy folk, or some such otherworldly beings, could steal what they didn't guard carefully, the people of Mosier frequently awaken to find what they work for has disappeared. In Mosier it is the invisible hand of capitalism, not the fairies, who pocket the gold. This hand directed most notably by Monarch Industries.

The majority of the town traced their lineage to Scotts Irish ancestors who believed in days gone by that fairies could steal the babes of humans and leave changelings in their place, the people of Mosier were accustomed to sacrifice. Sacrificing their children to fight the mythical 'war on terror' or the war on the working class right here at home. Offerings to the Monarch.

Jose and Analisa's son, Jose Hernandez, was taken as such a sacrifice. Oh, how they may have wished it was just a fairy mound, just a changeling. This is how we do it, the town will tell you. To enter Monarch Industries is to enter an inner chamber of the world of Mosier. A realm of its own, to which most of the rest of America is oblivious.

Behind the barbed-wired fence, inside the stone walls, the air is heavy with the reek of suffering. To walk the path through the entrance to the Monarch Abattoir as they may call it to pretty up the gruesome work which must be done...

Sacrifices must be made, and who will enlist to the army if not for the glamour of travel and college aid and training? Or the allure of the bloodlust to gain revenge and restore righteousness as outlined by Empire...

To enter the abattoir is to enter a world apart. It is the universal *but* to every sentence ever taught by every teacher, from the secular to the spiritual. Thou shalt not kill, but for the sake of a bacon double cheeseburger. All men are created equal, but for the wetback who will not complain when she loses a finger....

Who would resign themselves to this lowliest of rungs on the ladder to Hell without temptation that within its walls is the promise that only for a little while, the rules may be distorted, with the hope that the rent can be paid, the car will be fixed, the baby will have food, life will get better?

For one thing is known for certain within the walls of the abattoir, things couldn't possibly get any worse.

As Kashira was about to learn, this being her first day of work at Monarch. She sat in her car, in the parking lot, dialing a familiar number.

"Good morning," Joan's voice was like a chime. Kashira wondered how this woman, with all she had been through. Years in the trenches at the mercy of the God Crack Cocaine, could be so upbeat. She had heard Joan's stories in the rooms of NA. She wanted to emulate Joan's recovery. To have that serenity in her own life. That is why she had asked Joan to sponsor her.

"We'll see about that soon," Kashira joked.

"How many days today?" Joan went on, getting right down to the business of their daily calls.

"Seventy-five days. But I have today. So far, I have today. I'm at the new job. The meatpacking plant. I don't think I'm going to like this," Kashira admitted.

"One day at a time. Right? You can do anything for a little while. Have you heard back from that program about getting your nursing license back?" Joan asked.

"No, not yet. And I have to do something. PO has been on my ass and it ain't like people are lined up to give a job to a junky with my track record."

"A grateful recovering addict, you mean. Words have power. Choose them wisely," Joan corrected her.

"It's not fair. I've never committed a violent crime, and my record is because of addiction. If it's a disease, why do we get punished for being sick? My doctor started me on those pills when I was a kid. What was I going to say? No thanks, I will just sit here and suffer? Man, it's not right. And now here I am about to go to some shit job and that doctor, you know where he is? Nowhere around this stinking place."

"Fair or not fair you can only do you. Addiction may not be your fault, but the disease, and it's a disease, is now your responsibility to manage. And that means working your program. Learn from the past but don't live there. You got today. Am I going to see you at the meeting this evening?"

"Yes," Kashira assured her sponsor. Hanging up, she couldn't help thinking about the past. About the pediatrician who started her on codeine when she complained of menstrual cramps.

Her pediatrician didn't live in this town. He lived in the sprawling suburbs far from view of Mosier, or Greenfield, aka Shitstorm. And he would continue to serve opiates while many of his patients would go on to serve time. Kashira was desperate to stay on the outside, and Monarch was the best she could do. She could ignore the snide remarks and rude comments made by her coworkers among whom she was the only female. She could force herself to ignore the stench of the kill floor, the sight of blood. She had been trained as an RN. She could ignore the oozing sick feeling as her feet sloshed through blood on the floor. She could ignore the rats that scurried through the room, even on the chain itself, the ghosts of dinner yet to come. She could ignore the sight of maggots and the buzzing of flies. She could ignore the "locker room talk" the guys bantered in constantly, eyeing her sideways to glean her reaction.

But when her first day of working the chain was over, as she waded through the blood and mess on the floor, through the door to an area where pigs were herded into a holding pen, she couldn't ignore the sensation that suddenly came over her. Every hair on her body seemed to be standing on end. She couldn't explain the sudden sense she had that the supervisor, Mitch, a man twice her size and twice her age, stood smirking and speaking in a hushed tone to Ricardo, the guy with the weird reaper tattoo who was one of the Stickers. Another sticker, a guy named Tom, looked her way and sneered. He whispered something. The men chuckled, and the pigs in the pen nearby squealed. And the pigs that didn't squeal seemed to stand in terror.

A fear much like her own. Mitch grinned crookedly, glancing in her direction. As she headed for the door, the supervisor made a move in her direction and grabbed her, reaching one of his big, meaty hands into her pants.

"Get off me!" She yelled, pushing herself free. Both men broke out laughing.

The echo of their laughter and the sound of the pigs squealing made it seem as if for a moment she was surrounded by the sound of both hysterical laughter and cries of horror.

"I just wanna show you I agree with you people, Black lives matter!" Mitch mocked.

"All lives matter..." Tom added coolly, and with that he lifted a lead pipe and brought it down hard on the skull of a pig that had been standing at his feet only a moment ago. Ten minutes later

Kashira took out her phone, finger hovering above Joan's name in her contact log. Then scrolling and landing instead on another number. Kashira called her dealer.

The next day she turned herself in to probation. Because she couldn't bear the thought of spending another day at Monarch Industries.

CHAPTER 30

June 10, 2016

Cam

Cam couldn't park near the facility, and he presumed that was no coincidence. After what Matt had told him about the lengths places like Monarch would go to protect their interests, and the horrors they profited off of, Cam could understand why the slaughterhouse was hidden. On the outskirts of town. Not visible from the main roads, not easily accessible to the public.

He managed to park out of the way, on the side of the old dirt road off of I-83. Close enough to approach the parking lot's entry gate. He was dressed down today. More than usual. In his opinion, at least. His jeans were still ironed, it was a habit he didn't want to break, no matter how casual he was trying to be. He tried to conceal his steno pad and pen inside a pocket in a lightweight jacket that was still overkill for a hot North Carolina day. Maybe the jacket was a bad idea, he wondered, but then, carrying a notebook around wasn't the best thing either.

He walked into the parking lot. A man stepped out of his car. Cam approached the man, who held a cigarette in one hand. He looked worn and tired, and Cam wondered if the shift was beginning or ending for him. He had a tattoo of a reaper on a motorcycle on his left bicep, and his hands were marked with several nasty looking cuts.

"Hello, do you have a moment?" Cam asked.

"Very few moments. I can't be late."

"I don't want to make you late. My name's Cameron Burton, and I am a lawyer representing the interests of a former employee of this establishment. I was wondering if we can arrange a time to meet, I am just trying to get some information that may help my client's case."

The man squinted suspiciously. "I don't know. What kind of information you looking for?"

"Nothing that would put you in jeopardy, but I can understand if you're uncomfortable talking with an outsider. We can meet elsewhere; I want to get a sense of what my client's average workday would have looked like and if anyone knew anything about him. Client's name is Collin Griffen."

Cam couldn't be certain, but he thought a look of recognition crossed over the man's face. The man abruptly turned his face away, looking over both shoulders. Cam could tell he would get nowhere. This guy knew something or was afraid of something, but he wasn't going to talk.

"I can't help you," he turned to walk away, then turned toward Cam again. "You know whatever people say about this place, it's a job ok?"

Then he went inside the building and left Cam alone in the parking lot.

* * *

RICARDO

Nosy prick. Hanging around asking questions. Ricardo sat on the bench inside Monarch's changing room. He tried to shake the feeling in his gut that the dude in the parking lot. What was his name again? Fucking snitch. Ricardo couldn't afford to fuck things up. He was so close to being promoted. Mitch had told him that if he kept up the good work and kept his shit together, he could be a shift lead by next month. Maybe even get a transfer to a different part of the plant. One that wasn't so fucking painful, he thought, as he rubbed his aching feet before putting his work boots on.

"Hey, what's taking you so long? You writing poetry for your boyfriend?" Ricardo looked up to see his boss, Mitch.

"No, I'm coming," he wrestled with the decision for a moment, but before Mitch left the room, Ricardo knew what he had to do.

"Hey, boss, got a sec?"

"No, I'm not gonna suck your cock, stop asking," Mitch responded.

The jokes and innuendos made Ricardo livid, but he kept his temper because more than anything else, he wanted a promotion. He took a lot of shit. But at least he wasn't one of the pigs.

"I wanted to let you know, um, that guy Jose? There's no way that will come back to haunt us, right?"

"What with Jose?" Mitch asked. Ricardo knew he was playing dumb on purpose.

"Well, I wanted to tell you. Just now, on the way in, a guy stopped me in the parking lot. Says he is Colleen, I mean, Collin's attorney. Wanted to ask me questions."

Ricardo saw Mitch's face turn from ball busting humor to simmering anger.

"What kinda questions?" He asked.

"I don't know. I guess about Collin. About work here. I told him I didn't want to talk to him."

"What was his name?"

Ricardo strained to remember. He reconstructed the view of the middle-aged Black man with blue jeans and a jacket, reading glasses. And what was his name? Just then he heard it in the man's own voice.

"Cameron Burton," He said.

"I'm glad you told me about this," Mitch looked side to side. They were the only ones in the locker room, but still Ricardo thought he looked nervous.

"Am I going to be in any trouble for this? For anything?" Ricardo's stomach felt sick. All the days, weeks, months. Putting up with shit. Not complaining. Playing along. Joking along even with the racist shit.

"No, don't worry. You're fine," Mitch replied. But he left, and Ricardo thought he seemed to be in a hurry.

CHAPTER 31

June 16, 2016

Finch

Michael Finch didn't expect to hear Mitch Johnston's voice on the line; the call jarring him away from the video broadcast. One of his favorite new reporter, giving hell to some liberal professor.

"Mr. Finch…." Johnston had begun the conversation in his gruff barking tone.

"This better be good," Finch replied.

"You can decide on that when I'm done. Got a report this morning. Problem with one of the runts HR hired. Boy named Griffen. Had a little incident a few months back. He's in jail, but there have been murmurs, lawyer poking around trying to get information."

"Why are you calling me for this horseshit? Find someone else. Runts get locked up all the time. What is it this time, DWI? His wife accused him of beating her? Not my problem."

"He beat his kid to death," Johnston cut in.

"It's all over the news. Reports are coming out identifying him as a Monarch employee. Just thought you should know how this will effect-"

"No! No, you need not spoon feed me. I got it. Have Courtney prepare a statement. We're so sorry. This is an isolated incident, disturbed individual… not our values… blah blah blah."

"Courtney? Sir, do you mean Carmen?" he asked, trying to hint at his superior's error without directly confronting him.

"Right, Carmen, whatever, with the tits, yes, her," Finch shot back.

"We're a step ahead of you. Just wanted to put it on your radar; reporters may call you. They've been nosing around the plant. I'd recommend a gesture to the wife, maybe sending flowers, something like that."

"Got it," Finch replied, then added, "this kid, Griffen, talk to HR. Did he pass the personality assessment? Drug screen? How were his references? Light a fire under their asses, will ya? Letting loose cannons through and now I have this to deal with."

"He had no history to speak of. Checked on this already. As normal as they come. Quiet, no prior legal. No alcohol or drug history."

Finch paused for a moment.

"All right, well what the fuck. People don't know how to handle their shit, what can I do? If I had turned him away, I would have liberal whiners up my ass for denying people employment. Give a man a job and he isn't cut out for it and then they still want to blame you. What the fuck do these people want from me?" He was on a roll.

"Do they think when they go to the market and buy a slab of meat wrapped nice and clean packaging, that the animals rolled over and just gutted, skinned, and dissected themselves? Nobody goes out and picks pork chops off a pork chop tree. It's a dirty fucking business and if that isn't clear to someone when they apply for a job, when they accept the job and when they gladly take paycheck after paycheck after paycheck to do said job," Finch ranted.

"I just want to prepare you. Reporters may come calling. Give you a chance to prepare a statement."

"Ok, how is 'fuck off' for a statement?" Both men laughed.

"I will let you get back to your work, Mr. Finch."

"Call me back someday with good news, will ya? And hey, call Tammy down in HR, tell her to replace this kid with someone who has a pair of balls, ok?"

"Shall I ask her to add ball examination to the recruitment process?"

Finch responded in a slightly more optimistic tone, thinking of Tammy examining his own. "That won't be necessary."

Hanging up the phone, Finch shook his head. The employees always start up so naïve- fresh meat! Desperate for a job. They lie during the interview process, or they promise the world. *Yes, I can handle it, I'll do anything.* Maybe they've lost every job there is to be had in these little piss-ant towns. Maybe getting evicted, maybe got another kid on the way because by some bizarre universal law the folks who have the most kids seem to be the folks who are chronically incapable of feeding them…. but they are eager to work.

Do they think working in a slaughterhouse is supposed to be easy? Do they imagine that all they have to do is ring a little dinner bell and little Cows and Happy Piggies will come galloping over to stand in line like they are checking their fucking passports to take a ride on Uncle Noah's Happy Boat of Salvation before the fucking flood?

He was a businessman, and he understood that just like in any industry you need people who were the right fit for the job and if occasionally people came on board who weren't cut out for the job ….that wasn't his fault and nobody should stick their snouts in his business trying to ask questions about job stress and worker safety and whatever other bullshit. But it always happened. Eventually there would be an inspection, some audits, questions asked, and he would have to take care of it.

He cracked his knuckles and then rubbed his temples. The last thing he needed was to get those nosy reporters snooping around. Then PETA, then God knows who else. He picked up his phone again and scrolled through his contacts. It had been a while since he had played golf with Steuben, but the DA still owed him a favor for his company's generous donation to Steuben's campaign.

"Hello," Steuben answered on the third ring.

"Hey, Steub, how've you been? Still golfing like a little girl?"

"Well, I wouldn't want to hurt your self-esteem by not letting you win." He chuckled. "But in all seriousness, I am doing well, keeping busy, that's for sure. How about you, Mikey?"

"Well, I'm gonna let you get away with that annoying nickname you know I hate because I know you're busting my balls. And because I need a favor from you."

"What, you have a problem with some of the inspectors? Need me to talk to someone about an audit?" Steuben asked.

"No, no, it's not that. It's about a former employee. He's in jail now, apparently lost his marbles. Lawyer, guy named Burton snooping around trying to talk to employees."

"Collin Griffen, the Baby Killer," Steuben confirmed.

"I don't care whether who he is or what he did. I don't need people nosing around here. You understand what kind of losses that can mean for me, right? And I give a lot to the community."

"Will take it under consideration," Steuben replied. "By the way, how's your son doing? He getting back on track?"

"You know, I appreciate you pulling strings to get the charges dropped. He finished another rehab. Getting back to work. Hopefully it works this time."

"Glad to hear it. And I will see what I can do about your, umm, situation."

PART II

Man's Best Friend

Two Years Earlier

CHAPTER 32

2014

Bobby Ray

Dodger barked in alarm as smoke rose from the skillet. Oil splattered and the smell of sausage burning filled the air. Six months ago, the entire house could have burned down, and Bobby Ray wouldn't have known it. Thanks to Dodger he was alerted-reminded that he had been cooking.

He needed so many reminders these days. So much had changed. Being a straight-A student throughout school, he thought his prospects for college looked good.

He was one of only a handful of Black students in the advanced classes in his high school and was constantly reminded by his white peers and teachers that he would have to work twice as hard to disprove their assumptions about him. He did in fact get some scholarships for college. But not full scholarships.

He tried to make it a few semesters working, supplementing his scholarships, but it was never enough. When a recruiter had stopped he and his friends at the bus stop one day and talked to them about how his long-lost Uncle Sam could give him the opportunities of a lifetime if he would agree to serve, he was game.

His first tour of Iraq was an education of a very different kind. His second tour was when an IED scrambled his eggs for good. Traumatic Brain Injury, they called it, and any hope Bobby Ray had of going off to college went MIA at that point.

Instead, he was back in Georgia, disabled, brain damaged.

Appearing functional at a glance as long as you don't ask him who the president is, or whether he had taken his meds, eaten breakfast, finished cooking breakfast, or set the house on fire accidentally instead. On a good day he was almost like his old self, with the addition of constant nausea and headaches. On a bad day he would lose the ability to understand simple words, become emotionally reactive and have lapses in not only memory but judgment.

Minor details.

Dodger saved his life. A doctor at the VA referred Bobby Ray to *Mutts for Vets*, a program that rescued dogs from high kill shelters, trained them as service dogs, and matched them with service people in need. Dodger, a medium-sized pit bull mix, had been a loyal companion, faithful friend, roommate, and therapist to Bobby Ray for months now and both were grateful to have each other.

* * *

Application for Certification as a Therapy Dog Handler
 Wounded Healers Project
 498 Amber Dr. Helen, GA
 Applicant Name: Robert Ray Birch
 Applicant Age:31
 Address: 1704 Delaware St. Loganville, GA ZIP
 Phone: CODE 394-1297
 Email: dodger308@gmail.com
 Tell us about your Companion Animal Applicant
 Name: Dodger
 Breed: Pit bull
 Age 5 years
 Altered? Yes

Please attach confirmation of companion animal vaccinations if applicable. All dogs, cats, ferrets must be up to date on their vaccines in order to be considered for this program.

Tell us about yourself; why do you want to work with Wounded Healers, what makes you a fit candidate for Therapy Animal Handler? What specific populations would you and your companion animal prefer to work with?

I am a veteran and suffered a Traumatic Brain Injury in 2011 during my time overseas. My road to recovery has been long and difficult, but I am getting better over the last five years. Dodger, my service dog, has been my biggest helper as I make my life normal again.

I am very fortunate to be alive and while chronic disability prevents me from working; I want to be of service and to help others. Dodger is a patient, kind and loving dog. He is very obedient and good with people, even when they are stressed out. He has helped me a lot and I know we can help other people together.

Dodger would be good with most people but has not been around kids often. I would like to work with adults or elderly people, either veterans or civilians. I would like to work with people who have anxiety or PTSD. I have also been making progress overcoming PTSD from my time in service and want to help show other people that there is hope and life can be good again. Dodger is the perfect dog to make anyone feel better.

* * *

To Whom It May Concern,

I am writing on behalf of Robert Ray Birch, with his permission. He was a client in at my TBI recovery program for veterans from 2012 to 2014 and since graduating this program successfully has remained in contact on a biweekly basis to provide volunteer peer counseling in our Project Hope program. He has demonstrated a willingness to be of service and treats others with respect, professionalism and compassion. He has demonstrated the ability to form personal connections with others in the program and has been a reliable and consistent volunteer.

I highly recommend him for the Wounded Healer program with his therapy dog, Dodger. Please feel free to contact me at any time with any questions you may have about this reference.

Thank you,

Dr. Arnold Maxwell

TBI Unit

VA Hospital

Loganville GA ZIP 30052

May 17th, 2014

Mr. Birch,

Thank you for your application to the Wounded Healers project. We are excited to inform you that we have approved your application. Please contact this office at your earliest convenience to schedule an orientation and training for you and Dodger. We are happy to have you both on board and look forward to working with you.

Regards,

Natalie Richards

Volunteer Coordinator

Wounded Healers

To: Richardsnat@woundedhealers.net

From: BBirch@gmail.com

Ms. Richards,

I wanted to thank you for accepting Dodger and I into the Wounded Healers Program. We have enjoyed being part of this program. I have had to move and am now living at the following address:

498 Morris St. Mosier, NC 27007.

I could rent this apartment because Dodger, my dog, is in this program, otherwise the landlord wouldn't have allowed me to rent with a pit bull.

Thank you again,

Bobby Ray Birch

CHAPTER 33

June 2014

Ricardo

"I can work at the Slaughterhouse," Ricardo reassured his friends. "Dude, I love bacon!"

They broke out into laughter.

"I don't know, man," Max replied, "dudes go into that place, and it fucks with them. You remember Dante? He sat behind me in seventh grade math class. Fucker was a cool guy. We used to bust out laughing' at this motherfucker. He used to say the funniest shit, one crazy motherfucker. Anyway, he dropped out, you know? I think freshman, sophomore year, he got his girl pregnant, what was her name, Tanya or Tammy, or some shit, I don't know some shit like that. Anyway, he dropped out; you know? My man went to Monarch he's like 16 it's all good, he's got this job, they tell him you keep it in line, maybe you get some overtime, we take care of you, you know? It's like this is how we do it, we're going to hook you up, you know? Motherfucker thought made it big like Fuck, man, 'no degree no problem, I'm set' you know? But I saw him two months later at the store and he was just, man, he was fuckin', dead dude. He was like zombie apocalypse and shit. I mean, it was no joke. Motherfucker was gone. It was like that place made some bacon out of him, man. For real."

The group fell silent.

"So, what happened, he quit?" asked Ricardo.

"Quit. Yeah, he quit all right. He put a pistol in his mouth and called it quits right there."

After a moment, Ricardo shrugged his shoulders.

"Hey, man, some people just can't handle their shit. Not me. I'm doing my time, get my check, and maybe I will get some discount on the bacon because that's what's up."

They continued to laugh, joke and talk about the girls they liked, the jobs they hated, and in to the wee hours of the morning they had expounded on the ills of the world, and of Moser, and had collectively knocked off a six-pack and the rest of the pulled pork.

CHAPTER 34

August 2014

Ricardo

Forget that shit.

Ricardo told himself as he pulled his car into the lot at Monarch's meatpacking plant. Max, he reasoned, was just jealous. Only job he can get is a janitor at the hospital, probably cleaning some old man's shit. He said to himself. The image made him chuckle.

And fuck Andre. He thought he remembered Andre. He was probably fucked up, anyway. Jose thought he remembered rumors that Andre was a pussy. Who knows? People have all kinds of fucked up shit they don't show you. This was a good job. He would make it a good job and if Andre couldn't handle it, well, that was Andre.

"Fuck that," he said out loud to himself as he left the car and walked to the entrance. "I'm a man, and a man brings home the bacon!"

But he would learn that bringing home the bacon wasn't as easy as he thought. On his second day at work, Ricardo was gathering the pigs, herding them into the chute, which was like herding cats. Only these cats were three hundred pounds of obstinate screaming stubborn fucks! No wonder they called motherfuckers pig headed! He thought to himself.

It took Ricardo by surprise at first that the pigs so persistently disobeyed the prompts to follow his directions. They didn't cower in fear, and they didn't walk on a leash like a dog. The motherfuckers, he would swear to God, the motherfuckers would try to outwit him! Swear on his grandmother (rest her soul) and all things holy, these little fuckers were strategizing ways to avoid being corralled.

Well, he thought, I wouldn't come here either if they weren't paying me, and all things considered I get the better end of the deal. But on this day, it was one pig who caught Ricardo's eye.

When he was ten his dad surprised him one Christmas with a puppy. Pudge, as he would be called affectionately, was not only Ricardo's almost constant companion, he was all that remained of his father who died of cancer two years later. Ricardo shared everything with Pudge, would even give him the best cuts of meat from his plate when no one was looking.

Ricardo didn't get all sentimental over dogs in general, but Pudge, he could tell, was a thinking, knowing dog. Pudge could do something Ricardo hadn't known a dog to do before or since. He would look at you and it was clear he was in the know. They had entire conversations, he and Pudge, without saying a single word. Pudge had this look that said, *"I got your back, and I know you got mine."* It was a look that also seemed to say, *"stick around, I got things to teach you."*

Ricardo did stick around, and would have stuck around longer, but the day came when Pudge, at the ripe old age of eight and a half, also succumbed to cancer, Ricardo was devastated. His decision to euthanize the dog was an act of mercy, as poor pudge was now anything but pudgy. And even then, Ricardo would have continued to hand feed his dog the canine equivalent of a Boost shake, had the day not come when Pudge used that special stare to look Ricardo in the eye and say "Enough."

And it was this pig. He thought, I swear to God this motherfucker is looking me in the face. In the eyes. The way Pudge used to. The look that says *"We can come to some kind of arrangement here; we are both reasonable men."*

He stopped, just for a moment to consider, but it was a moment too long. A middle-aged white man in a Monarch Industries shirt spotted his hesitation.

"I'm a tell you straight, m'kay?" his supervisor laid it out for him. "This here is a serious high-volume operation and we don't got time for anyone slowing it down. You pussy out, you going to get all soft and start backing' down, then you best better leave and let someone with the balls to do the job step in, m'kay?"

Ricardo cringed at the resemblance between his supervisor and the annoying cartoon character from a show his brother used to watch, *South Park*.

The man with the annoying voice went on.

"The minute you start thinking that pig is some cute little pet, that sombitch going to maul your ass over, and you'll slow down the whole line. This is how we do it here. You ain't Cesar Milan, and this ain't the Pig Whisperer. You get it out of your head that this is Old MacDonald's little farm, m'kay?"

Ricardo's hands began to sweat. He didn't want to get on this guy's bad side, but didn't think he was really expecting an answer. He stood, frozen, waiting for the supervisor to just back off. He didn't.

"You are here to make bacon and pork and sausages and not to play with the little farm animals. And you're going to see some shit, and hear some shit, and you best better leave it where you found it, m'kay?"

Ricardo nodded, eyes down. He felt his cheeks getting hot. His coworkers were glancing at him. The supervisor was zeroing in on him and continued to rant relentlessly.

"You better learn fast. You take charge of the animal. So when you need that sombitch to run in the direction you need him to run, this is how we do it, you take this here…" he said, picking up something that looked like a tuning fork, only wider, and jabbed it at the pig.

Jabbed it right into the eyes.

The staring pig. The pig with Pudge's wise, sentient eyes. The pig who just a moment ago held Ricardo's gaze pleading. But now there was no pleading. Only electricity and shocks, and blood and screaming.

PART III

Metamorphosis

Summer 2016

CHAPTER 35

June 25, 2016

Ricardo

The memory shook Ricardo, and he realized then that he had been sweating. Lost in recollection of his first days at Monarch. How did he managed to get so fucked up that he would lose his values, everything he believed in, to try to be one of them? And that fucker had canned his ass anyway, he thought now.

The call had come in last night. Mitch. *Two faced bitch*, Ricardo thought. "Don't bother to come in tomorrow." The little bitch had said. Tried to throw him under the bus for "sexual harassment" and the entire time he was the one fucking around with Kashira. Ricardo thought now that he should have known better.

"And don't go running your mouth either," Mitch had said.

Well fuck, Ricardo thought, what did he have to lose?

He picked up the phone and dialed.

"Cam Burton here."

"Hello, Mr. Burton. My name is Ricardo. I met you outside of Monarch Industries a while back?"

"Yes, thank you for calling me."

"Yeah, I'm ready to talk now."

They planned to meet at Ricardo's. Fuck those little bitches, Ricardo thought as he hung up the phone.

CHAPTER 36

July 14, 2016

Dierdre

Dierdre was excited about the hospital's new initiative, bringing therapy dogs in to interact with the inmates. It was the initiative of the week much like the soup of the day over at the PigPen Bar and Grill and so whether you wanted Beef Barley or Clam Chowder if Pork and Bean stew was on the menu then it was Pork and Beans you would have.

Dierdre loved dogs, she had a maltipoo back home and would carry Bella around in one of those designer handbags. She would take Bella to the store, even to a movie once. She left Bella behind when she got married. Her husband was more of a cat person, and so her parents now kept an eye on the dog.

Dierdre reviewed the backstory on the team assigned to the Forensic unit. Team in this case referred to the therapy dog and the animal's handler. A man from the deep south with a head injury-what were they in for? With a flash of shame, she scolded herself mentally for being a snob. Bobby Ray's dog, referred to by the *Wounded Healers* program as his "teammate" was named Dodger. She was not sure what kind of dog Dodger was, but imagined him to be some kind of hunter. Hunting dogs were big in Georgia, weren't they? A sleek, cuddly hound. The professional in her was eager to see how inmates would respond to this animal-assisted therapy, and part of her looked forward to having a dog in the office because who doesn't love dogs?

Approaching the unit's entrance, she heard the commotion.

"You can't bring a dog in here!" came the booming voice of a man Dierdre considered one of the more belligerent COs, Hank. She felt her blood pressure rise. The staff had been briefed on the new initiative. They knew what to expect.

"I'm here as a volunteer," Came a calm reply.

"Oh, is that right? Because visiting hours didn't start yet, and you don't just get to bring your dog in-"

"Hank," Dierdre cut in, "this gentleman is part of the new program. You got an e-mail about it. He's got authorization to come with me."

As she looked up and saw their first volunteer a sick feeling came over her. She understood now why Hank had chosen to pretend he didn't know about the program. She couldn't prove it, but from the jokes she heard him tell the other officers, and the way she had seen him treat certain inmates, she could safely assume he had deliberately feigned ignorance to give this man a hard time.

Standing at the desk, confirmation letter in one hand, leash in the other, stood a young African-American man. Dierdre felt ashamed of her colleague's behavior, but didn't know what to say in response.

"I'm Bobby Ray. Nice to meet you," He remained calm and stoic.

The leash moved then, and her eyes shifted. She noticed for the first time that beside the man walked a lumbering porky dog with shiny black fur and an enormous head. It was perhaps the ugliest dog she had ever seen, she thought to herself.

He was square and meaty and had a mouth like a Pac Man. Huge jaws that she imagined could devour a person leaving nothing but slobber behind. They made the expected introductory small talk while she walked with him back to the area where he would meet with Collin Griffen.

"What kind of dog is umm..."

"Dodger," He began, saving her the embarrassment of stumbling through her memory to recollect the dog's name. "Pit mix. He was rescued from a shelter and trained as a service dog." he said beaming with pride. She winced at the reference to the dog's genetics. Pit bulls, she had always heard, were dangerous. Her reaction had been instant and then hoped he hadn't noticed.

Whether he had or had not noticed he didn't say. One thing she would come to learn was that aside from any of the stereotypes she was told about the deep south, it was still a land of manners.

"They actually let pit bulls become service dogs?" she asked in astonishment, regretting the words immediately.

"Yes ma'am. Pit bulls get a bad rap, you see. They are extremely smart, obedient."

"If you were of a certain character, you want to make your living by fighting animals, who you going to pick? You find yourself a nice, loyal, intelligent, strong dog, and you teach him to be a killer. He will obey you. He will kill. Now you take that same dog and you teach him to be a second brain to someone like me, and he will still serve you faithfully. He will be the second brain. That's what Dodger has been to me, you see? He is true to his breed, patient, loyal, and teachable."

Dierdre tried to appear polite though skepticism loomed. Bobby Ray didn't seem to notice. He went on.

"I got him through *Wounded Healers* a few years back. Five years to be exact. He's saved my life a million times and aced his Therapy Dog training, didn't you boy?"

As if on cue Dodger looked up at his man, panting through a smile so big Dierdre thought for a moment that it might sever the top half of his face from the bottom half.

"This here is the best dog you ever want to meet, but I'm partial to him. I think he'll do a great job here. He was in jail, in a way. Being at the shelter and all."

"What was his crime?" testing her hypothesis that deep inside pit bulls were killers waiting to unleash their fury on the unsuspecting. To end up in a shelter, she assumed. He must've done something really bad. Bit a kid's face, maybe, or threatened his family.

"His crime was being a pit bull. A family had him. Then they had to move. They couldn't get an apartment anywhere that would allow pit bulls. It's a shame. They probably loved him and all. I can't imagine what I would have done if I had to make that choice. Did you know there are entire cities trying to ban pit bulls and ordering veterinarians to euthanize all the pit bulls in the towns? It's like Nazi Germany or something!"

Dierdre hadn't heard that, and despite her continued mistrust of this big galumph of a dog, she had to admit the notion of mass extermination of a species seemed wrong.

"You can go on ahead and pet him if you like. I can tell you're a dog person," Bobby Ray said.

Dierdre tried. It was an awkward moment. Like when, as a child, she had been commanded to kiss her great Aunt Hildy. She remembers approaching with some trepidation, not wanting to offend, but also not knowing just what would happen if she got too close to the wrinkled face of her aunt. Only now the wrinkled face wasn't a kind elderly lady with whiskers on her chin and perfume wafting from her neck, but a wrinkled black face. A snouty, toothy grinning wrinkly black face with perky ears... all the better to hear you with...

She approached the dog, becoming fearful that even fear itself would give her away and trigger the dog to respond with aggression. But he continued to sit patiently, smiling up at her. There was something about his eyes. They seemed to speak to her and say.

"Yes, I know you don't really trust me. It's ok, I'm not offended, you don't know any better. You're just doing what you've been told... It's all good, I forgive you and I love you, anyway." And it was this realization that made Dierdre realize she was acting on the same ignorant assumptions as Hank. She felt disgusting.

CHAPTER 37

July 2016

Collin

"Hon....?" Collin heard his voice echo down the hallway. Had the house always had that echo? He didn't notice it until now. "Babe? Where's Quinn? I can't find the baby, hon, is he with you?" He heard his footsteps echo one at a time. Walking down the hallway, when did the hallway become so long? Collin wondered. It was a small house, all they could afford to rent. A reasonable rent because Collin had agreed to make some upgrades.

The hallway had only connected two bedrooms upstairs, but now it went on and on, doors on both sides. Had they really had all these extra bedrooms? He wondered how he failed to notice it before. Pretty lucky to have a house with so many rooms. Maybe have a bigger family. Some day. Why wasn't Jolene answering him?

"Hey, babe? Jolene? Quinn? Where are you guys?"

He heard a noise on the other side of a closed door. The door hadn't been painted in some time. It was cracked and chipped. I need to fix this. Collin told himself. My next day off, I'll fix this.

He swung the door open. Nausea overtook him. The room was filled with bloodstains. On the walls. Puddles of blood on the floor. Little plastic farm animals, Quinn's toys, soaked in blood. On the floor, Quinn sat with his back to Collin, whimpering.

"Baby? Quinn? Little man? What's wrong?"

Quinn turned to face his father. Collin saw that in his hands he was cradling the lifeless body of a pig.

Collin was startled awake.

He turned side to side and screamed for Jolene. Screamed for his son. They didn't come. Strangers came. With clipboards. And a needle.

CHAPTER 38

July 14, 2016

Bobby Ray

When the stress of his losses caught up with him, Bobby Ray would hear his therapist's words in his mind. "Think of the last time you really felt happy. Remember what gave you hope."

Returning home from the Forensic Mental health unit that day, he played the video through in his head. The last time he felt hope. It was earlier that year. April or March? He couldn't recall exactly. But he remembered the important parts of the scene. He remembered the excitement as he stood in line. The line stretched out the door and around the block on an unseasonably cold spring morning. The wind howled and at times rain was even coming down, but people stood in line. They gathered, and they waited.

They were here to see Bernie Sanders during his campaign trail for the Democratic primary. A candidate for president stopping in this small city in Georgia, no one could remember someone so important coming to this town, he made the trip all the way back home from Mosier for the event. He was thrilled that Sanders would be in his hometown, talking to regular folks. Working class people.

Sanders was either Christ or antichrist, depending on who you might ask. Dave Williams, the owner of the local bed-and-breakfast tavern and gun store hated the man. Called him a no good fuckin' commie and insisted any pinko sombitches who were crazy enough to vote for that motherfucker had best better pack their bags and move to Russia. But Bobby Ray also know full well that he was also the subject of Dave Williams's foul vocabulary. Though Williams wouldn't dare utter some of those words to his face. Still, Bobby Ray thought he had noticed a new boldness coming over Williams, and others like him, in recent months.

But today, that didn't matter to him. He was inspired already, just by the number of people from all walks of life, who stood with him in line to hear the Senator speak.

To Bobby Ray, Sanders was a hero. Whether he won or lost, it was enough to know that somebody big, somebody important, somebody who could influence and change things, was listening. He got it. He called out the bankers responsible for the vacant boarded-up houses that were now a common in this part of Georgia. He might wear a suit, and he might be a Yankee, but he talked about the working people in the voice of the working people.

It had been cold, unusually cold for the season, as Bobby Ray, and Dodger had stood in line. Over time Bobby Ray had learned to pace himself so the migraines and nausea were less frequent, and his fatigue better controlled. With Dodger's help he was reminded to take breaks, naps and rest periods. But on that day, he had ignored much of Dodger's pleas to take care of himself. He had been standing in line already for an hour and was starting to see double.

He cupped his hands over his eyes, squinting and cringing and doing his best to keep his pounding head from deterring him. A woman nearby noticed his growing discomfort.

"Sir," she said gently, "are you ok, sir?"

He couldn't make eye contact; the daylight was now piercing his eyes.

"Yes ma'am. It's a migraine comin' on, but that's ok. It's worth it. I really want to see Mr. Sanders."

"Yes, it's a great day, ain't it. Tell you what, I'm not trying to be nosy, but I see you got your service dog with you. Did you know there is a separate line for folks with disabilities to get right in?"

Bobby Ray hadn't known. With the exception of his service dog he didn't like to make a big deal out of his limitations, believing that the more he focused on what was wrong with him the less he could move ahead with what was right with him.

But the thought kept nagging at him. If he didn't take care of himself in advance, he would be in worse shape later. He might not even be able to drive home if it gets bad. Sometimes in the past he had to sleep an hour here or there in his car when it got so bad, he couldn't see or drive. He thanked the woman and went in search of the line for people with disabilities.

Once on the inside someone from the Sanders campaign led he and Dodger to a section reserved for the handicapped. This section was right in the center of the arena, the three rows directly behind where Senator Sanders would speak were largely occupied and as he didn't know how people would respond to the presence of a service dog, a pit bull no less, he took a seat toward the back of the section and Dodger settled in at his side.

He took some of his emergency headache medicine and closed his eyes while the music blared from speakers and the arena filled up around him. As he listened to the music, Burning Down the House it was now, Revolution the song before, he felt a tap on his shoulders.

"Excuse me, sir" the woman began, "this seating is only for people with disabilities."

"Yes," he replied politely, "I know, ma'am," He gestured to Dodger sitting at his feet sporting his "Service Animal" vest.

"Well, I'm sorry… but you don't look disabled."

No, he thought. He recalled how for so long it had been a struggle to adjust to his brain injury and PTSD because they were significant conditions which left only internal scars. No one who saw him one moment to the next would not understand what he lived through and what he lived with every day.

It used to make him angry, having to justify, to prove himself to others, then having to prove his limitations to others, just to have his voice heard. The story was familiar enough. Being a Black man required constant justification. Why are you here? Where are you going? Were you aware that you had a license plate light out? Just what business do you think you have loitering in the library parking lot?

If it wasn't terrifying, the irony would have been laughable. The cop had been called because he "looked suspicious" as he stood outside the library one day when he was sixteen. Waiting for it to open.

It was hard enough having to constantly be reminded of his need to justify his existence, his presence in places white people didn't expect him to show up in. Now, because of his disability, there was more to explain. More to justify, and more to test his patience. To have the doctors at the VA, his primary care doc, his boss at work, anyone understands why he suddenly wasn't acting like himself.

Finally, he stopped trying to prove anything to anyone. He had come a long way and owed much of his progress to Dodger. The noise that filled the stadium was deafening, yet it filled Bobby Ray with a kind of hope, exhilaration and joy he hadn't known in a long time. This man with the crazy white hair was telling them, all of them, he was telling him, Bobby Ray, this is our country, this is our revolution.

"Whether I get elected," Senator Sanders had said, "it's up to all of us, all of us to take action....to build a better America..."

Bobby Ray took in everything Mr. Sanders had to say. He took in the crowd's cheers, the messages of love and hope. And it was one of the happiest days of his life.

His time in the service taught him a lot about the world and about things he didn't care about before he enlisted. He always wanted to help people and would spend extra time after class helping his friends with their homework or listening to their problems. He wanted to give people some hope.

He didn't know how to give hope to a psychotic man potentially facing the chair. A man who had lost everything, and by his own doing. Yet if one man could try to inspire a nation to not give up, no matter how bad things had gotten, he could find some way to get through to Collin.

He had to.

* * *

July 25th, 2016

Mr. Cameron Burton, Esq.,

It has come to our attention that you have made several inquiries of Monarch Employees. Your client is now a former employee. His incarceration is a result of an incident which occurred outside of work hours and off of the premises of Monarch Industries. Therefore, we order you to cease and desist any further contact with our employees.

Please note that if you are found on the grounds of Monarch Industries for any reason, you will be charged with both harassment and trespassing.

Regards,

Anita Thompson

Monarch Industries Legal Director

Chapter 39

July 27, 2016

Finch

"Hello?"

"Hello Mr. Michael Finch, please?"

"Speaking."

"Mr. Finch, thank you for taking my call. My name is Belinda Tyler and I am with the *Mosier Tribune*. I am calling to get your statement on the arrest of Collin Griffen…"

The line is silent for a moment.

"Mr. Finch?"

"Yes, well, comment, what comment, what can I say? I don't know who you are talking about."

"He is one of your employees."

"Well, we are a very large company Miss, uhh, Miss.."

"Tyler, Mrs. Tyler"

"Yes, we are a very large company, and I am a very busy man and so you will have to get to the point…"

"Collin Griffen, the Mosier man who is accused of killing his baby, I want to get your…"

"Well, I hardly see what I have to do with this unfortunate tragedy. We are a large corporation, we have many employees, and we do thorough screenings, but what can I say? There are some unstable people out there…"

"Would you say there is a high turnover rate?"

Silence.

Then, "I am a very busy man with work to do"

CHAPTER 40

July 30, 2016

Ronnie

Ronnie slumped down on the barstool. Covered in sweat from the late July heat, he had walked to his home away from home to drink in peace and reminisce about the anniversary of the moon landing. He didn't give a second thought to the fact that he was over a week late. All the days had flowed together. Beatin' them commies to the moon was all he had on his mind this afternoon. He wanted to feel good about it. To feel good about something.

The surrounding conversations quieted. He looked out of the corner of his eyes to see his fellow patrons, What's-His-Name with the Harley, the Lady-with-the-Cowboy-Boots-and-No-Tits, and ZZ-Top-Bearded-Man, to name a few, looked to each other, then to him, then to each other. It reminded him of the awkward glances people make when someone farts in an elevator.

"What'll it be today, Ronnie?" Jimmy, the bartender, broke the tension.

The crowd of familiar no-names went back to their chatter and Ronnie's eyes met the gaze of the younger man tending bar.

I wish a buck was still silver, if you really wanna know, Ronnie thought.

"Today ain't special. I'll take the usual," Ronnie answered.

Jimmy turned his back for a moment, returning with a tall glass of Yuengling.

"Here you go. How you holding up?" Jimmy asked.

"What, like anything's new?" Ronnie croaked. He took a generous gulp of his favorite medicine, turned toward Harley-Man and No-Tits, and belched.

"Glad the situation hasn't caused you to lose your charm," Jimmy replied, more teasing than sarcastic. "But if there is anything you or your family needs, you let me know."

"What I need," Ronnie replied, "is another beer."

In a small town, reputation is its own currency, yet his motto since childhood had been "fuck 'em if they can't take a joke." But now that his son was incarcerated, his grandson, dead, he had begun to notice. He couldn't help noticing the accusing stares and awkward silences that followed everywhere he went.

This is Collin's doing. He told himself initially. Boy ain't been nothing but trouble. But recently a new voice began to creep around the edges of his mind. Maybe he had brought some of this on.

From the overhead speaker, Merle came to the rescue. Back to not caring about what anyone thought of him, Ronnie's hoarse voice belted out, "*We don't some marijuanaaaaaaa in Muskooogeeeee ....*"

CHAPTER 41

August 1, 2016

Cam

"Something wrong with the way I cook now?" his wife's voice cut like a knife, pulling him back from the obsessive thoughts of his client, the web he had become entangled in. Cam hadn't noticed that he barely touched his plate as he sat staring into his work. He had promised Donna they could barbecue. Low key, just the two of them. Yet he had been unable to pull himself away from his research and she had prepared all the food. All of his favorites, potato salad, corn and greens, sausage, all sat untouched.

She had even made up his plate just the way he liked, all food separated, nothing touching anything else. Each portion measured, spaced evenly apart. Clean. Orderly. But uncustomary for Cam, becoming cold.

Summer isn't over yet, he reasoned to himself to assuage the guilt. Yet the ribs no longer looked appetizing to him. He didn't like the way the Griffen case had begun consuming him. It was bad enough his wife hounded him about sleeping with his Steno book under the pillow in case an idea came to him.

Cam himself didn't care for the laptop. He preferred his trusty steno pad. He didn't entirely trust new technology. he had so many questions since his visit with Matt. It was as if he had stumbled into an underworld hidden yet so essential to the world everyone inhabited, except those hippies who didn't eat meat.

His conversation with the young animal rights attorney had haunted him. Like a dog with a bone, he devoured a stack of library books. *Slaughter, The Chain, The Meat Racket, Project Animal Farm.*

What he found was so startling, so amazing, so blatant…how could it be real? He was making a strained effort to be present. To even remember the remark his wife had just made.

"No no, it's not your cooking, its, this is fascinating. Just incredible…."

After a moment, she prompted him.

"What's incredible? Obviously not the ribs I made you because you haven't touched them…and they're your favorite!"

"It's incredible. Meat production. A whole world, Donna, and its hidden. Think of that! In 2016, when no thought is private, when meals debut on social media newsfeeds, how is it possible that this industry has pulled the wool over people's eyes?"

If what he read was true, and his Inner Lawyer held tight to the supposition that no information is valid unless it can be proven … he may have a case implicating Monarch in Collin's behavior. Nothing else seemed to make sense. The boy's dad was a drunk and a bully, so were many people's parents. He had wandered again. Her voice brought him back.

"What does that have to do with anything? You joining PETA now?"

"What? No. The Griffen case. He worked for Monarch. From what I am learning, it's possible he developed PTSD from the working conditions there. Look, right here is another article, 'Growing evidence suggests long lasting psychological disturbances in those who work in abattoirs.' So many correlations, So much that it was being compared to the damaging effects of combat and PTSD in veterans. It's just incredible!"

The underworld of meat production both fascinated and disgusted him. Documented accounts of exploitation of illegal immigrants, sexual abuse of both human workers and animals en route to their deaths. Reports of injuries, deaths even. Accounts of substance abuse, suicide and increases in violent behavior.

He was lost in thought again and didn't notice the flat look on her face. She had no sympathy for the young man who killed his own child when her own baby had been born dead. Cam had deduced this, though Donna hadn't gone so far as to say it outright.

He knew the case was weighing on their already strained marriage. As had become customary, he didn't notice her expression and continued pouring through the stack of books he had checked out of the library. Scattered in with the various titles on slaughterhouses and industrialized farming were piles of papers, studies from around the world.

"One study correlated the opening of a slaughterhouse with ensuing increases in violent behavior and aggression toward humans in that town."

The sound of metal clanging snapped him out of his soliloquy, and he realized he was now alone in the room.

CHAPTER 42

August 5, 2016

Cam

The cigarette hardened voice on the phone had described the location of Cam's next interview as just outside of Mosier, a town he never heard of, it might as well have been called Deliverance. Cam pulled up to a trailer with so much stuff piled outside he couldn't imagine what would be found inside.

A kind older woman answered the door and identified herself as Dottie. Numerous holes in Dottie's smile revealed missing and stained teeth, the mark of a heavy smoker and one who likely didn't have dental insurance. Cam reminded himself that he was overdue for a trip to the dentist, although he this dialog internal. Dottie led Cam into the trailer. His senses adjusted to the heavy smoke and a sharp scent that greets all who enter with a message- "Welcome, cats live here." Dottie's husband Brian was seated in a recliner in their living room.

While smoke dimmed the light in the room, the wood paneling on the walls also created a dark atmosphere. Any light that came in the windows did little to further illuminate the interior. Still, Cam could see photos hung on the walls. A much younger and more vivacious looking version of Brian and Dottie on their wedding day. Another photo of Brian standing proudly amidst what appeared to be the rest of a bowling league.

Looking at the weathered face of the man who now sat before him, Cam wondered at what kind of unrelenting storm had taken away that glint of pride and vitality.

Brian now looked withered, as if something had eaten him up and spit him back out. He recognized the look. Often the beast responsible was poverty, the storm, industry.

"I'll give you gentleman your privacy," Dottie said and with a slight bow slipped into a back room. Cam reflected that Dottie hadn't given him the snapshot look. She hadn't seemed afraid or confused to see a Black man standing at her door. Brian was a different story. Cam could read suspicion in his wary gaze.

"I appreciate you taking the time to meet with me," Cam hoped his calm demeanor would put Brian at ease.

"Nobody can find out I talked to you. I don't know if you understand how important it is," Brian's fear was palpable. Was he having second thoughts now after I drove all this way? Cam wondered. Hoping the answer was no.

Cam took a breath to steady himself, conscious to eliminate the urgency from his voice before proceeding.

"I intend to keep your statement confidential. This is a commitment I take very seriously. You don't have to answer any questions you don't want to, but I would greatly appreciate it if you would."

"How is it that this is going to help you anyway?" Brian asked.

"I am representing a man accused of a violent act. He has no prior history. Like you, he worked in meatpacking. I think there is a link between the job and his breakdown. You and as many others as will come forward, even confidentially. If we can establish a reasonable link between the duties performed in the slaughter-house and psychological decline, it can make a big difference not only in this case, but potentially in future legislation."

Brian snorted.

"Forgive me, man, I don't mean any disrespect. It's just that… you don't know Monarch."

Cam thought he saw the frail looking man tremble as he uttered the name of his former employer. Brian continued.

"They own the town. They own the world for all I know. They have a net cast wide. You have no idea how much is caught up in their net."

"I didn't say he worked for Mon-" Cam started.

"You don't have to tell me. Who else? Look, would I love to make the world a better place? Sure. Do I think there is a snow-ball's chance in hell of it ever happening?"

"Luckily for you," Cam cut in gently "it will be my uphill battle to fight. All I need is a sense of the duties. The day-to-day work-ings of the slaughterhouse. What were the responsibilities…"

"You got it all wrong," Brian interjected.

"You're thinkin' these guys got a tough gig, cutting up animals. Dealing in blood and shit. But a nurse sees blood. A doctor, cops, lots of people see death. But not everybody stands in the position of doling it out."

Cam remained steady as if his own energy could ground the man as he began to tremble. Brian lit a cigarette with unsteady hands and Cam waited for him to continue.

"It's a big fuckin' machine. All of Monarch. no heart. No…." he struggled for the right word before continuing. "No reverence," Brian began, then he paused for a moment. "Can you imagine the worst dive bar? Where ain't nothin' off limits. Where there's rules, but no one pays attention. Like the wild west." Cam was grateful to only be able to conjure such a scene in his imagination.

Brian continued.

"So yeah, Its hard slitting an animal's throat. Everything in you resists doing it. It's as fucked up as French kissing your sister ok? You hold that knife or the stunner or an electrical prod in your hand and you face off with someone. You know that pig is no fuckin' toy, man. Its alive. And you see all kinds of thoughts and feelings in their eyes."

He took a drag.

"You have any pets at home?"

"No, not now, but I did growing up."

As if on cue, one of what Cam's olfactory senses told him were many cats sauntered into the living room. Grey and hefty, the long-haired cat peeked at Cam from behind a table and then darted over to join Brian in the recliner. The cat jumped into Brian's lap and settled in, large yellow eyes set on Cam.

Brian pet the cat thoughtfully and continued, as if he had just been given a prop to continue his story.

"You ever have to take one of 'em to the vet, but he won't go? Cause he's like 'I got my own agenda and I don't give a fuck about some vaccine' right?" Cam nodded his head as Brian continued.

"When that cat or that dog doesn't want to do what you want him to do, he's going to fight you, man. He's got a will of his own. But, hey, you love the little fucker, you spend all day getting him to go poopy on the papers or get into the carrier to go to the vet. Maybe you pick him up, right? If he's a good pet and you're not a total asshole, you work with him because you think you're doing something for his own good, right?"

He gestured to the grey mass of fur in his lap. "Take Sheila here," he continued, "when she needs to get checked out, it takes a good two days of catnip and treats just to get her ready, then we gotta chase her and get her into a crate. And she's only ten pounds."

Cam nodded. "I bet it takes some maneuvering. Herding cats, as they say."

"You bet! And even then, I'm lucky if she don't take my whole hand off," Brian let out a husky laugh, then a series of deep coughs.

Brian went on.

"Well, imagine a thousand little Sheilas," he scratched under her chin and she purred audibly. Cam tried to imagine replicas, Sheila clones, roaming through the living room.

"Except," Brian voice pulled Cam's attention back, "except instead of ten pounds, they're eight hundred pounds. A thousand pounds. That's how it is at Monarch they bring thousands of animals. Each day. The pigs are enormous, bred to so big it ain't good for them. A thousand pounds. You aren't picking them up and putting them nowhere. And pigs aren't like pets. They aren't there to serve you like a golden retriever, you know? They are smart sonsabitches, they'll run you over to get free. We've even had one pig break free and you know what he done?"

Cam didn't,

"That little sombitch turned right around and unlatch the other pens trying to set all the other fuckers free! Can you believe that?" Brian cackled and the coughing fit returned. He took a drink of water and steadied himself before going on.

"So, you start off doing a job no man, anywhere else… well maybe a man who goes to war. They train a soldier in a war to kill. A man in a slaughterhouse is there to kill, and that's probably the only times in a man's life that he is called to do a job that is unnatural for a man to do."

Brian took another drag from his cigarette and stared off in the distance for a moment. Then he continued.

"At least a soldier on some level it's like they know they are being of service. They are heroes. But a man whose existence is about takin a life. What the hell prepares a man for that? In the army you get basic training, right? But at Monarch, you kill and strip all reminders of life from a thousand animals per hour for ten, sometimes twelve hours a day."

He took another long drag on his cigarette and Cam wondered if he was really jonesing or if he paused at this time to let it sink in, or both. Cam did the math. One thousand animals an hour. At ten hours, that's ten thousand to twelve thousand animals per day.

"You ever do something you didn't like at first, but you had to do it so much that it just become, I don't know, it doesn't faze you anymore? Like you don't even feel it anymore? I don't know what a man who ain't never been there could even think of to understand. It's so… unnatural."

"Indeed," Cam said softly, taking notes. Brian went on.

"Back in the day the farmer might kill some cows and chickens, maybe some pigs. He knew not to get all sentimental, but there was a sense of connection. My granddaddy was a farmer, my man, I know it. But when you speed things up…you just get a different feel to it. It's like the way these kids drive these days, you know? Like when you first get into a car and you're all careful you obey every single rule, and you have pride in your car you know? But then traffic keep speeding up. It keeps getting faster; you stop caring and you get sloppy…it's not a clean job and my man we don't get no training but here's your prod, have a nice day. It's not just Monarch, it's everywhere. No training. Guys quit the chain on all the time. You got an entirely new team every three to four months, you understand?"

Brian shifted in his seat, his face becoming more solemn. He continued now in a monotone, his eyes stared vacantly through Cam, no longer looking at him.

"So, these pigs don't obey you just because you're there for a paycheck, you know? So, there's things you gotta do to get em in the chute. You stun em or you kick em or you shock em. I saw dudes stick a prod into a pig's ass. Is that necessary? Hell no. But you already playing the reaper. Some dudes, a lot of dudes, they play worse than the reaper, they turn right into the devil."

Cam nodded silently to encourage him to continue.

"First you got to decide that the pigs aren't your friends. You got to ignore how smart they are. Maybe you got to even see them as your enemy. Do you think a single soldier could fire a gun at his enemy if he didn't first learn to call him a red or a gook or a rag head?"

After a moment, Cam spoke.

"How long did you work at Monarch before becoming desensitized?"

"Before what?"

Bad move, Cam reminded himself.

"Before you got numb to all the killing."

"It wasn't but my third, maybe fourth week there that I realized that it isn't just the pig that became a thing. I was nothing better than a thing too, man and that was what fucked me up."

Then Brian asked a question of Cam.

"How long did your man work at Monarch?"

"Almost a year," Cam answered.

"He use drugs? Drink?"

"No, not that we can tell, not to any great degree."

Brian pondered this and said.

"Your man worked for Monarch and it took him a year to lose his shit? I don't know what he did, but he must have been a saint."

* * *

Mosier Tribune

Family, Police asking for help in the disappearance of Mosier Man

August 15, 2016

Jose Hernandez, a 24-year-old Mosier resident, has been reported missing by his family after he did not return home from work Tuesday night, August 13th, 2016. Jose is 5 foot 6 approximately 130 pounds and has a short goatee. He was last seen wearing a navy-blue hooded sweatshirt, blue jeans, work boots. He is described as a quiet man and is not suspected to be involved with drugs or illegal activity.

Police were told he worked his shift at Monarch Industries meat processing plant on Tuesday and was last seen at approximately six p.m. by a peer as he left the facility. "He is a quiet guy, no one here hardly knows him, he keeps to himself, not really. Sometimes people come here, and you work beside them, but you know, they aren't really part of the team," Robert Foley, a supervisor at Monarch, told the Tribune.

If you see Jose Hernandez, pictured above, or have any information as to his whereabouts please notify police immediately at 1-555-9785.

* * *

Cam flipped through the pages of the paper. He didn't just read the news like some folks did; he liked to savor his time with the news. He hated scrolling through the flashy headlines online like so many of his peers. Cam had sensibilities from an older generation and he needed to hold the paper, smell the ink, and engage in his perfectionist's ritual of turning the large pages while trying not to have the bottoms of the pages wrinkle up on him.

His wife laughed at this habit, but it was this ritual that brought him a gift from the law Gods this morning. Cam wasn't didn't give credence to woo-woo much, but he believed in what his grandmother called 'the Chill'.

When he got the Chill, he knew it was an alert. Like a notification from God's universal social network. He would get the Chill and it would run down from the base of his skull to the small of his back and he knew it was time to stop, look and listen.

Something is here, the Chill would tell him, and he never doubted it.

He got the Chill while reading the article about Jose Hernandez he knew not to dismiss it as a coincidence.

* * *

Cam pulled up to the house on Peachtree Lane. He recalled the words of a stand-up comic "If you live on 'Fox Run' then you know they killed off all the foxes that used to run there to build your house…"

It wasn't funny now. No peach trees in sight. The block lined with houses built in the 1930s. All needing repair, but unlikely to get it anytime soon. *Just like the rest of us,* he thought to himself. The Hernandez home was a two-story in a row of other buildings lined up tight as if preparing to board a truck to greener pastures.

Rosa met him at the door.

"Can I fix you some tea or coffee, Mr. Burton?"

"Please, call me Cam, and coffee would be great."

Cam noticed the religious artwork and candles depicting various saints and the Virgin Mary. A corner table held a photo of a young man Cam recognized as Jose, surrounded by lit candles, a rosary hung from a corner of the picture frame.

"Mama's old school," Rosa commented apologetically.

"You are more of a pragmatist?"

"I believe God helps those who help themselves. I would do anything to find Jose. I know something bad happened. It's not like him to just go off somewhere."

"Ms. Hernandez…"

"Rosa, please."

"Rosa, I have to ask you some difficult questions. Did Jose use drugs, or drink excessively?"

"No, no. He would not," Rosa poured coffee into a mug and handed it to Cam. She gestured for him to sit at the table in the kitchen cluttered with knick-knacks and old family photos.

"Addiction can be hidden. I have represented many young people who, for example, have gotten into the grips of pain killers and these are good kids from good families. How can you be sure about Jose?"

"Our dad. When he drinks, he becomes a monster. Jose goes out of his way to be the opposite of my dad in everything. I mean, they ended up working for the same place, but that was because Jose couldn't get any other jobs. But he's anti-alcohol, he's anti-drugs. Even as a kid, he would sneak around when Dad passed out and he would dump out the bottles. Only the open ones, though, so dad would just assume he forgot that he drank the whole thing the next day, you know?"

Cam nodded, making a mental note of how similar this sounded to how Collin's family had described him. Rosa continued.

"Jose didn't go to parties, he never had a girlfriend, he stayed, always close to home. He's afraid for our mom, you know? He always wanted to be around to keep an eye on things and he would never go off on a trip, especially without letting anybody know."

"Think back over the past few months. Anything strike you as unusual, at all, about Jose? Change in mood, interests, stuff like that?" Cam tried to be encouraging without unintentionally planting seeds.

Rosa took a deep breath and seemed to strain to remember.

"It's hard to say. I've been away a lot. When I came home for a visit last Jose seemed different, but until you mentioned it, I didn't think of it. He's always quiet, but this time he seemed edgy. Like he was carrying something on his shoulders he didn't want to talk about. We aren't as close as we used to be."

"What happened? Any argument or falling out?" Cam tried to sound reserved.

"I assumed he was mad at me because everyone knew he was smart enough to go to college, but I got to go because I got a scholarship. He didn't do that well in school. He could have but it was like, you know, there was this one point, way back in middle school? Maybe earlier, he just seemed to give up. He didn't do it to impress his friends, because he didn't have too many friends anyway, and he really seemed happier that way."

Cam thought for an instant he knew better. He recalled going in to seventh grade and being placed in the honors class, the track for students who showed a high aptitude. He remembered how his friends, his cousin and his brother had given him the cold shoulder, rather than celebrating his good news.

"Oreo cookie," he recalled the insulting term his brother had called him when they were kids, "you're Black on the outside, but trying to be white on the inside."

It would be years before Cam would feel comfortable being himself, an intelligent Black man with high aspirations, without feeling deep down like he was just an imposter. But in those formative years, as he discovered what it meant to be a man of color in America, Cam recalled, he would find great solace in being invisible. Hiding with his books.

"How does Jose like his job?"

Rosa seemed taken aback by this question.

"I don't know.... he doesn't really talk about it. I mean, he didn't really want to work there. He always loves books, loves to read, used to write stories in his notebooks when we were kids, you know? I think he wanted to be a writer or something. He wanted to go to college, to be an English teacher, or a biologist."

Cam's face gave away a hint of confusion.

"Yeah, I know, the two don't really seem to go together. Jose, it's like, he always needs to know why things happen. He wants to see what is under the skin. He reads about so many things. I know he reads. He hides it a lot, tries to act dumb. I think it disappointed him because he didn't get a full scholarship, but then, I mean, what do you expect? He doesn't play a sport, and he floated through school getting a C average."

Rosa looked to Cam for confirmation and he nodded. She went on.

"It was a disappointment to him to have to work at Monarch. He only planned on being there a few months and then he's going to maybe move near our cousins if he can't find another job. Jose doesn't show his feelings much though. Our Mama was more upset, though. She tried to talk him out of it. She was afraid he would end up like our dad. He works for Monarch and she always said the job made him crazy, made him drink all of that. She cried for Jose. She is convinced that Jose will turn into a raging drunk or worse. I guess it's very stressful work."

"Is there anyone you can think of who might want to hurt Jose? Did he owe anyone money, try to move in on some guy's girl? Someone at Monarch who might have a bone to pick with him?" As soon as he spoke the words Cam recoiled at the unintended pun. Rosa didn't seem to notice.

"He got picked on a lot in school, for being shy and for hanging out with the kids that weren't popular. Mostly theater kids."

"Jose liked to act?"

"He didn't really get into the acting, but he liked to work on the scenery. Jose works very hard, but he likes to be behind the scenes. That is why this is so strange. Who could he have pissed off? I mean, since he got to junior, senior year no one bothered him anymore that I know of. By then the bad dudes dropped out, and if you don't bother anybody, nobody bothers you, you know? So recently, I don't know. I went through his room. I know it was wrong. I just wanted to see, like you said, if maybe there were some drugs, or some clue or some note or something. But nothing. I didn't see anything unusual."

"You mention that your dad works at Monarch too. Did he see Jose before he left work Tuesday?"

"Oh, no. Papa works the late shift now. He's on the cleanup crew now. He didn't see Jose Tuesday, but that is normal."

"How has your dad been managing this?"

Rosa sighed. "The way he handles everything. He goes to work. Comes home, sits in his chair and drinks."

Cam thought of an earlier conversation with Dierdre. Drinking aside, it was the same scene she depicted. Collin returning from work. Sitting in the chair. Zoning out. He decided to take a chance, trusting his instincts that some connection he couldn't quite see existed here.

"Rosa, this may seem like an unusual question, but did Jose ever talk about a young man, a few years older than him named Collin Griffen?"

Rosa's face changed to both deep sadness and recognition.

"I read about Collin in the paper. Jose knew him. I knew him too."

"From Monarch?" Cam had a feeling he knew the answer would be no.

"Not only Monarch. We went to the same schools. Collin was in my grade. I knew him but we weren't friends. He only had a few friends and they were kinda," Rosa hesitated. "kinda losers, I guess that's a bad thing to say." Rosa started to cover her mouth as if pushing the words back in. She smiled as if embarrassed. "Let me try that again. They were the kids who didn't really fit in. Kinda nerdy or awkward, you know?"

Cam nodded; he could picture Collin as the tagalong in a small group of outcasts.

"Did he get in trouble at school? Collin, I mean? When you read in the papers, you knew of Collin before. Were you surprised at all?"

"Surprised is an understatement. I know it sounds like a cliché, Mr. Burton... Cam, but the idea of Collin being violent is the last thing. I mean if you told me Jesus just arrived in a spaceship with the Easter Bunny and they're parked in front of our house, I would believe that easier."

Cam noticed her tone become more intense as she spoke about Collin. Something is there. Something else, what?

"You seem pretty determined but you didn't know Collin that well. How can you be so sure? It's a long time since High School."

"I know. But it is totally out of character for him. I know this. He would get bullied by other kids. Never spoke up. Never made trouble. He wouldn't push back at all. Except once. Jose wrote about it in his diary. Yes, I know I told you, he was a geek, right? But he kept a diary. And when he disappeared, I read it. I know it was wrong. But I read it. I was just so desperate for clues. I didn't want to turn them over because it was no one's business his private life, the police I mean. He had an entry about his work. It being stressful and people having a sick sense of humor. It almost sounded like he was scared of some of the people there, but he didn't come out and describe why."

Cam made note of this in his steno pad. He gulped the remainder of his coffee.

"Cam, can we make the police investigate Monarch?"

"That gets into tricky territory unfortunately. We don't have evidence of a crime, first of all. We don't have anything more than a hunch that people from Monarch were involved even if we both suspect something ominous. We have to stay vigilant, be open to connections or things that turn up. And stay in contact when more developments occur. Sometimes it turns around in a day or a week, sometimes years. My hope, is that he comes home and has an interesting story to tell," Cam tried to reassure her.

"Do you really think that will happen?"

Cam thought for a moment. "If I am being totally honest, No. But I will be in touch if I learn of anything you need to know."

CHAPTER 43

August 18, 2016

Cam

"You're late again," Donna reminded Cam. What could he say? She was right. But he was exhausted and didn't want to argue.

"I know. It's been a long day. I'm leaving the office now. Don't wait for me. Go on and have dinner. I'll make something when I get home."

"I didn't bother to wait. This is the third night this week, Cam."

"I'm sorry. I'm heading out now. I'll see you soon," He knew he should say something more. I love you or I'm doing this for us or some other more meaningful way to apologize. He wasn't good at these things. If she had said I love you, he would have said it back. But he couldn't bring himself to say it first.

He had probably earned that but what could he do?

He hoped she would say it. Instead she just said "Ok bye," and hung up before he could reply. He stacked the steno pads on his desk into several piles and placed them in his briefcase. Each notebook was dedicated to a different case. He shoved a few folders, overflowing with reports into the case as well and leaned on it hard to ensure it would close.

As he locked up the office, juggling keys, and briefcase, he replayed the conversation. In his mind he had the right things to say. He reassured his wife and cracked jokes that made her laugh, the edge in her voice disappeared.

He was distracted by the mental scene of what didn't happen, and so he almost overlooked what was happening. What was out of place. No one else was in the office this late, but there was a car parked just outside of the parking lot. Concealed mostly in darkness, he could make out the profile of a figure behind the driver's seat.

Fumbling with the radio, he pulled out of the parking lot and headed home. When he checked his mirror several blocks later, the car was still there. How long had it been? At least two commercials, one for the local Bingo Pizzeria and another for a Fish Fry. Also, long enough to hear a Twofer from The Grassroots on his favorite oldies station. Was it the same car? He tried to read the license plate but even through heavy glasses it was still unclear. The car was following too far behind him. He turned a corner detouring from his normal route.

A few moments later headlights turned behind him. He felt uneasy, his stomach turned. He hadn't eaten lunch but a burning acid from anxiety crept up to his throat. He swallowed hard. Not usually easily scared, there was no one else out on the street. He turned again, now meandering without a specific direction.

He thought, now I will be even later. Donna will kill me.

He wondered who would be following him. Maybe he had a light out? He didn't dare pull over to check. He circled back around to Main Street. The headlights pursued him still. He decided to make a stop at the PigPen. It was a public place, there would be others around.

When he pulled into the tavern's parking lot, his pursuer passed, slowing but then drove off. Maybe, he thought, maybe I had just made it all up?

He called his wife. "I'm running late."

She started to voice her disappointment and he cut her off. "Donna, I think someone was following me. Lock the doors."

CHAPTER 44

August 20, 2016

Cam

"I'm sorry, Mr. Burton, nothing has gone according to schedule," Dierdre sounded harried as she walked Cam from the front lobby back to the Mosier County Jail's Mental Health Unit.

"I can understand from watching all the traffic in and out that it has been quite a day."

"I'm not superstitious, but I swear there is a Full Moon coming or something." Dierdre pushed open the conference room door and with a clumsy gesture cleared scattered paperwork so that Cam would have a place to set his files on the table. She took a seat across from him and tried to get her bearings.

"Well, not to argue with your theory but we are actually coming up on a New Moon tomorrow. I'm as addicted to checking the Farmer's Almanac as I am to old music and work," Cam smiled.

"Nothing like a little light reading, I guess," Dierdre responded.

"Yes, especially in our line of work. So, tell me, how is our mutual friend Mr. Griffen fairing these days? It has been a while since I stopped in to see him, but I have been trying to piece some things together on the outside."

"Well I would love to know what you've learned. I'm afraid I have little news to report. He's displaying traumatic reactions. Appears to have restless sleep, nightmares, and a lot of anxieties.

Startles easily but has not really been interacting with anyone, including me."

"The trauma is exactly what I wanted to talk to you about. My research has uncovered some interesting skeletons in Mr. Griffen's closet, pardon the bad pun."

"You mean he's killed other people?" Dierdre tensed noticeably, unable to suppress a tone of shock.

"No. Not people. Pigs. It was his job. He was working for Monarch Industries in their slaughterhouse."

Dierdre flipped open Collin's file and paged through the various medical reports and notes. "Ok, that I did have documented, maybe from a conversation with mom? But I don't understand. Monarch is a huge company. Having a difficult job isn't an excuse for murder."

"Excuse, no. But I there are documented studies of increased rates of crime, substance abuse and violence among slaughterhouse employees."

Dierdre looked up at him, a puzzled expression on her face. "But, does the work create violence in the person.... Or does it take a violent personality type to be drawn to that line of work?"

Cam laughed. "I guess we can see the type of analyzing that draws you to the line of work you do. It's an interesting question. There's probably no way to know for certain. Except I've talked to a lot of people who know Collin. Know him well. They can't account for this from anything else in his background. The more I learn both about Collin and about Monarch, the more I am convinced that this was a kind of job someone with Collin's temperament had no business doing."

"Collin's temperament?" Dierdre asked.

"Well, it may be hard to envision because you've seen the after picture. Like I have. That's all we've seen. But his family, his wife, people who know him, they describe a shy, smart, passive kid who got caught up in a difficult, violent, gruesome job. I'll be honest, it's a weak defense and I can't guarantee a jury will sympathize. But I am learning more about cases like Collin's."

"Of people who were traumatized by working in slaughter-houses? Who go from killing animals to killing people?"

"That kind of a link would be a golden puzzle piece that I don't have. Not yet. May not get it either. But I have found a recent link to one of Collin's coworkers. Man named Jose Hernandez. Disappeared recently. No reports of depression or other problems. Other instances of things like suicide. Changes in personality, similar to what happened with Collin, but not the same crime, as far as I have been able to find."

"I guess it makes sense. I mean in my profession burnout is high and people can be vicariously traumatized by dealing with intense situations with patients."

"Yes, and you're in a position of empathizing with them. Imagine how the dynamic changes if it was your job to kill them."

Dierdre shook the image out of her mind.

Cam changed the subject. "This may not be something you can predict, but how long do you expect it will be before meds or something starts working? Before he clears up enough to communicate?"

"It's hard to say. We are trying a new medication and if it's going to be effective, we should see some improvements in a week or two."

"Has he shown any violence or agitation since being incarcerated?"

Dierdre flipped through her notes. "Not that I recall, at least as far as aggressive or threatening. No, I don't see that here. It's more like, agitated, excitable. Out of nowhere. But that is only on a few occasions. He has called out for his family a few times, likely a hallucination. Sometimes he seems to know where he is but not why. Sometimes he thinks he's somewhere else."

"So as far as we know he still doesn't know what happened to Quinn? Does he realize he killed his son?"

"We've agreed not to go into that detail with him in the state he's currently in. So, we're keeping explanations general for now.

Things like 'you're in a mental health unit at the Jail' if he asks where he is. We don't want to lie to him or feed into delusions. At the same time, he's definitely not ready for the truth just yet. Fortunately, he hasn't really asked about why he's here. Honestly, I am not convinced that he is registering what he's being told."

"I don't know what I am going to be able to do for him, even if he does clear up. This is going to be a tough one to get any empathy from a jury. I've already started proceedings to get the case transferred to a bigger city, someplace where small-town biases won't come into play."

"Well, as much as jail has become the new mental hospital in too many cases, it really isn't the ideal place for the kind of care someone in Collin's condition needs. I have connected him with a new initiative. He gets a volunteer visitor with a service animal, a young man named Bobby Ray and his dog, pit bull, Dodger."

"How has that been going?"

"He tolerates it, he is able to remain calm during the visits and we only allow the visits on days when Collin is relatively calm. Recently he's had more good days than bad, just some nightmares most nights or if he falls asleep during the day. But he seems to like the dog and so they chat, and Bobby Ray is not a professional, but he seems to be making small talk with Collin. We're hoping the social enrichment will help."

"Interesting. Collin had a dog back home, so maybe the connection will spark something," Cam said, reflecting back on his notes.

"I can't imagine how anyone could work in a slaughterhouse," Dierdre suddenly blurted out. "Sorry it just popped into my mind. It must have been awful."

"Desperation, from what my research indicates," Cam replied.

Dierdre considered this. An old memory surfaced in her mind. Her college roommate back in Boston had been a character. Didn't eat any meat, dairy, anything from animals. Put herself in a cage, nude, painted orange to protest the circus. Always doing things like that. Without fully understanding why, Dierdre pulled out her phone.

"I just thought of someone who may be able to provide some more information to help you build your case. Can I give you her contact info?"

"Sure. I'm open to any leads," Cam readied his pen and steno pad.

"Ok, her name is Gillian. She's into the whole 'free the animals' thing. She does some of the wacky street protest stuff but she's also a professor, she's studied a lot about animal issues. She may be able to give some added fuel to your fire."

Dierdre found Gillian's contact information stored in her phone and read off the number.

"I'll give her a call. Thanks."

* * *

Professors, Cam thought to himself as hung up the phone after his call with Gillian, were a fifty-fifty bargain. In his experience, they were either arrogant, in a world apart, speaking a language no one outside their specialty could understand and out of touch with reality. The other grouping, he had observed, were the kinds of professors he had liked best in school. Those who were intellectual enough to be helpful and smart enough to know how to not flaunt their genius.

Gillian turned out to be the likable kind.

She was able to confirm the suspicions of slaughter related cases of violent outbursts, though her statistics were more pertaining to domestic violence and cruelty toward family pets, not specifically murder of a family member.

"I suspect the cases are much more prevalent, but it isn't something that is widely looked at. The criminal justice system may look at someone working in a slaughterhouse as no different from someone working in a gas station or shoe store."

"Understood," Cam was taking notes quickly to keep up with her fast talking.

"The problems are really all interrelated," She affirmed.

"What do you mean by that?" Cam had asked.

"Think of any of the biggest contemporary problems in society. Any of the people on your caseload. Some theorize, and I agree, that all of the issues, from drug addiction to domestic violence to theft and more, all relate to a paradigm, a mindset that has, at its core, animal agriculture."

Cam had been caught off guard and abruptly stopped writing.

"Can you break that down for me? I'm afraid I don't follow that logic."

"Sure. People think that just because animal agriculture is the norm now, that this means it was always the norm the world over."

"Ok," Cam noted her words, he was slowly digesting the possibility that maybe somewhere in the world at sometimes there had lived a scrawny tribe of leaf-eaters.

"But the idea, the very concept that it is acceptable to not only eat an animal but capture and enslave and then exploit an animal for their body, milk, meat, bones or what have you is not a right of nature. It is a human made construct."

Cam felt uneasy. "You say enslave. As a Black man, that word doesn't sit well with me when used to describe pigs or cows."

"I hear you," Gillian replied and then continued, "but context aside, I don't mean to imply that enslavement of humans is any less significant of an issue, but if you set apart the social acceptance of it, the normalcy of it, confining any being against their will, forcing them to work, whether a person thinks they are 'well cared for' or not, is at its core, a process of enslavement."

Cam could see her point, but it still made him uneasy to branch into this terrain. She continued. "At some point in ancient history, humans decided it was our right to completely dominate another species. We built it into our society at every level. Capitalism itself, even the term 'capital' is traced back to this. It refers to a head, specifically head of cattle, as being a measurement of value. The earliest monetary value."

"I hadn't made that connection," Cam was again hurriedly writing to keep up with her.

"Not just that, other terms, normal to us, the Stock Market, right? It's the core belief that owning a living being and having the right to have complete control over every aspect of that being's life. Where they live, how they live, whether or when or how they reproduce, what happens to their children, how they die, these are acts of control. Domination, violence. Those who work closely in this industry are brought right up to the front lines of this violence. It disconnects them from the morality and empathy that we all have as humans."

What she had said next was sticking in his mind now more than anything else.

"Animal agriculture is the basis of all forms of violence against people and animals, it is the hub of capitalism, patriarchy, even racism. It is the core belief behind any presumption that one person or group of people should have the right to control, exploit and ultimately kill, another. Simply by first calling them *animals*."

CHAPTER 45

August 2016

Collin

Collin tossed and turned in the cell. His body ached, but his mind was elsewhere. He was out in the yard, behind the shed, knees covered in mud as he sat in the dirt.

"Here Ace! Come here Ace!" he called, trying to not startle the dog or alert his daddy. He was ten. If his daddy came out on the porch, the old shed would block his father's view. He could stay here all afternoon. He could skip having to try out for the kids' football team. He hated the idea of playing ball. Instead, he focused on Ace.

The old hound was smart and knew his name. He trotted over to the chain-link fence where Collin waited for him. Peanut butter cookies crumbled in his hands. Ace snouted at the fence. Collin grinned. "Hey boy. Look what I gotcha? These are the best. You can have mine."

Ace's muzzle poked harder through the fence, and Collin reached a hand filled with cookie through the opening. Ace backed up and sniffed his hand eagerly, then licked his fingers and nudged his grip open, devouring the treats. Collin refilled the crumbled cookies until his shirt pocket was empty. He loved Ace and hoped that he could have a dog someday.

"Good boy, Ace, good boy!" Collin scratched at the dog's ears and patted his nose. He had become so lost in the moment he didn't see the shadow appear behind him.

"Collin!" He jumped.

Ace jumped and cowered back. Collin thought he was in for it now, he turned to face his father. Hovering above him was his boss. He was no longer a child. The smell of peanut butter turned to the smell of blood. Iron and the stabbing odor of bleach. He looked down at his hands. Now a man. He turned to check on Ace.

The dog was no longer there.

In his place was the body of a pig.

Cut to shreds.

The knife at Collin's feet.

CHAPTER 46

August 2016

Cam

While Collin was haunted by a montage of memories and nightmares, on the outskirts of town in the suburb surrounding Mosier, Cam Burton's sleep was disturbed as well.

Shopping locally, even in his sleep, Cam was inside the local market. He looked side to side, eyes focused intently as he scanned the aisles of the corner grocery. Something should have been there, what? It was there, on the tip of his tongue, a bad taste in his mouth. He reached his hands out as if scanning the shelves would make it appear....

"What are you looking for?" a voice asked him.

It was his wife, then his grandmother, and it seemed normal, as if people morphed before his eyes every day. He didn't have time to think. He just had to find.... to find... what?

Was it toothpaste, toilet paper, had he stopped in for eggs? Milk? Cam wondered. The store lights were dim. Was the store closed? Had he broken in? Would he be caught? Disbarred?

No time to think. Scanning the aisles.

He noticed a newspaper on the stand. The date caught his eye. September 21st, 2016.

"You looking for Jose, Cammie?" his grandmother asked. He realized he had ignored her and felt ashamed of himself. Then wanted to sit down with her. To talk to her. To ask her about Heaven and if she was there when the stroke took his mother a few years back. He wanted to cherish her presence, smell the scent of her cooking on his clothes, hear her stories but he couldn't.

He couldn't. No time, no time, no time left for you… he heard the guess who taunting him in his mind…Nanna I'm looking for, I'm looking for…

"You looking for Jose? He's not here now. I'm sorry, Cammie. He ain't here. The pigs got to him."

He froze.

"The pigs got to him, but you still got time if you hurry. You still got time for that white boy. He's a good boy that white boy and it's not too late. He's awake now. You go and talk to that white boy."

He felt the chill.

"What do you mean the pigs got to him?"

The temperature dropped. His throat dried up. He looked around as if expecting the police to crash in through the storefront windows.

He had turned his head just for a moment, but when he looked back toward his grandmother, her face held a sinister appearance. She looked sick.

Grey. Like a character in a Stephen King story who was alive … enough, but dead. Under the skin. Dead. She was holding something out to Cam. His eyes dropped, and he gasped. Balanced on both hands, a large silver serving platter. Garnished with kale, maggots crawled on apple slices, centered on the platter, the bloated head of a pig.

Cam woke with a start.

* * *

Mosier Tribune
   Body pulled from Mosier River, Identified as Missing Man
   August 28, 2016

A body pulled from the Mosier River on August 21st, 2016 was identified as Jose Hernandez, the Mosier man who went missing Tuesday. Preliminary reports suggest Hernandez may have been the victim of an assault, no word yet on possible motive.

CHAPTER 47

The Next Day

Cam

"Dr. Decker speaking."

"Decker, how you doing? It's Cam"

"Cam! Great to hear your voice, haven't seen you in church! Was going to give you a call. You having a good time bringing justice to mankind?"

"Well, I'm working on a pretty interesting case right now, I might need your professional opinion."

"You moonlighting as a detective now, too?" Decker joked.

"No, I guess you could say I've taken a special interest in one of my cases though, and it's got my curiosity piqued. I've been asking around as a result."

"Well, how can I help you?"

"Have you performed the autopsy on Jose Hernandez?"

"The kid they found in the river?"

"Yes, that's him."

"Your timing as always is impeccable. You got the bad guy already?"

"No, no, I don't know how to explain it other than a lawyer hunch that something Hernandez was involved in might somehow be related to a bad element. A situation that one of my guys got involved in."

The line went silent.

"Well I'm not sure what you're looking for exactly. A bad element, you say. Yep, pretty bad."

"What do you mean?"

"This young man had injuries. He had tearing of the rectum and traces of metal. The final report is not yet finished, but from what the team saw, he had been beaten and sodomized with some type of instrument. Whether he lived long enough to throw himself in the river or whether his body was dumped, we can't quite say yet. You think… you think your client is the perp?"

"No," Cam thought a moment.

"You see some difficult stuff, Decker. Does it ever give you nightmares?"

"All the time."

Chapter 48

September 8, 2016

Finch

Michael Finch had gotten a solid month of regular sleep before the nightmares returned. The recurring dreams always began in mundane circumstances. Black and white, Dorothy and Toto before their grand entrance to Oz. He would see himself checking the mail or making coffee or opening the bathroom door to take his morning shower and then it would hit him.

Night after night, dream after dream, with the image of Aiden turning blue on the floor, haunted him. He would see the needle protruding from his left arm. Now in technicolor. In tonight's dream the surprise climax bomb had dropped when his dream Self had opened the door of his red Bentley to find Aiden sprawled over the passenger seat turning what Procol Harum would have called a Whiter Shade of Pale.

And there was the needle.

Before waking, Finch always had the sense the needle was shouting at him.

"Gotcha!"

Which is why at three in the morning on a Thursday Michael Finch was not sleeping. Nor was he up early to get in a morning workout like he used to before the addiction had taken his son- and vicariously him- hostage. He sat staring at his net worth report on the computer screen. He scanned the list of numbers and felt the stabbing pain when the line of data went from black to red. And stayed in the red.

Aiden's first rehab had was covered by insurance, but that had been a year and a half ago. He had since tapped the managed care well one too many times. When that well ran dry, he had borrowed against his retirement. Inpatient rehab, outpatient clinic, an interventionist, a hypnotherapist, legal fees, long term residential treatment agencies.

Not to mention the times he had bailed his son out by paying off his dealers.

Aiden's addiction was hemorrhaging Finch's bank account. If this kept up, he might be forced to sell one of his son's cars, or perhaps put a second mortgage on the summer home.

Or your son might just end up dead, you selfish fuck.

Finch shuddered at the thought and felt shame surge in the pit of his stomach. How many times can you find your own kid overdosed and passed out in a heap before the prospect of death becomes strangely routine?

This month would be worse than usual. Hurricane Matthew hit productivity hard. Flooding had wiped several farming operations. The flood waters had drowned thousands of pigs and cattle trapped inside each warehouse like structure.

Finch smirked to himself, thinking if he had one thing to be grateful for it was that he didn't live downstream where gallons of shit had flowed into the drinking water.

CHAPTER 49

September 2016

Jolene

Jolene's head throbbed.

"Are you coming out of there?" Jolene's mother called, rapping on the bathroom door.

Buzzkill. Jolene thought. Pills were getting harder to come by and the last thing she had wanted was to have her freaking mother ruin this… this… it wasn't even a high. It was a relief. Couldn't she just take a moment to get some relief without pounding on her fucking head….no, her door. Mom pounded on the door, but her head had been pounding anyway, and this was just too much. She wasn't trying to get high. She was just trying to make her head stop pounding so she could get through today.

"I'm coming mama," she grumbled.

She washed her face in the sink and stared at the apparition of a young woman who had found her way into the mirror.

Who the fuck are you? And what have you done with my life?

The apparition staring back at her had creases, dark circles, sharp edges. Jolene had always been average weight, but her face always had a roundness that one would associate with cherubs.

Or babies. But there were no babies here anymore. Not even crybabies. Jolene had been doing much better in therapy. Doing much better at self-medicating. A voice emerged from her head to correct her. Who the fuck invited you? Jolene asked and then started. Had she said that out loud? She didn't know; she didn't hear the echo of herself, or had she…

That fucking knocking.

We'll finish this conversation later, she said to the pointy, haggard specter of herself. This time she knew she only had said it in her own mind.

Jolene emerged from her escape in the bathroom, taking one last glance over her shoulder. Clean. Really clean. Thanks to her mom, God knows she hadn't been able to clean in how long? But the loo wasn't just washed down. It was cleaned out. Empty. Every shelf cleared, the shower empty, no towels, no toilet paper, no tissues, no cosmetics. Had the room always been so white?

It's amazing how different a room looks when it's emptied, she thought. Emptied. How white her life must look now that it's been emptied. Almost emptied, she corrected herself.

"Hand me that marker, will ya, hon? You ok? Sick to your stomach?" Her mother was labeling the last of the boxes. Some were "To Be Donated" others were marked "Collin" and others "Take" indicating that these lucky items would find their home back at Mrs. McGurn's house, where Jolene would also now be making her home for the foreseeable future.

"Yeah. Stomach," Jolene mumbled.

"What did you use for toilet paper?" her mother inquired.

"Huh?" Jolene was headed for that special altered state in which she had lost track of the feasibility of her excuse to hide what she was really up to with her frequent trips to the bathroom. She had a vague sense that her mother was onto her, but she couldn't quite place where she had slipped. She caught herself starting to instinctively reach to run her hand over the bottle of pills in her sweatshirt pocket but managed, somehow thank goodness, to catch herself and pretend to scratch at her arm instead.

She averted her mother's hawk-eyed stare and began to absent-mindedly place a few remaining items into boxes.

"This will only be for a little while," Her mother tried to remind her in a tone meant to be comforting but which came across as patronizing.

Only a little while. You will lose everything of any importance in your entire life. But don't worry; it will only be for a little while …Only a little while until…

What?

Until your baby comes back from the dead and continues his life? Until your husband invents a time machine in that fucking prison cell of his and finds a way to go back in time and keep himself from single-handedly destroying three lives?

What will only be a little while? Because the secret Jolene had discovered, and which no one else, not her mom, her therapist, her friends; well, she didn't have to worry about friends! What a laugh that was. They came around for the initial drama and then drifted into the woodwork. It seemed sending sympathy cards and posting little "prayer" icons on Facebook was about all the heavy lifting her friends could do to help her get through this. No one understood the secret. Jolene was the only person who could see what had really happened.

Everything had stopped. There was no "little while" because there was nothing to come next. Nothing. The highway she had been cruising down had disappeared. It reminded her of something her friend Crystal used to say. When she was first learning to drive, Crystal had told Jolene that driving over bridges in the dark made her anxious.

"I drive up to the bridge, and it's like, just for a split second, I say to myself 'what if this bridge is under construction and I missed the sign? What if I just drive onto this bridge and there is nothing there? Like if it doesn't go anywhere?'"

Jolene hadn't understood then, but she understood perfectly now. Crystal clear she thought to herself and chuckled at the pun.

"What on Earth is so funny?" her mother asked.

"Huh? Oh, nothing."

"This is only for a little while," Her mother repeated. Jolene began to wonder if this was a chant her mother had to tell herself to keep herself from realizing the bridge had in fact disappeared. That the whole fucking scaffolding of life had been under construction all along and oops! You just took a wrong turn, and now you are going to drop into nothingness.

Maybe her mother had to convince herself that it would only be for a little while. Because she needed this mantra, the way some people need God to make sense of the world. Jolene understood, she had been one of them. Needing God and Jesus and church and a choir and hymns and songs and prayers and stories. Nursery rhymes for the faithful.

Jolene hadn't intended to be so moody, especially since her mother was doing her a favor at great sacrifice to herself. Which is why you should just kill yourself. Now. The thought, it was a thought not really a voice, not in the sense of a hallucination, had been there just beneath the surface for so long. It popped in from time to time, driving home its self-destructive directions like a politician harping on their bullshit platform with trite slogans and soundbites.

"Make America Great Again, off yourself."

But she couldn't. Like a politician, she thought. All talk and no plan, no action. Just inertia. Emptiness.

She remained in a fog of grief and Xanax as her mother toted the last of the boxes into the car, now filled to capacity, with barely room for her to squeeze into the passenger seat.

The BMW pulled up just as Jolene's mother emerged from doing one last sweep of the place, looking for any forgotten items. A woman in a pantsuit emerged from the car, all business, all smiles. Maybe this woman had a clue about Jolene's circumstances. How could she not? Even if she wasn't from around here, and her stylish and high price suit suggested she was in fact not from Mosier, surely, she had seen Jolene's picture in the paper, on the news, the constant barrage. The woman's demeanor betrayed no foreknowledge of Jolene's circumstances. She carried a clipboard and Gucci purse.

"I'm here to pick up the keys from you," She began.

Really? Jolene thought to herself. I thought you were my fairy fucking godmother. Isn't that a pumpkin you were driving?

But Jolene couldn't bring herself to speak. She was afraid she would scream, tear this bitch a new one.

Liar! Ok, she was lying. She was afraid she would burst into tears and never stop crying again. She kept her mouth shut, eyes down, and fumbled for the keys. Without making eye contact she handed the keys to the well-dressed woman who worked for the absentee landlady who was so busy, or self-important, or both, that she had to send one of her minions to enforce her eviction.

Jolene slumped into the passenger seat of her mother's car. Her own car had been repossessed already. No one expects to find out the highway they were driving on is subject to randomly disappearing into nothingness and so in spite of the sage advice about nest eggs and 6 months safety savings, the Griffens had not been financially prepared for the loss of one income.

Or more. Even if they wanted to take that advice seriously, who the hell can square away six months savings? She would have been lucky to save fifty bucks with the wages she and Collin had been able to pull in. She was paid decently as a CNA when she had been able to put in all the overtime and bonus shifts.

But how long had it been since she had been able to work more than a few days in a row? Before her boss had called her into the office and explained that although they understood the horrible trauma she had gone through, they couldn't use her services if she was not able to be consistent.

If she couldn't be consistent. If she couldn't forget it all, put it behind her, get over it all quick because the hospital needs a warm body to wipe asses, take vitals, and serve lunches, so can you just hurry up and get over your baby's murder? We have shifts to cover!"

Jolene wasn't fast enough to bounce back, so they had bounced her right the fuck out of a job. Out of a car and now out of a home. As her mother's car pulled away from the curb, Jolene couldn't resist one glance in the side mirror.

She burst into tears.

CHAPTER 50

September 19, 2016

Cam

It had been a long time since Cam lived in a neighborhood that didn't have manicured lawns, tidy fashionable homes, and multiple car garages. He hadn't forgotten where he came from. Growing up, mom, aunt, cousins, siblings, and grandmother had lived in an apartment in the type of neighborhood his colleagues did not venture into if they could avoid it. What would his neighbors in the cul-de-sac on Winding Brook Drive think of the cluttered porches, scant yards, visibly deteriorating buildings the likes of which he spent his first 18 years occupying? They would probably do that thing people do, cringe just enough to notice that they are betraying physical signs of their disgust and try to cover it up before anyone notices.

Cam always noticed that look when various county social service workers visited his neighborhood. Thankfully, they never visited his house, but their presence was intimidating to him as a child and it was this fear that kept he and his siblings and cousins from saying a word about mom's drinking, or the belt, or the time she fell asleep with a lit cigarette after working a 16 hour shift. "What goes on in this house stays in this house," mother and grandma always said, and so it did.

Cam wondered, as he approached a run-down building here on Jefferson St., what went on in this house, the home of Ricardo

Melendez. This building, barely an echo of its former pre- WWII self, reminded Cam Burton of the people he grew up with.

This is how his mother had appeared by the time Cam was ten, beaten down by years of working on the lowest tiers of whatever dead-end job was available to an uneducated woman. The alcohol hadn't helped, nor the cigarettes, nor the day when her beloved walked out, leaving her with a house full of bills, kids, and little else. It was how his childhood home had grown to look, and it was how Ricardo's house looked to him now. A house of broken dreams someone had once called it.

He rang the bell and checked his reflection in the windowpane to make sure there was no trace of that disgusted look he so reviled. Ricardo was prompt, although not fully dressed. Cam noticed how, as he was led into Ricardo's home, to a place at his dining room table, Ricardo's attitude seemed to say, *you're in my house, you're on my terms*. Having noted this subconscious establishment of power, Cam thanked Ricardo for making time to speak with him and proceeded with his questions.

"What can you tell me about your typical day working at Monarch Industries?"

"Nothing anymore. They canned my ass."

"I'm sorry to hear that. What happened?"

"Slimy motherfuckers is what happened. A month away from a promotion they were promising me, suddenly, out of nowhere trying to call me up and say I made certain people feel uncomfortable. This from a man who was assaulting staff, with witnesses. But, he's the Boss. He's a white guy, and he's got shit on everyone. Mostly everyone."

"What are you going to do now?" Cam asked out of genuine concern.

"I thought you said your investigation wasn't about me?"

"True enough. Ok, so let's start over. What was a typical day at Monarch like?"

"Bringing home the bacon. That's all. You do your time and people have their sausages. Me, I don't even eat the shit no more.

How can you? You ever go to a restaurant and then one day you see some shit, maybe a bug on the floor, or you see back into the kitchen? Then you're like 'fuck that, I'm not gonna eat in that restaurant no more!' Well I tell you what, that shit on the chain? That shit is worse than some cockroach running across the floor at your favorite pizza parlor. That shit make you lose your appetite for bacon."

"How long did you, or most people on average, work at Monarch?"

"Depends. A day. A year, six months. Depends on how much someone could keep their shit together. That skinny white boy, he didn't have it in him to do the job. Neither did I at one time. Neither does anybody, you know? We saw his picture in the paper. That's how we knew him. None of us really knew his name. The bosses have nicknames for people and that's how we get to be known so half the time no one knows a dude's real name. But Colleen, that's what the bosses used to call him, get it?"

Cam frowned but nodded his understanding, and Ricardo went on.

"Colleen... Collin, we saw his picture in the paper. The boss couldn't wait to show it to everyone. Said 'this is what happens when you got no balls and try to do a man's job.' That's what he said. Motherfuckers were laughing, making jokes. There's some bad shit on that chain...what do they call it, 'gallows humor' but man, fuckin' kill a baby, your own fuckin baby. That's fucked up."

"Did it surprise you to see the picture in the paper?"

"Yes, and No," Ricardo began.

"Yes, because no matter how you cut it that is some fucked up shit, you know? And yes, because when you know a dude, I mean hell, do you ever know a man? You think you do, though. You stand next to him. Do a job, see him most every day, and it's like no way. No way can this little scrawny guy they call Colleen to his face, dude they fuck with openly every fuckin' day. No way could he really hurt anyone. But then, that is the job. So no, I can't really be surprised."

Cam nodded and kept quiet, hoping Ricardo, now loosened up, would continue. He did.

"People come through that door who wouldn't hurt a fly, but your job is to slaughter. Your job is to hurt something bigger and more human than a fuckin' fly. So, you become a killing machine. Its intense and I feel sorry for the dude. It could be any one of us."

"Do you really think so?" Cam asked, trying to keep his tone neutral.

"When I first started at Monarch, no way in hell I would have thought I would do some shit I done. I'm still realizing now that I been out, man, it's still coming to me. Some of the shit I had done. Some I had to do, some I didn't have to do but you can do a little bad then hell one day you are doin' a little more bad and then suddenly you're ass deep in doing bad and you don't even fuckin' know it. I'm sure that's what happened to your boy there."

"Is it common that employees develop violent tendencies?"

"You know what my dad used to say? If you sleep with dogs, you get fleas."

For a second Cam saw Ricardo's eyes glaze over. Something about the dog reference seemed to take him somewhere else in his mind, but only for a second and he was back.

"You sleep with dogs, you get fleas… what do you think happens when you spend all day, every day, electrocuting, slicing, cutting, takin' the guts out of squealing pigs? You don't get fleas then, you get fuckin' crazy."

Ricardo looked Cam in the eyes and when Cam didn't respond right away, Ricardo continued. "Yes, a lot of violence. They gang up on each other worse than high school. Lots of dudes beat their girlfriends, their kids. You know it. Everybody knows about it but it's one of those things. Everyone keeps quiet about it. Probably like how every cop knows the other cops are dirty, but when they're all dirty together, then they just stay quiet about it."

"Why do you think you really got fired? I mean, being so close to promotion and all. Did something happen?"

Ricardo glared at Cam, then breathed a sigh and proceeded.

"That is your first mistake, right there. You assume a man does something wrong to get his ass canned. You got a lot to learn about Monarch if you're going to help your client. I haven't done shit to deserve being fired. But to Monarch I committed the biggest sin in the industry."

"And what is that?" Cam asked, pen poised at the ready to take notes as if the secret of life was about to be revealed.

"I caused the line to stop. Just for a minute."

Cam squinted, showing his confusion, and Ricardo continued.

"See them fuckin' pigs, they get loose all the time. They're alive many times when they come in, you know? So, some big old pig is doing a mad dash through the place, and who can blame him when there's an electric prod heading for his ass and he knows he's a dead man, or dead pig. We aren't all that different in the ways it counts, you know? Motherfucker was running for his life and gets his chunky ass stuck in one of the machines. Then he starts to shriek in pain."

Cam could see that Ricardo's face has changed as he recounted the story. Cam noticed a pained look on the younger man's face, but kept quiet as Ricardo went on.

"Everybody is yelling at me 'Just stab him in the head, stab his fuckin' eyeball man! Hurry up, he's going to jam the machine!' and you know what? I've killed more of those motherfuckers than I can fuckin' count," Ricardo seemed to be almost reliving the scene. Cam noticed he was staring into the distance, no longer fully present.

Ricardo continued.

"I've sliced more of those motherfuckers than I can count. I've done it all, the taser, prod 'em in the face, in the eye, in the mouth, in the ass, it's just what we do you know? And no one's going to understand it unless you been there, unless you worked there and see how it is how normal this sick shit is, it's not even sick when you're there, it's just as normal as walking through a fuckin' metal detector at the airport. Thirty years ago, motherfuckers would be like 'damn what's with all these metal detectors' but then 9/11 and now it's just normal. That's how this crazy sick shit is. It's just normal. So where was I?"

"Pig stuck in the machine, people wanted you to slice him up."

"Right. Pig was stuck and screaming. So, I did what you're never supposed to do. I shut down the chain. I stopped operation. It was too late to save the pig. I don't know what I was thinking. But I tried to pull him out. No doubt in my mind that's part of the reason they looked for something to pin on me. To fire me. They allow a lot of shit to go down. But when it's convenient, they'll throw your ass under the bus."

"Would you be willing to testify against Monarch? About the conditions? About your experience? If you were guaranteed protection? Would you be able to tell a jury what you just told me?"

"I would do whatever to show those bitches they don't own me."

CHAPTER 51

September 21, 2016

Cam

The smell of baby back ribs wafted in from the kitchen and filled the PigPen tavern. Cam noticed how the smell didn't produce the Pavlovian response he had been used to. No matter, he thought to himself, I could stand to lose a few pounds.

He surveyed the room, looking for signs of Daryl Thorpe, Dr. Thorpe, Cam had to remind himself. He had been referred to Dr. Thorpe, DVM, who had served as an expert witness. Expert in Animal Husbandry.

The man in the polished leather shoes, dress shirt and slicked back hair entered the PigPen scanning the tables where peppered with those who found themselves free to patronize the restaurant mid-day, professionals, students, and those who while unemployed, still found the means, or the credit to eat their lunch out.

Cam rose from his seat with a preliminary wave. Wait for it. He thought to himself, another "snapshot" moment as the good doctor realized he was meeting with not just a criminal defense lawyer, but a Black man.

In fairness, Cam had to acknowledge he was expecting the good doctor to show up in a lab coat with a stethoscope around his neck, and for some reason, cowboy boots.

We all have our biases, he thought to himself. He extended a hand to Dr. Thorpe, and the two shook hands professionally and took their seats.

"What're y'all having today, sirs?" The amiable waitress swooped in just as Cam was adjusting his chair. Swarming in right on cue, he thought.

"I'm good with just a coffee," Cam replied.

"I will just have a salad," the doctor replied.

"Mister- I'm sorry, Dr. Thorpe, thank you so much for meeting with me today."

"Please, call me Bill, or anything but late to dinner," he laughed at his own joke before continuing, "these days I answer to many names, no offense taken."

"I am curious to know about the focus of the work you do, Bill."

"So am I, my friend! Seems there is less focus in the work I do year after year. But to your question. I am a veterinarian and spent most of my early career providing routine care to some local farming operations within the three counties surrounding Mosier. Dairy at first, then I branched out and worked in a few different hog operations. For a while I was a professor, now I maintain a small veterinary practice, but I have grown more exclusive about my clientele. More selective. I serve on the board of the FFP, the *Fairness in Farming Project* and have been called in as expert witness both as a veterinarian, these days mainly in animal abuse and neglect cases, although I have also given expert testimony and consultation on environmental issues."

Cam was already hurriedly taking down notes.

"This is a part of the scope of the FFP's work. We cover labor, animal rights, and environmental advocacy. More of my work these days seems to be in education and advocacy as opposed to traditional Veterinary Medicine. I guess that is why I was referred to you."

"Yes, thank you. I am unable to discuss the details here in a public setting, but what I can say is that the case is requiring an inside view of the processing end of the industry."

Cam observed the good doctor cringe slightly. "I know this is not the best lunch conversation…"

"Oh, no, believe me, I have seen and done it all. If I made a face just now, it isn't because the topic grosses me out, it's frustration you're seeing."

"Your familiar with some of the uh… issues, in this industry?"

"Yes. The issues. We got issues all right," he said with a dry chuckle.

"Have you ever been close to a bona fide farm, Mr. Burton?"

"Yes, although not recently. Growing up, my uncle's family had a small farm outside of Allendale. Chickens, goats, nothing large like cattle. They were small time but had enough to survive. But we're going way back now. My uncle was an old man when I was a kid, I was probably ten by the time he quit farming."

"Did he quit? Are you sure?"

Cam considered this.

"Well now, I guess I am not sure about that after all, funny you mention it. It was one of those things you take for granted as a young person, you know? They had a farm, and we would go visit, get eggs, harass the chickens, play in the field, and then one summer, I ask my mother 'when are we going to Uncle Jeremiah's farm?' and she just said 'they quit the farm' and that was about it. Come to think about it, we didn't really see them much after that."

"I hope I wasn't intruding, it's just that farming is a way of life and people who have done it all their lives, they seldom quit without a really good reason. Most are bought out or go bankrupt. Hence my frustration. The big-league farmers, the corporations, they aren't content to have their own successful operations. It's like they're out to monopolize. They have empires and their empires swallow up the surrounding small farms."

He paused to take a sip from his ice water, then continued.

"Place's like your family's farm, they're stuck like a mom and pop shop trying to compete when a Walmart moves into town. And they got a lot going for them. Lobbyists, regulations, did you know that Monarch Industries has patented their GMO seeds and will turn around and sue small farmers if the wind blows the patented seeds into a farmer's crop?"

"Seriously?"

"No lie. And the Monarch always wins. Whatever your client is up against, I hope it isn't that behemoth."

"Well, tell me about the view, from the inside, what is normal in this industry?"

"The truth is stranger than any fiction you could read. If you wrote a story about the slaughter industry, you would have a best seller, but no one would believe it was true so you would have to put it on the shelf labeled "Fiction" next to the Stephen King books!" He laughed.

Cam chuckled too, in spite of himself. Dr. Thorpe continued.

"What doesn't pass for normal in those hell holes? Let me take it back a way, and I apologize for the history lesson, but you have to understand why things are the way they are, not just the way they are. A woman named Cecile Steele is in some ways responsible."

"I've never heard that name. But how could it have been a woman? The corporate tycoons of the twentieth century were men, at least until recently," Cam reflected.

"No tycoon at all. Story goes, she made a mistake, ordered five hundred chicks instead of fifty. Had to think fast and build up a bigger operation to house them. Was in the 1920s. She ended up with five hundred chicks to try to make into meat. So, she built an operation of indoor broiler feeding and housing. And while we love to blame the woman... first Eve, then Cecile Steele, and today, Hillary...."

He trailed off momentarily and Cam wondered what the nominee for president had to do with Eve or Ms. Steele, but he refrained from asking. "We really have to move to Perdue or even Henry Ford to understand how the chickenizing process."

"Chickenizing?" Cam asked.

"Yes, that is what they call it, because it started with the chicken operations. So, Purdue takes a cue from Henry Ford, the assembly line. He applies Ford's assembly line concept to chicken farming. Now mind you, Perdue's got his name all over poultry, but he wasn't like, like your Uncle, you see? He wasn't a farmer. He was a businessman who tapped into the market of farming and brought in the priorities of a businessman. Profits, efficiency, he made it like Ford's assembly line, and others followed suit not only for the poultry industry but to all of farming. Let me ask you, Cam, can you estimate how many chickens your Uncle had on his farm at one time?"

"Oh, boy, I don't know, it seemed like they were everywhere, but I couldn't begin to estimate."

"Rough guess? Or let me ask you this, where were they kept?"

"Well, there were maybe a few dozen, it seemed, maybe more. They ran around outside in a fenced in area, then at night they went into an enclosure."

"Were they in cages?"

"Not that I recall, no."

"Most modern farms, even the so-called organic or small family farms of today and really the past several decades, most of them have been using battery cages, for chickens. You ever go out on a lobster boat?"

Cam nodded that he had.

"The little lobster crate gives you a visual of the size of these cages. Sometimes seven to ten chickens are kept in each cage. In a modern operation cages are stacked floor to ceiling, several rows deep. This is what Perdue started. A mechanized farming system that has grown larger and more expedient, a machine which has sped up significantly in the past thirty years or so."

Cam nodded, imagining such a horrific scene of stacked cages filled with chickens the way one may find stacked shelves filled with books in a library.

The doctor, finding his stride, continued with his story. "And it affects everything. The quality of life for the animals, the environment, labor, even nutrition and spread of disease. Do you think it's any coincidence that of all the influenza strains we have had outbreaks of swine and avian flus?"

Cam hadn't thought of this, but the more Dr. Thorpe provided details, the more Cam could imagine the setting. He could imagine the pungent ammonia from chicken waste, it almost made his eyes sting. The thought of potential for disease made perfect sese.

Dr. Thorpe went on.

"We can trace this to the conditions of the farms. The farms aren't what you saw at your Uncle's, I mean in some pockets here and there you have your small farmers like that, and the backyard farms and homesteaders and whatnot. But the food you buy in the store, even in the gourmet health food stores, chances are it comes from a CAFO and a slaughterhouse that is tied in with the CAFO operation."

"You said, CAFO?"

"Yes, sorry, Concentrated Agricultural Feeding Operation Concentrated, meaning high volume of animals confined in close quarters. It's run like a mill, like a sweatshop, so to speak. Then you get to the processing- the slaughter units, they're no different, the grand finale is run in much the same way. Emphasis is on profit and appearance of the final product, so measures are taken to speed up the line. So, it's discovered that if you can keep an animal subsisting on the bare minimum- the more you profit. Chickens naturally are territorial. You've seen that at your uncle's farm I betcha. So, they begin cutting off their beaks. That way no pecking, as in the pecking order, as we have come to say."

"Sounds awful," Cam admitted, feeling guilty about his dinner the night before.

"They are kept basically just existing for the bare minimum to get eggs, and eventually meat. The same goes for any of your modern farming operations. They become a machine. It was 1980s that chain speeds began to skyrocket, this is a recent phenomenon, the intention is to 'feed the world' vs. 'feed your community' but read between the lines, the objective is not to feed the world, it's to dominate the industry worldwide. You may recall a time when the average person didn't eat meat, but maybe once a day, or a few times a week, depending on their wealth. Why do you think the push for more protein… more meat protein in particular has become such a modern… staple of our diets? The lobbies between cattle and pork and meat industries and the USDA and the FDA."

"So, it was economics, not nutrition, that influenced the food pyramid and the methods of modern farming," Cam said, pondering how his own beliefs about diet had been influenced by conventions he never questioned before.

"Indeed. They boosted supply and speed. And to profit the speed is now key. Speed trumps safety, sanitation and defies logic on these production lines. The line speed only goes up. It may be announced monthly or several times a year, but it's inevitable. Going back, it's not an option. One of the hog plants went from 950 hogs an hour to 1300 hogs an hour. We aren't talking about pushing paper, we're talking repetitive, fast movements, with knives. Smaller operations like your family's farm can't compete. They fold or get bought out."

Cam nodded. He barely recalled hearing some talk about the struggles of farmers in some of the local rural communities. Now it made sense.

"There was a time," Dr. Thorpe went on, "that USDA inspectors had some handle on the industry, but all the inspection slows things down, so things have changed. The inspectors these days, half the time they don't even get near the meat. They may look through a window at a distance, and they will not do a thorough job because this would slow down the line. If they do get near the chain, the assembly line, it's moving by so fast, no way they can really see anything. This is mass production. Many houses are now relying on internal inspections, that is, the company inspects its own meat."

"Isn't that a conflict of interest?"

The doctor smirked. "Who's going to stop 'em?"

"Would you say this is how Monarch operates?"

"This, my friend, is how modern meat operates. Monarch, they are at the top of the pecking order and I pity anyone who goes up against them."

"Why do you say that?"

Dr. Thorpe stopped to consider his words, then replied, "Anyone going up against Monarch, they're liable to get their beaks cut off."

Cam felt a chill, recalling the blinding headlights on an otherwise dark street. The car that had seemed to follow him the other night. Why was he risking his career, possibly his safety, for a lost cause?

CHAPTER 52

September 2016

Ronnie

It had been an hour at least since the man in the suit left the household of Ronnie and Maggie Griffen. Maggie had been at some church something or other. Ronnie couldn't keep track of her.

Now he sat alone. In the dark, skipping the glass, drinking out of the bottle. No need for formalities here, gentleman, it's just me, myself, and I and all of us are fucked. Ron wasn't gulping now. He was taking slow pulls from the bottle, the style of drinking reserved for deep thinking moments.

If Rodin had set out to sculpt this thinking man, he wouldn't have a statue of a composed, dignified form, chin resting on hand, brow slightly furrowed. No. This thinking man held the posture of one who just realized that after giving a speech to an audience of thousands, his fly had been down the whole time.

Worse, the composure of a man who, head held high, left his father's home to make something of himself, his family name, who served his country and was served nothing in return. Well, that wasn't true, was it? He had just been served, hadn't he? Served a big, steamy turd on a silver platter by the man in the suit.

What the fuck had his name been? The suit said he worked for Collin's old employer. Damn kid, causing him even more grief now. The suit also said Ronnie would work for them. Be their man… but what can a man be when he bows to call someone his master?

The message was clear. Ronnie would testify, in court, against his son. He would take the stand, place his hand on the Holy Bible and swear before the jury, judge, prosecutor, God, St. Peter, John Wayne, Elvis Presley, John F. Kennedy and who-so-ever-the-fuck-else was watching down from that great TV room in the sky, eating popcorn and marveling at the clusterfuck down here on Earth….

He would testify that his son was a problem child. A monster. That in spite all Ron and his wife had done to raise him right he was incorrigible. That he pulled the legs off spiders, set cats on fire, fingered little neighborhood children behind the back shed.

"Make it up," the man in black had told him.

"Be creative. Here's a bottle of Jack to get your juices flowing. I know it's your favorite. We know a lot about you. And your family. You just keep that in mind. Because we know a lot about you, and we know lots of people. We even know your landlord, and unless you and your family have somewhere else to go, somewhere very, very far away to go… you want to do what you're told."

But there was also a silver lining, wasn't there? This nice anorexic Santa Claus from Corporate Hell had assured Ron that if he co-operated, he and his wife would never have to work again. They would be put up in a fancy house, in a nice part of town.

"Isn't that what an honorable veteran like you deserves, after all?" The man in black had asked.

Ronnie sat haunted not only by the words of the man in black, but by his conversation at the PigPen with Bert Tillinghast earlier this week. Or had it been last week? He couldn't recall. Bert used to work for Monarch. A sorry arrangement lasted all of two weeks. Bert wasn't a quitter per se; he had been disabled when a cow that had been sent down the chain to be disassembled, alive.

"They can't kill 'em all proper," Bert had told him, "because the boss hollers at you faster you're slowing the chain- and so that fella who's supposed to knock em in the head and the fella whose s'posed to make sure they're dead? Well, they're in a hurry just like you are so they jab once, move on, jab once move on." The cow that did Bert in, it turns out, had become quite animated and as workers tried to stab and slice and slash, he had some slashing and tearing of his own, this cow did.

"Fucker thrashing about so bad he tore himself down from the hook, begins running through the kill floor, knocked me the fuck over. Can't say as I blame him, I would fight for my life too, an' so wouldn't you, Ronnie, just like them days when we were in the jungle."

A fellow veteran, Bert's words held with Ronnie in a way that few others did. And that was when he realized. His weak, pussy of a son had gone to war. He had served his time. He didn't enlist in 2001; he enlisted at birth, right here in Mosier. Signed on to the army of the working class to fight for life, survival and the American Way meaning profits for the wealthy.

And just like Ronnie and his fellow soldiers, Collin had been funneled into the chute, lead to the slaughter, hung up on a chain, he had been chewed up and spit out and now the machine that had created this monster wanted to clear its good name. Wanted to deny any wrongdoing...

Te Absolvo, you are forgiven, keep it moving folks, you got nothing to see here, pay no attention to that sweatshop, that battleground, that slaughterhouse, that prisoner of war camp, that concentration camp... behind the curtain.

They wanted to call his boy a baby killer. Ronnie recalled. He thought back to the hippies with their flowers and long dirty hair. They called him baby-killer when he came home, and what did his Commander-in-Chief do? To honor, remember, thank, commemorate those who gave all for the US? For the cause of... of... of what? Of an open door letting all the jobs out and terrorists in? For the right of Wall St. billionaires to play slot machines with the earnings of people like him? For Patti Jo down the street to die of cancer because not only did she have to drink water poisoned by Monarch Industries but the plant she worked for didn't offer insurance and the best she could do by the government wasn't enough to aggressively treat her illness, an illness that was given permission to eat her alive from the inside out.

Eaten alive led to the slaughter.

Baby killer.

But Ron knew better. He knew his son wasn't no baby killer.

The bottle shattered on the ground loud enough to cover the sound of Ron Griffen weeping.

The next morning, he checked himself in to Mosier Hospital Detox unit.

CHAPTER 53

September 23, 2016

Collin

Collin didn't fully understand where he was but accepted it in that strange way that one adapts to being thrust into a Twilight Zone so removed from his inner workings it might as well be another world. He vaguely remembered a book in which a man woke up in prison. What was it called? He couldn't remember, but thought it might have been the man's birthday. Sometimes you just had to accept things and work with it. A shitty town, an alcoholic dad, a lousy job.

A quiet man.

He appeared suddenly; it seemed to Collin.

He appeared. And sometimes he talked. But mostly he just sat.

The man had a dog. A black dog.

At first Collin thought it was a pig, and maybe it had been. In this strange world, things can happen. You can be in different places all at once.

A pig can be a dog.

He had a dog, Collin suddenly remembered.

Suzie.

Suzie was definitely not a pig. She was a Beagle. The least piggie looking dog you could have. Could the black dog be Suzie? Could that be the kind of world this was?

The man was speaking.

"How ya doin' today, sir?" He was younger than Collin, but not by much.

Collin waited, watching, waiting to see what the man would turn into. In his anticipation, he forgot that the man's question deserved an answer.

He had not been in the habit of answering questions, but he liked this guy. This guy visited before a few times. Was it real or a dream? It was hard to tell sometimes, but Collin was sure it was real. At least once. He liked the dog, pig, dog no it was a dog.

The question, what was the question? The man was watching him with a patient, soft face. Not grinning, not scowling, just soft and patient.

"My name is Bobby Ray. This here is my dog, Dodger."

"Kafka," Collin murmured, not because it was his name but because he finally remembered the author of the story about the man who woke up in prison. The man's eyebrows raised. He began to shrink, shrink back, away from the man and the pig, but caught himself. It felt ok. The man felt ok. He didn't startle, he didn't stand, or yell. The pig didn't squeal because it was a dog and Collin could see that now. The air hung heavy for a moment, and the man with the dog spoke.

"You like Kafka?"

He sounded like the song that sang about the man who stopped loving her today. That song was like a joke, except instead of a happy ending, it had a sad punch line.

Collin didn't know how to answer. It occurred to him it might have been a long time since he had spoken to anyone, though he couldn't remember exactly. This was a world of sounds and smells and sights, but it was a world his own voice hadn't entered until just now.

"Your dog. It's a dog. Does he stay a dog?" Collin asked, not even sure what it was he was trying to learn, only that for a moment reality would stop changing. It would just hold still and the pigs and the screams and the nurses and the bosses and the fathers and the cell doors would just stop. A dog needed to just stay a dog.

"This here dog," Bobby Ray began "he saved my life. I was a sad, confused, lost man. Is he just a dog? I don't know, my friend. It seems he is sometimes more than a dog. He is a guardian angel. I guess he is only a dog because that is what we call him. Maybe he would call himself something else, who knows?"

* * *

The man with the dog returned the next day.

"You look good, my friend!"

After a moment, Collin realized this was a reference to the fact that he showered today.

When did he last shower? He couldn't recall.

"You brought your dog," Collin replied.

"Yes, and he is still a dog. Would you like to pet him? He is mighty friendly."

Collin approached the pair. Man, and beast. Both patient, friendly and smiling. Was it a trick? No, it didn't feel like a trick. It was a dog. A good dog. Collin sat down on the ground.

He lifted a hand and placed it on the dog's head. The dog waited patiently as Collin tested the limits of his trust. A gentle stroke on the dog's head, then over his snout.

Pig.

Snout

Pig.

Squeal.

Dog. The dog remained a dog.

And Collin, the man, burst into tears.

* * *

Bobby Ray returned a third time that week, even though his volunteer work only required him to visit weekly. He couldn't get Collin out of his mind. He knew the man's story and read the articles in the paper. He couldn't believe that such a kind, quiet man could have murdered his baby.

Until he remembered what he had been forced to do. In the war. Collin hadn't been in a war, but Bobby Ray knew there had to be something. He was fighting a war with something. He had been transformed.

Kafka

Prison

Transformation. Metamorphosis.

Bobby Ray had returned with a book from the library.

He and Dodger entered the visiting room, and again Collin was clean and showered. He was even more alert than the day before. The tears had scared Bobby Ray at first. What should he do? He recalled waiting on his last visit. He just waited, taking a cue from Dodger, who just sat and waited.

Did the dog stay a dog? What had the man been trying to make sense of? Eventually the tears had stopped, and the man retreated back into himself, but Bobby Ray could see something inside him was awakening. Bobby Ray recalled how it felt when his awakening began. Both as a veteran and a man with a brain injury.

Bobby Ray sat down with Dodger, a tattered book at his side.

"Hello, my friend," Bobby Ray said. The man nodded his head as if he was nudging the words out.

"Hello. Hello again. I brought a book to share with you. It's by your man Kafka."

The dog stayed a dog this time, too. Collin was sad to see them leave, but the man… the man… Bobby Ray, left the book for him to read. In the book, a man woke up one morning and was a bug.

A giant bug?

A cockroach?

A dung beagle… no dung-beetle…. It seemed important to Collin, though he couldn't say why, to grasp the size of the bug. If the man was a small bug, it would somehow differ from if the man was a big bug. Would the result have been the same? The man had been a man. Then he was a bug, and life went on. Except that his family regarded him with disgust. Then they forgot about him.

Collin had been treated with disgust. Why?

And he felt forgotten about. Had Jolene been to visit him? Where was Quinn? Were they ok? Were they here too, some place he couldn't see them?

Had they turned in to bugs? Or Pigs? Or Dogs?

Why hadn't they come?

CHAPTER 54

September 29, 2016

Collin

That night in dreams Collin heard pigs squeal, he heard doors slam; he felt a floating, vague sense of terror. He was on the Kill Floor at Monarch Industries. First the room was empty, save for the pigs, squealing and screaming, huddled masses yearning to be free, he thought. Or had he seen that written somewhere?

A dog entered the room, his paws padding through the blood smears on the floor. A happy little black pit bull. Dodger. The dog was Dodger, and he stayed a dog. He was a good dog.

Even with the pigs around, he only stayed a dog.

Collin's fear gave way just slightly at the sight of the dog, but where was the man? How could the dog be here without the man? But he was a man, Collin realized. He was the man and here was a dog, a boy and his dog here with the pigs. The dog looked at him knowingly.

"It's ok," the dog seemed to say. "Brace yourself, hombre."

Collin heard the squeals grow louder, closer. He wanted them to stop. And a child's voice singing *Olllld Mc Dooooonaaalld's haaaad aaaaa faaaarm.*

Collin followed the voice, and he saw himself. In his living room with Quinn and the plastic farm animals. He saw himself worn and beaten down. He saw the purple caverns below his eyes. Saw himself rubbing his head to try to smooth away the migraine and erase the sound of the pigs squealing.

But the pigs weren't squealing now. They were silent. They too were watching.

And the dog sat faithfully by watching as well. Saying, "You're ok, it's ok, you gotta see this."

And Collin saw himself screaming at the pig, the child, for it was a child. It wasn't a pig. It was a child. He screamed at the child and the child screamed back. He saw himself throw the coffee table. He saw it break. He saw himself pick up a leg of the coffee table and run for the screaming child who was not a pig, not a pig a child a child who would stay a child except he wouldn't because he was dead.

CHAPTER 55

September 30, 2016

Cam

Cam was just leaving the office when the call came in. Dierdre, from the jail, sounded excited, but something was off.

"Cam, he's had a breakthrough."

"What does that mean?" Cam had asked.

"The good news is, Collin is lucid. He seems to be out of the psychotic state. The meds apparently are working. The bad news though is that he is talking about suicide."

Cam knew that even in a secure facility, inmates could take their own lives. Dierdre said they were putting him on constant observation and isolation. Cam could visit, if he wanted to try to reintroduce himself, but Collin's state was fragile. As Cam drove to the jail, he wondered at the futility of the social worker and staff who would work to keep Collin alive, knowing he was likely to be put to death by the state, anyway. It seemed kind of pointless.

As pointless as fighting to defend someone you know is guilty of murder and is going to lose? A voice in his mind asked.

Yes, he answered to himself, that pointless.

Then why do it? Why work late, why further destroy your marriage? Why take time away from other clients when you know this boy is dead meat?

Cam thought of Collin, sitting in a cell, being convinced by well-meaning do-gooders to stay alive, only to await the time when a judge and jury would sentence him to death. Lead him to slaughter, Cam thought. Like one of the pigs. Cam shook the image out of his mind.

I'm spending too much time with the PETA people. He told himself.

* * *

Dierdre met him at the front desk and Cam was relieved because the guard on duty was the same man who had given him a hassle back when this whole thing had started. He wasn't in the mood for games today.

As they walked to Collin's cell, Dierdre prepped Cam with further details.

Collin was oriented to place, but not date, which was reasonable considering the length of time that had passed. He may not remember the details of the ordeal that lead to him killing Quinn, but he understood that Quinn was dead, and he was responsible.

Cam jotted down notes as he was briefed on the situation. Approaching the cell, Cam noticed that for all his remaining distress Collin was at least better groomed than before. He appeared to have showered and shaved at some point. He still looked gaunt and showed signs of insomnia recently. His thumb had healed and was no longer bandaged. He sat with his knees pulled up to his chest, arms wrapped around his knees, head down. Like a child trying to hide,

"Collin?" Dierdre tried to get his attention. This time, he responded. Looking up, his gaze went to Dierdre, then to Cam, then back to Dierdre.

"Yes, ma'am?" he asked.

"There's someone here to talk with you. This is your attorney. His name is Cameron Burton. He's been doing a lot of research on your behalf. He's going to try to help you."

Collin took this in with momentary silence. His eyes watered and he turned to Cam, a pleading look on his face.

"Why?"

"Because it's the law. Every person in this country has a right to be represented in a court. I'm going to do the best I can to make a case for you. To advocate for you, but I need your help. I need you to help me paint a picture of what life was like…."

Collin shook his head.

"I don't want to paint a picture of what happened. I don't need a defense. I don't need to waste your time. Let them kill me. For all the things I've done, it's what I deserve."

The trio fell silent. Cam and Dierdre eyed each other awkwardly. Collin put his head back down. Dierdre began, "Collin, you have a chance to prove that you had a breakdown. That this wasn't you, you love your son and would never have done this if not for this illness and other circumstances. You can help Mr. Burton convince a jury of that."

Collin looked up again.

"How am I going to convince a jury of that, I can't even convince myself of it?"

* * *

Cam was mostly silent during the initial meeting because his frustration was brewing just beneath the surface. He knew the last thing Collin needed was to be further berated, but the aggravation, all the time and energy for someone who wouldn't be bothered to even try to help himself, Cam found it infuriating. As he and Dierdre walked out of the tier, he tried to explain this as professionally as possible.

"I guess I am at a loss for words when it comes to convincing someone that they should care about their fate, when that fate is about to be decided by people who won't care. How do you convince a suicidal man facing execution that it is worth trying to prove their innocence?"

"The team here will work on the mental health part," Dierdre tried to reassure him. It wasn't convincing, though. Still, Cam agreed. They would work on stabilizing him with medication, Cam just needed to work on his defense.

There was something deeper that both irked and intrigued Cam about this case. He kicked himself for pouring so much time into it. He knew Donna resented him for being away so much and especially for trying so hard to help someone who killed his own kid when their child, the one they had been so eagerly anticipating, had been born dead years before. It felt like a betrayal to her, Cam knew. Maybe it felt that way to him, too. But something kept him focusing on this case even though it felt like a monumental waste of his time and skills.

Was it selfishness? He challenged himself. The desire to stick it to Steuben and the Judge? Was he actually entertaining some fantasy in which he could amaze a jury with his ingenious connections, set a new precedent in legal proceedings? Was he hoping to sit there, smugly admiring his job well done when a jury finds his client not guilty against all odds?

A young man's life was on the line. Had he really been making this all about him and his career? Or was he just a sucker who couldn't help rooting for the losing team?

* * *

As he left the building, Cam noticed a young Black man walking with a sleek, grinning pit bull. The dog wore a vest that read 'Service Animal, Friendly.'

Cam approached the young man.

"You must be the fellow who's volunteering to visit inmates with your dog, correct?"

"Yes sir. My name's Bobby Ray, and this here is Dodger. You can pet him, he loves people."

Cam wasn't much of a dog person, but Dodger was enough of a people person that before Cam could respond, the panting, grinning dog had firmly planted his body on top of Cam's right foot. Dodger leaned against Cam's leg and nudged him with his heavy snout. Cam couldn't help laughing and bent down to pet the dog's smooth head.

"He's a happy dog, it appears."

"Yes, he loves everybody, and he loves coming here."

"Well, I think it's a fortunate thing, my running in to you here, I'm Cam Burton, Collin's lawyer. I understand you've been meeting with my client for a bit. Do you mind if I ask you some questions about your visits and your take on Collin and his personality and all?"

"Sure, I would be happy to help, but I'm not a medical professional," Bobby Ray answered.

"Sometimes, I find it's better to have a novice perspective. Someone who isn't biased by professional experience. Someone who is on the outside, looking in," Cam replied, then went on. "How would you describe Collin in the time you've gotten to know him?"

Cam flipped open his steno pad and grabbed his pen. He tried to balance with Dodger's weight still heavy on his foot.

"Well, I know of what he's accused of doing and all, but I can say if I didn't know that in advance, I would never've guessed it."

"I'm hearing that a lot," Cam noted. "Have you observed any violence or aggression in your visits with him? Even in the things he says? Threats or anything?"

"Not at all. We talk about books. Mostly Kafka."

Cam looked at the young man over the rims of his glasses. "Kafka? Really." But hadn't Jolene said Collin loved to read? That was one of their earliest connections as teenagers.

"Yes, it's strange, isn't it? People bond over the most random things. But he's a smart guy. Seems like it anyway. Seems like he come up on a rough time in his life. Made choices he thought he had to make, I mean about his work, not about the murder. That just seems like he was out of control. I'm not a professional, but that's my opinion at least. Guy sitting in that cell? He wouldn't hurt a fly."

Cam pressed on, testing Bobby Ray's theory. "Perhaps not. But he killed a child and was responsible for hurting a whole lot of animals from the work he was doing."

"Yeah. That's true. But that wasn't him. It was, or it seems like it was, a situation. Like me. I'm a veteran. The last thing I ever wanted to do was to hurt anyone. Some kids I enlisted with were flag waving, just excited to go off and kill people. Not me. I just wanted to get an education. Had no other option. It was the only way I was going to see the inside of a college, or so I thought. So, I enlisted. I hated it. I did what I had to do, not proud of it. I killed people. May have killed children. It messed me up pretty bad. Brain injury, PTSD, whole bit," Bobby Ray looked off into the distance for a moment and then turned back to face Cam.

"But you know what, Mr. I'm sorry, what did you say your name was again?"

"Cam, you can call me Cam."

"Ok, you know what, Mr. Cam? I could easily have been sitting in where Collin is sitting. That could have been me, no doubt. Could be anyone. No offense meant, sir, but it could even be you, if you're put into those circumstances. Could be any of us. Forced to do what is unnatural just to try to survive."

"But you're out here. You're contributing to society. What do you think the difference is?" Cam asked.

"Lots of therapy, maybe. Maybe just plain luck. Maybe some twist of fate that turned me onto a different road and Collin onto another road. 'There but for the Grace of God go I', they say."

"They do say that," Cam replied.

"I don't think badly of Collin, I feel bad for him. He's as average Joe as you get. If he can go down a path that leads to something so horrible, so could anyone else. Since I started talking to him, I actually started learning more about where he used to work. I stopped eating meat. In the store, even my favorite foods, hot dogs, all I see is Collin sitting in that jail. I know what's behind the scenes now. How it ruins people's lives. Their families. I think of it like a boycott. For inhumane conditions or something."

Cam couldn't argue there. He, too, had lost his appetite for most of his previous favorites.

"Bobby Ray, I appreciate you talking with me. I'll let you go along with your day, but just to give you the head's up, Collin is having a rough day. They have him on suicide watch. He's become lucid, you may know, and the recent events are catching up with him."

"Thank you for the heads up. I sure hope they keep him safe. He has to testify. He's gotta tell his story," Bobby Ray's passion struck Cam.

"Why do you say that?" Cam asked.

"Because people have to know. Even if it's too late for Collin. Think of the others who can be saved by his story coming out."

CHAPTER 56

October 2, 2016

Cam

Cam was led to Collin's cell for the second day in a row. This time by a CO who stood a short distance back, looking bored. It's ok, Cam told himself, at least he's not interfering. Cam had a folded newspaper under his steno pad today.

Cam noted that Collin, for whatever loss of hope he was feeling, had continued to maintain his grooming. At least, as well as could be expected while in jail. Collin was reading a book today. Another guard sat watching from outside the cell. Constant Observation, Cam thought, 24-hour suicide watch until Collin's mental status improved. He noticed Collin wasn't curled up in a despondent posture today. Instead he was pacing, trying to avoid eye-contact with his observer. Cam thought he seemed anxious today.

Collin responded to Cam's greeting. Cam was relieved by this and thought he saw some relief in Collin's eyes. Happy to see a familiar face? He wondered.

"Good morning, sir," Collin responded.

Cam froze. What do you say to a suicidal man who is likely to be dead soon, anyway?

"How was breakfast?" Cam asked. That was stupid. He told himself.

"I haven't had an appetite. I had some of the hash browns. They were ok. I guess."

"Ok, that was a dumb question to lead with," Cam admitted.

Collin smiled. Cam felt like he could breathe easier. A smile was something. He tried again.

"How are you holding up?"

Cam thought for a moment before replying. "For a few moments, I feel like maybe I'll be ok. Then I don't care if I'm ok or not, I just wish I was dead. I hate myself for what I did. Miss my wife and," his voice began to crack, "my son."

Cam waited patiently as Collin stopped pacing and sat heavily on the bed inside his cell. All blankets had been removed. Most everything except a paperback had been removed. Additional safety measures.

Collin wiped away tears and struggled to slow his ragged breaths. He wiped his nose with the back of his hand and hiccupped.

"I'm going to be really honest with you, young man," Cam began. "I don't have the answers for you. I don't know if a jury will redeem you. I can't make you see yourself as redeemable. But in the short time I've gotten to know you, and what I've heard from those who know you, I don't think you're unworthy of redemption. I don't think you're unworthy of bringing something good from all of this."

Collin didn't respond. Cam thought he appeared to be listening, his gaze looking just past Cam's shoulder. Cam wondered if he was seeing things or just avoiding eye contact. He got his answer then, Collin shifted his gaze to face Cam directly, but then averted his eyes. Behind Cam, a door slammed further down the hallway. Collin's entire body shook but Cam saw him steady himself again.

"This is what we're talking about," Cam began again. "Your response, the vigilance, that's all a part of PTSD. Are you familiar with the symptoms of Post-Traumatic Stress Disorder?"

"Yeah, kind of. I know about it from books. I think my dad may have some signs of it from the war. He drinks so much though, he covers everything. Bobby Ray talks about it."

"I met that young man yesterday. He thinks well of you. He sees good in you."

Collin was silent but seemed to take in Cam's words, so he continued. "It's not just you. Cases of PTSD in slaughterhouse workers are well documented, Collin. Maybe you've even seen it yourself. In your coworkers?"

"I guess. I didn't pay much attention, tried not to anyway."

"I can't guarantee this will hold any water with a jury, Collin, but there are others out there who are being destroyed by the work you were doing. The work that destroyed... a part of you... at least temporarily. That destroyed your family."

Collin seemed to be with him so far, Cam thought. He weighed whether to push further, then decided in favor of taking the risk, even though it could backfire, badly.

"Collin, did you know a man named Jose Hernandez?"

"Yes. Sort of. We weren't close friends. We went to school together. He was younger though," Collin's attention seemed to go somewhere else. He turned his head slightly as if he was watching a scene replay.

Shit, Cam thought, I pushed too hard; I lost him. But his assumption was wrong. Collin began to recount the memory replaying in his mind. As he told the story, Collin ran a hand over the side of the bed as if scratching at an itch.

"When we were kids, I don't know how old, I was coming home from school. Some kids older than me were beating on him. I don't know why. Probably just because his family was from Mexico. I should've broken it up. I thought about it. I wanted to. I wanted to be like my dad and just run up on them screaming, not afraid of anything. But I didn't. I ran into the gas station and told the guy working there. He broke it up. I saw Jose around here and there, and then he was at Monarch when I started."

"Collin, I've got some bad news. I'm not sure if telling you this is a good idea or not. But I'm going to because I want you to understand why this could be an important case for a lot of people."

Collin took a deep breath and looked Cam in the face.

"Ok. I guess you can tell me."

"I spoke to Jose's sister. Let me back up. There was an article in the paper. Jose was missing. They mentioned Monarch in the article. I thought maybe worth looking into. I talked to Rosa, his sister. She was suspicious of your, his, coworkers having something to do with this."

Collin closed his eyes as if he was expecting what came next.

Cam went on. "They found his body. It's being called a suicide, but Rosa isn't convinced and the medical professionals who examined him found evidence of abuse. Do you understand where I'm going with this?"

Collin nodded his head slowly. He covered his eyes with both hands and took a deep breath. When he lowered his hands, Cam thought he saw a different person where a scared young man had been sitting. Collin's expression showed resolve, toughness even.

"Ok. That doesn't surprise me. I mean, that he's dead, yes. But not that he was being bullied. They do it. With everyone. With the animals even. It's a horrible place. I just wanted to get through it. We were so close to having the credit cards under control," Tears began again, rolling slowly down Collin's face.

"I knew it was wrong to do. The first day there. You know it's unnatural. But you also think, if I eat meat, if my parents, grandparents, the Pope, everyone, eats meat, then this is where it comes from. It's got to be done. And when you're desperate. You've got to make money. I never imagined it was as bad as it is. How can anyone imagine it? I told Jolene maybe just a few more months. She wanted me to quit then and there. I couldn't have that. I couldn't avoid doing my job as a husband," he closed his eyes tight as more tears escaped. "As a father. I was so close to just being done. Once the cards were paid off. I would have been able to quit. Now it's too late."

"Perhaps," Cam replied. "Perhaps too late for that plan. Too late for Quinn. Maybe even too late for you, Collin, if I'm being totally honest here. But not too late for another Jose. For another, Quinn. For another young man out there, whose only option is to go to a place like Monarch. Not too late, Collin, because the whole world is going to be paying attention to this trial. What you bring to light, it could ripple out. It could reach far beyond Mosier. Beyond Monarch. Maybe that's the only good that can come from it. For people to understand what their appetites are costing, to others, to the animals even."

Collin nodded his head slowly.

"Collin, I just ask that you think about this. Ok? Just give it some thought. No matter what, I'm going to advocate for you. I'm going to try to convince strangers you deserve another chance and that this industry is brutal and evil. You can make that easier for me to do by believing you deserve a second chance to, but I'm going to represent you no matter what."

Collin smiled. "Thank you. I don't know why you're doing it, but I guess I can think about it."

"I'm not sure, other than I have a job to do. And so do you."

* * *

Cam tried to make it home at a reasonable time that evening. He was close. Only a half hour late. Would've been on time, but once again he had the strange feeling he was being followed. This time the car was too far back to see clearly.

CHAPTER 57

October 3, 2016

Cam

"This is Matt," the Animal Rights Lawyer always answered the phone just as Cam was certain he was headed for voicemail.

"Matt, Cam Burton, am I catching you at a bad time?"

"Not at all, just editing some scenes for the documentary."

"You'll have to let me know when you have it all completed, I'd be interested in seeing it. I was wondering if I could get your opinion on the profile I put together for potential jurors? People whose sympathies may be more like, you know, the animal people."

Matt chuckled. "It's not that simple. You could get twelve card-carrying members of PETA and seven of them will want to see him killed for having a part in animal agriculture, while four may see him as a victim of the industry. Maybe not that exact breakdown, but you get my point."

Cam scribbled along in his steno pad, beside the notes he had outlined.

"Ok," Cam replied, "I follow you, but here's what I'm thinking so far," Cam skimmed through his notes. "Collin's age, I think just based on appearance and personality, will possibly draw sympathy from other young people, A younger juror may empathize with the difficult job market and taking work out of necessity even if they hate the job. Also thinking, working class, favorable over affluent.

I was wondering about dog or cat owners, though, could go either way. Sympathize with him for being put in a position of having to kill animals or hate him for the same thing."

"That's going to be the issue no matter what, Cam. It can go either way. A working-class jury may be more concrete, less interested in psychological explanations and excuses, also more conservative and less inclined to give people a pass for what they see as bad behavior," Matt pointed out. "Also, someone who loves animals but still eats them is going to have a hard time being convinced that Collin is no different than they could be in his shoes. It's the same battle we have in the Animal Rights community every day. Animal shelters save animals while having hot dog cookouts to raise money. People will call for your blood if you kick a dog but will look the other way while others cut pigs, chickens and cows apart. You've got to make a compelling case, I don't have to tell you that."

"Do you think a more liberal juror may sympathize? Who are the majority of the Animal Rights crowd from your perspective?"

"It varies but historically speaking there have always been more women taking the lead in Animal Rights. Many SPCA's were founded by white women with means to be philanthropic. There are also communities of people of color who are spreading the message that animal agriculture perpetuates racism, food scarcity and is a byproduct of colonialism."

Cam jotted down as much as he could. Matt continued.

"Still, getting people to see the truth let alone empathize with someone who is responsible, in part, for partaking in this industry triggers their own cognitive dissonance. It reminds them that they too are responsible as consumers. You want to take the approach that it's not their fault, they didn't know better, but as they learn more, it will make them feel uncomfortable about some of their choices and the like."

"Ok I'm taking this all down this is great, thank you."

"Younger people who are inclined to look at the broader systemic injustices, which right away implies liberal or college educated, and of means, though not so affluent as to be out of touch with the harsh reality Collin and people who end up doing the work he did are living in."

Cam's stomach was in knots. In Mosier, this was going to be like trying to fill the jury with unicorns.

"I'll give it my best, but you've been to Mosier. This will be a tall order."

"Aim as close as you can, do the rest with your powers of persuasion. You want to go for people who are open to working through their own cognitive dissonance. A jury full of black-and-white thinkers who believe that something is either good or evil will not be moved by your argument."

"Thanks a lot, Matt, I appreciate it," Cam was about to hang up, but one more question had been hanging in his mind. "Matt, can I ask you, on a more personal note."

"Sure."

"If you were one of the twelve PETA members in the imaginary jury, based on your own feelings, would you be one of the seven who wants Collin to suffer for what he did, or one of the four who see him as a victim?"

"If I were one of the seven, I wouldn't be helping you to advocate for him. This industry kills everyone and everything it touches. It just kills some beings faster than others."

* * *

The mid-autumn sun was unforgiving the afternoon Cam sat in the Mosier County Courthouse for jury selection. Though the building had an air conditioner, they used sparingly it. Cam, who relied on fans and open windows in his own office and home, was accustomed to this. It appeared the prospective jurors were not. They'd dressed in layers, expecting the typical indoor blast of cold air to offset the raging midday heat. Proceedings hadn't even begun and already people were getting antsy.

He could tell. A middle-aged woman in the front row was sighing and huffing in dismay. Her blonde hair matted to her forehead with sweat. She brought a fashion magazine to read and was now using it as a fan. This seemed to annoy the young man with a five o'clock-shadow who sat next to her. He must have come from work. His T-shirt had the logo for the local grocery mart and as was customary of this uniform, he wore long black pants and black sneakers. His clothes were stained, and he looked underfed. Cam guessed he was in his mid-twenties. Grocery kid tried to scroll through his phone but continually looked up to give blondie the side-eye.

Cam jotted a note. Grocery Clerk, maybe?

An older woman sat on grocery clerk's other side. Her t-shirt caught Cam's attention. Paw prints and the phrase 'my cats walk all over me.' Cam took notes. A young Black Woman with reading glasses in the row behind them was busily turning the pages of a book. Cam squinted to catch the title. *Mr. Mercedes* by Stephen King. He had seen this on sale at the store but hadn't read it. He preferred historical fiction.

Cam scanned the crowd for further clues. The majority of the forty or so assembled appeared middle-aged or older. A few younger people in their twenties.

The Bailiff spoke. "All rise, Honorable Judge LeClair presiding."

Cam stood as the judge, face red and puffing for air, took his place at the bench. Judge LeClair leaned down and plugged in a small table fan, wiped sweat from his brow, and the process of jury selection began.

First called was Latina woman. Possibly in her late forties, Cam thought. He methodically began asking the questions on his list. "What do you do for a living, ma'am?"

"I own a salon."

"Do you have a college degree?"

"Two, cosmetology and business administration."

Cam jotted down notes.

"Do you own any pets?"

"I have a dog. His name is Maxi."

Cam smiled and took down the reply.

"Do you have any dietary restrictions or special dietary needs?"

She looked at him quizzically and answered, "I'm a vegetarian."

Cam didn't get too excited. This was likely a lucky break. But he made a note of it.

Cam had a hunch this would not be easy. As the day went on, he found little in the jury selection process that met his profile. Grocery Clerk was not a vegetarian. His favorite foods were hot dogs and bratwurst. He was still in college, studying Criminal Justice. Cam thought that may be an advantage. The young woman reading Mr. Mercedes had an interest in the thrillers genre, but did not seem to have much empathy for those involved in real-life horror stories.

"Have you ever been convicted of a crime?"

"No."

"Do you know anyone who has been convicted of a violent crime? If so, what is your relationship to that person?"

"I had an ex who beat someone up bad. Sent them to the hospital. When I found out I broke up with him. We don't talk anymore."

As the day wore on Cam became irritated by some of the prospects. He tried to hide it. Probably just the heat, he told himself.

They called another number. A young man who Cam guessed to be about Collin's age came forward. Cam was hopeful. Maybe someone who would empathize with someone his own age just trying to get a break. The young man was clean shaven and well dressed. Cam guessed college educated.

"Do you have a college degree?"

"No."

Strike one.

"What do you do for a living?"

"I'm assistant manager at a convenience store."

Promising? Cam thought. He tried not to stare but caught sight of the spine of the book the young man held in his lap. Jordan Peterson. Strike two, Cam thought.

"Do you have any pets?" Cam asked, trying to sound casual.

"I don't."

"Do you believe there are cultural, social or environmental factors that influence people's behavior?" Cam asked.

"I believe people know right from wrong and act accordingly. I don't subscribe to such Cultural Marxist ideas," he replied smugly.

Strike three. Cam had studied economics and was sure Cultural Marxism was a recent invention. Either way, he crossed the young man off his list.

The woman with the sweat soaked blond hair was college educated, but Cam couldn't tell if it was the sticky heat of the afternoon or her disdain for being interrupted from her work as a Social Studies teacher that was to blame for her flippant attitude. He jotted some notes but wasn't altogether hopeful.

Mary, a Black Woman in her seventies, caught his attention. Cam's questioning revealed that she was a retired English teacher whose hobbies included rescuing cats and riding motorcycle.

"How many cats have you rescued?" he asked.

"In total, about eighty. Right now, I got about ten living with me."

"Are you a member of any animal rights organizations?" he had asked.

"I give money to the ASPCA and to local rescues."

"Do you have any biases against animal abusers or those accused of domestic violence?" Cam had to ask.

"I don't have a bias until its proven. Accused can mean a lot of things. They can accuse a hoarder of animal abuse, but mental illness, and not underlying cruelty, is the actual issue."

Cam tried to conceal his excitement. The others weren't so promising. A white man in his forties who worked as a freelance web designer and part time DJ wearing a Make America Great Again hat flat out responded that he and his brothers had a 'special way' of dealing with people who were accused of being violent to their families.

Cam crossed his number off the list.

Is this really the best of empathy and intellect in Mosier? He asked himself as he looked at the shrinking list of ideal jurors. Of all those interviewed, he could identify three that minimally fit his profile.

CHAPTER 58

October 9, 2016

Bud Jennings

"You're listening to the voice of Mosier County, the Bud Jennings Show! Thank you, patriots, for joining me for another episode of the Bud Jennings Show. The Voice of Reason for American values in North Carolina. I'm Bud Jennings, and today I will be speaking to Doctor Neil McDermott, who will help us understand why good people turn bad. Dr. McDermott, welcome to the show!"

"Thank you, Bud, I'm a big fan of your show!"

"So, Dr. McDermott I'll get right to it, there's a killer in our midst. Every day you hear reports of violence, terrorism, mass shootings, school shootings, and now right here in Mosier, a violent infanticide, a horrific crime. What is it that makes these sickos tick? Are murderers….is there a gene… or something… is there a profile of a mass murderer or a terrorist?"

"That is the million-dollar question, isn't it Mr. Jennings? My research suggests that it's a little of both. For example, we saw the case in Pattersburgh, you may recall, where a young man opened fire on his college campus. This was two, maybe five years ago. Well, Marques Jones, the young man convicted, it turns out he had no history of violence… no real… nothing you could pinpoint and say 'that man's a kook' right? But then you dig deeper, and what do you find? You find a young man from a broken home, a young man who was involved in drugs, and some suspicion of homosexuality."

"And it equates, or wouldn't you say…" Bud jumped in, now more animated, "back to broken homes which we all know, this all began, with women leaving the home and getting into the work-force, wouldn't you say?"

* * *

"This is bullshit! These are totally separate cases! One has nothing to do with the other!" Cam exclaimed.

"Amazing what passes for news these days," his wife concurred, one of the few things they had agreed on lately.

"News?! Even what passes for facts! Research? What research is this nut talking about?!"

"Don't overlook this 'nut' and those like him. These will be your jurors."

Cam turned up the volume on his vintage radio. It was part of his work process. He considered it advantageous to seek news sources from both left and right wing outlets, but found television news to be the most trite form of media. His preference was print, but radio gave a pulse on the community invaluable to his work. Potential jurors and judges.

"Dr. McDermott? Let me guess, he downloaded the degree from a website?"

His wife just rolled her eyes, then took a seat to listen in to what could have possibly riled her husband so much.

The disembodied voices continued.

"So, you agree," Budd went on "that if Collin Griffen's mother had been a stay at home mother, his baby would still be alive? Is that it?"

"Well, I don't know if it is fair to say that one factor is to blame for this case, it's usually several factors but when you boil it all down, the common ingredient is the disintegration of the family."

"How often do you see, in your experience, a case where a young person will have a sudden outburst of violence, with no history?"

"Well, it's common. I mean, it's the quiet ones you have to watch out for, right? That's what they say, and I believe it. In fact, it's my observation that the louder, the more dramatic, let's say, the more aggressive a child is, for example, you have, today, you have a lot of people jumping the gun and getting all excited about every little thing… so you have the mothers and the teachers and the counselors who want to crucify a child for, let's say, getting into a little rough and tumble, let's say, for going out on the playground and doing what kids have done for a long time. When you and I were kids, right? Do you remember?"

"Boys got to be boys. It's the whole PC culture that we have been brainwashed into- the liberal agenda- that is making kids too soft …" Bud chimed in.

* * *

"Jesus Christ, are you kidding me?! This guy is comparing the Griffen case to Marques Jones! Are you serious? Marques Jones committed a mass shooting because he had been bullied his whole life, you gun loving quack!" Cam was now engaged in a heated debate with his laptop, the sight of which would have been amusing if the content had not been so tragic.

"Its people like this," Cam continued, "Its people like this who get the public all riled up and twisted up. All these Bible bangers! Collin's a white guy so they can't blame it on Black culture, or Islamic state so what's next? Homosexuality! Can you believe this?"

"Its people like this," Budd Jennings' voice seemed to echo, mockingly "people like this who reinforce the importance of the second amendment."

"Right! Some diligent NRA toady down the street was really going to stop Quinn Griffen getting killed."

"Its people like this that remind us how low we have fallen as a country. All the liberals and their rhetoric, but here we are, economy in the toilet, immigrants rushing through the borders, thousands, a day, and shootings, every day all these shootings."

Cam was now gripping the arm of his chair, clenching his fists. He yelled at the men who couldn't hear him. "Griffen used a coffee table leg, you moron, maybe you should mention that, then we could make IKEA address the IKEA agenda permeating liberal households!"

He saw Donna try to stifle a laugh, she was unsuccessful.

The commentary continued to emanate from the ethers.

"It's indeed troubling," Dr. McDermott continued, "but if we are ever going to reclaim the values that make us the greatest country in the world, we need to stop coddling. We need to stop excusing the mentally ill and pardoning them."

"Do you think Griffen should get the death penalty?"

"Yes! If he is found guilty, I believe he will be found guilty and he should get the death penalty. We need to send a strong, clear message. Mental illness is not, look, some people have a mental illness, right? They have a case of bipolar disorder or depression and they are able to get treatment, which is the responsibility... by the way... if I have heart disease, you know the liberals love to compare mental illness to heart disease so if I have heart disease it is my responsibility to manage it, right? It is my responsibility to cut back on the sausage and bacon and not for others to feel sorry or coddle me or that kind of thing. So, we have facilities... we have great institutions and if a mentally ill person refuses to go to these facilities to get help and they commit a crime, they need to be held accountable."

"Never mind that Prisons have become the new treatment facilities!" Cam yelled at the radio in rebuttal. He snapped off the switch, something Donna had never seen him do. Grabbing his steno pad and pen, he headed for the door.

"Where are you going?" Donna asked after him.

"Going for a walk down to the library, try to clean my head from that nonsense."

Out in the fresh air, his mind was beginning to settle. He didn't often lose control of his emotions this way. The case was getting to him. Or something was. His peace of mind was returning until he rounded the corner of the serene suburban block and gasped.

He was facing his neighbor's newly remodeled house. Manicured lawn, children's bicycles out front, abandoned. His neighbor who had celebrated July fourth with his family only a month and change ago. Whose children had sold Cam and his wife countless orders of Girl Scout cookies and candy bars for various school fund raisers.

The girls' bike now rested on the grass between two signs. One read "Make America Great Again" the other, handmade, read "Fry in Hell Collin Griffen."

CHAPTER 59

October 2016

Cam

Cam had received countless death threats and menacing letters since it became public knowledge that he would be defending Collin Griffen. He had been focusing his efforts on hunting down potential leads that would help his client, seeking out former Monarch employees, expert psychologists and psychiatrists who might give testimony. Harassment from the general public was becoming routine He had begun screening his calls. "My name is Raol Gutierrez, and I would like to help you," The voicemail began.

Intrigued, he returned the call immediately.

As the phone rang Cam wondered who this man was and what he could possibly have to offer his case, or what he wanted in return. Cam had learned that those who volunteered their help were not always benevolent souls looking for justice. Sometimes they were crackpots looking for attention, or people with an ax to grind who wanted revenge.

"Hello," the man's voice sounded level, calm.

"Hello, this is Cam Burton, returning a call to Raol Gutierrez. Sorry I missed your call just now."

"Thank you, Mr. Burton, for returning my call, yes. I think I can help you. I have been following the reports, in the news, about the young man who worked for Monarch. I used to work for Monarch, and represented the local Meatpackers' Union, Local 29."

* * *

Raol's house was on the other side of Mosier, in a neighborhood that managed to maintain some of the façade of working-class achievement. No boarded-up houses, no graffiti, Raol's neighborhood was frozen in time, a 1975 American working-class haven, modest and sturdy.

Like the pig who built his house of bricks... Cam thought, unsure why the reference to the children's story had surfaced in his mind.

Pigs.

He blocked out the images that had become prominent in his mental landscape since the day he first met with Davenport, first learned an unsettling truth.

Raol greeted him on the porch and being a calm, breezy summer evening, the men took seats on rocking chairs, cold beverages provided by Gutierrez's wife Natalie.

Gutierrez had a noticeable limp when he walked, and when he sat the rocker creaked under his stocky build, and creaked again in protest as he shifted his weight to extend his leg. A position Cam thought looked uncomfortable, but which he assumed the man would not have taken if the alternative had been any more pleasant.

"You like history, Mr. Burton?" Gutierrez asked thoughtfully.

"Yes, Mr. Gutierrez, I am very interested in history. It's one of the aspects of this job that I most enjoy actually, reconstructing a picture that explains events. Understanding the factors that lead people to end up in the system."

"We have this in common," Gutierrez spoke with thoughtful deliberation. Cameron was used to waiting, a habit born of practice, not wanting to miss discrepancies or leads. The law had taught Cameron a degree of patience he didn't have growing up.

"I have been a student of history, unofficially," Gutierrez continued.

"Officially, for just a few semesters. History, sociology, I went to the community college for a few semesters."

Cameron waited with the uncomfortable feeling he sometimes got when he sensed he was being tested, or shown up. It was his experience that people, men especially, would compare their credentials, life experience, college, accomplishments, as if to imply "I may not be a fancy lawyer, but I have read a few books in my time" Cam didn't sense that Gutierrez was showing him up, but something in the man's tone conveyed grief and regret.

"I had a scholarship in 1974, a year later I was drafted."

By reflex, Cam's gaze drifted to Gutierrez' bad leg.

"Oh, this, no, this was a gift from Mosier. No, I never made it into the service."

The man pointed to his thick-lensed glasses.

"I didn't pass the eye exam. Unfortunately, by the time I got my rejection notice, the semester had already started, and I had let my scholarship go. So, no community college for me."

Gutierrez looked off into the distance for a moment, as if he was scanning the horizon for the education that had slipped from his grasp.

"But I also didn't have to go to Vietnam. So, all in all, I got a good deal, right?"

Cam waited for him to continue.

"In 1977 I went to work for Honsinger's Meat Processing plant. Back then, Honsinger's was the big cheese. It began as a family operation in the 1940s and was by the time I got in, it was under the management of Honsinger, Bob Honsinger, that was the original founder, well when I got in it was under the ownership of Bob's son we called him Jr. Well, Jr. was not in the business from the ground up the way his dad was. Honsinger Sr. worked his way up and then started his own company, he had experience in agriculture, in some other big-name companies. Jr., well he came in as some bullshit consultant or another, came in at the top. He inherited it from his dad, but he didn't have the sense or the knowhow."

Cam nodded. Gutierrez sat back in his chair and continued.

"Now when I first got in just as this transition was happening, I had the best of both worlds; I started my career when the Union, Local 29, when we were strong. But we had a good relationship with the management under Honsinger Sr. he was a real innovative type. Now, you won't hear most other union folks talking this way, but to me it isn't us vs. them, we're all working for the same thing, really, and as far as I can see Honsinger Sr. had the insight to recognize that he wasn't making his fortune, we, his workers, were. I don't know where Honsinger Sr. got his brains from, but he didn't seem to leave 'em to his son! Jr, he came in, guns blazing. He was all swept up in the new race to compete, to take on the world, to be the best, and he was not interested in the workers, in the union. His dad stayed in the background as an advisor for the first few years. It was ok. Then, in 1985 Honsinger Sr. dies, Jr. has the whole operation to himself and even though the company was posting record profits, he got greedy. Like they do, you know?"

Cam knew. He acknowledged this with a nod and quiet 'mmm hm.'

"So mid 80s he comes in with a new plan. We were making $10.80 an hour, a good wage for hard and dangerous work. Decent. For a guy like me. So, he comes in and says, 'new plan, this is no longer skilled labor, therefore we are cutting wages to $8.00 an hour'. Non-negotiable. By the way, you wonder what this has to do with Monarch and your young man?"

Cam appreciated the history lesson and didn't want to interrupt. He nodded for Raol to continue. "Well, after the strike ended, Jr. comes in and he lays another bomb. Says he is negotiating a merger with a new company, Monarch Industries. Says that he is laying off half the workforce, and that the jobs done by that arm of the company, those jobs will be outsourced to Monarch, in the same building! Can you imagine? But by now it's late 1980s. Unions in this country were beat badly by then, and our union was no different. We had been fighting. I mean, this was a war zone. The strikers, and the scabs... because that guy, that's the guy who will cost you your job, and it's all downhill from there! So, guys lost their tempers. That same scab who gets escorted into work for the morning shift, he's going to come outside at the end of his shift and his car window smashed in, his tires slashed. I never condone this, but you got to understand your actions have consequences, so you got to do what you got to do, but don't be surprised if it doesn't make you any friends you know?"

Cam nodded.

"So here we go into the 90s slowly Monarch Industries spreads like a cancer, devouring any trace of the company I started out in. The union, forget it, all but demolished. Monarch workers were not eligible for union membership. They were crafty about that. But that wasn't the worst of it. Monarch didn't post jobs most of the time. They didn't need to. Men would show up in vans, then the guys would get off the vans and unload people. Mexicans. They kept people like me around because we could translate, I swear that is the only reason I was kept on. I was Union president at one point, and if there had been more Spanish speakers, I would have been fired much sooner."

"Was this common knowledge? Right out in the open they did this?" Cam asked.

"Pretty much. The new Monarch employees, they are brought in from Mexico. I assure you, there was no one sitting at a desk making sure work permits check out if you know what I mean."

Cam nodded.

"Fast forward to 2008. People around here didn't have much to begin with. Now they are being squeezed even more. The workers at Monarch, they are used to being at the bottom of the food chain. The inspectors and administrators are used to being a little more secure, but not by much actually. But everyone, from the low-wage worker, to the middle managers, to the inspectors, they got one thing in common they're losing. They're scared, they're feeling short changed. Retirement, benefits, all of it being cut. Layoffs, it's bad. People losing what little they had. The middle class cries bloody murder, but they forget. This recession was just another day in the life of those under them on the ladder."

Cam took in this visual, he hadn't given it much thought, but it was true. Even in his circle of progressive professionals, he could recognize how little the downturn of 2008 impacted many of his friends who didn't work with the underprivileged as he did.

"Anyway, the immigrants are on the bottom and shit is rolling downhill. People didn't complain too loudly before, but now it's like a volcano erupting. Someone vandalized my car. My family has been citizens here for three generations. It didn't matter. If you weren't white, you were on the shit list. People around here lost it, some of them haven't gotten it back. They don't realize it's the bankers, the millionaires, the people on Wall St. who should be the subject of their anger, not their fellow worker, not their neighbors. But people panicked and looked for scapegoats. You saw more 'accidents'"

At this, he made air quotes with the first two fingers of both hands.

"People, mostly brown people, started falling more, pigs were accidentally let out onto the kill floor, people were being harassed. It was intense."

Cam leaned in closer, taking down notes. Raol continued.

"Someone sabotaged part of the machine, or that is what I believe at least. Got a pig stuck in it, half alive. The last thing you do is stop the chain, so I jump up on instinct, to fix it. And suddenly, just like that, it's working again, and it grinds up my leg. I can't prove it, not to a court, but I know what I saw, and I saw the white men in the corner, laughing to themselves. This is the world we live in at Monarch."

CHAPTER 60

October 15, 2016

Pastor Billy

"Satan walks among us. While we allow innocent children to dress up for Halloween, a Satanic holiday, I wish to remind you. Only he doesn't wear horns like in the stories. He doesn't have a pointy tail like in the movies. He walks among us in many, many guises.

He is the political candidate who will bring distract our nation with the temptation of sins of the flesh, sins against God, take God out of our schools and out of our homes, and out of our minds and hearts.

Satan is alive and well. He comes to you on the TV set and social media. Nothin' social at all about that! He is the harbinger of our antisocial society! He will steer you away from the foundation of your church. Look around you, ya'll."

He paused for dramatic effect, wiped sweat from his forehead and surveyed the congregation. They were on the edge of their seats. All eyes on him. Not a one looked away or down at a phone. He loved knowing they were hanging on his every word. He knew just how to keep their attention.

He continued.

"Will you see Satan coming when he plants his seeds of hatred in your heart and poisons you against your neighbor? When he whispers in your ear and tries to take you away from Jesus Christ, your Lord and Savior? Will you know him? No. No, you won't. Because he is already here."

He paused again. The congregation members were uneasy now, he could see. Good. They needed to be uneasy; he thought to himself. He watched as some warily gave the side eye to the person seated next to them. Some shifted their heads clearly as if they expected to see a man in red seated in the back with a pitchfork. Some looked confused. He went on.

"Satan walks among us. He is the learned man who tells you your stories from the Bible are no more than fairy tales, and sways you with his fancy hoity toity scientific talk. He is the quiet man. The quiet man in the background. The man no one would believe capable of the most heinous of deeds."

His eyes scanned the room, he tried to appear as grim as possible, but he was enjoying the crowd's attention.

Now I know you all know who I'm talking about and out of kindness for his dear mother, God be with her in this miserable time,....I will spare his name and spare her the shame of hearin' it for she is a communicant of this church. Satan has visited her family, has brought Hell into the heart of her son and has twisted a young man so that he would take a life."

He let the words hang in the air now for a moment.

"And not just any life."

He turned his head from side to side, soaking up the transfixed gazes of the parishioners who stared back at him.

"The life of a baby, his own baby, his own flesh and blood."

Soft murmurs echoed through the church. He let the stirring pass through the crowd like electricity before continuing.

"And we ask ourselves, how? How, Lord? How Jesus Christ, Savior our own Savior how? How could this happen here in this small, humble town, among such God-Fearing Christians? For I know, I know we are a God-fearing people here in Mosier…How did Satan gain his hold among us?"

Pastor Billy Brannigan addressed the crowd, pausing again, not expecting a single soul to rise up from the pew and respond, but giving the time as if this were to be the case.

"Because doubt has entered the hearts of the people of Mosier, of North Carolina, of America! Doubt, doubt in God's plan, doubt in God's will, doubt, even in God's existence has fallen upon the land and it chips away, doubt does it chips away at the hearts of women and of men, and even of little children. It breaks the foundation and like weeds that grow up through the cracks in a sidewalk, so comes Satan. So, this leaves us to ask, is this man to blame? Is he, as a henchman of Satan, deserving of God's mercy?"

The tension was palpable now. The crowd hanging on his every word.

"And God said to me, yes. For thanks to Eve we are all born with the capacity to sin and must be brought out of the grips of the serpent and back to our Lord Jesus Christ. So, let us pray for our community, for the family of our poor lost young man and the soul of his child, may he be received into God's loving arms in Heaven."

His face turned solemn and stern, like a father about to half lecture, half scold a child.

"Now more than ever we must be vigilant and confront the serpent before he is given a chance to strike. And let us fulfill our civic duties to vote in this election for a candidate who will restore God's righteous order here in the schools, in the communities and in America!"

CHAPTER 61

October 17, 2016

Cam

"Cam! What the fuck! Cam wake up!"

Donna's terrified voice startled him from sleep. Before his eyes were fully open, the brightness seared into his vision, jarring him …did she have every light in the house turned on? What the hell was with the…

Fire.

The realization that his house was on fire brought Cam to his senses. No, not his house, his lawn. He grabbed his robe and ran out the front door, his wife a few steps behind.

A cross was burning on his lawn.

After the police and fire crew had done their preliminary questioning and taken down their notes, after the flames had been extinguished, Cam found himself on edge in a way he had not felt since childhood.

It wasn't just the burning cross on his lawn, a shock enough on its own. It was also the reaction of his neighbors. It was as if they had been operating under a gentleman's agreement that all would pretend they had gone to the same country clubs, the same prep schools, the same summer camps. As if the cul-de-sac had been pretending that all were part of the same club until the rude awakening at 3 am reminded them that he was an outsider.

An outsider who had brought his trail of... of what? His dirty secrets? His legacy, his race? He had moved discrimination into their peaceful little neighborhood. The Patenaude's, usually a cordial crew, had eyed him with utter disgust as they herded their 14-year-old son Caiden away from the spectacle. Caiden had run out of the house across the street in his pajamas and stood, transfixed and staring, before the fire crew had arrived. He seemed to have been eyeing Cam and his wife as if a spaceship had landed delivering an alien where his neighbors used to be.

Cam's blood surged with fury and beneath it, shame.

Shame, when he had done nothing wrong. The kind of shame that makes you at first doubt your own accountability. It was the attitude of his neighbors, he could tell, that he must have done something wrong. He must have gone too far out of the sandbox he and his people are allowed to play in...he must have done something to deserve this retaliation.

Like the guys at PigPen talking about the numerous police shootings of young black men. Never once asking his opinion, only assuming that he must be living a white enough life to agree with them, or perhaps he was so dark they hadn't even remembered he was in the room. They would talk in front of him about whatever trumped up news was being reported, that the victim must have been in the midst of a crime or must have been noncompliant. Not that it could be possible, they couldn't accept it, no, it couldn't be possible that corruption exists, racism exists, abuses of power exist.

Even the cop, Officer Bradley, a man Cam has seen hundreds of times in the course of his work, seemed to regard him suspiciously. Or was it annoyance? As in 'seriously, Cam? You gotta drag us out in the middle of the night with this? Can't you just keep your head down and avoid trouble? It's bad enough you have to move into a white neighborhood, do you really have to bring this riff raff with you?'

Cam didn't expect the investigation to yield any results. He racked his own mind… who could have done this? A former client angry about the outcome of a case? But who?

To his surprise, his first clue came with a phone call the next day.

"You Mr. Burton, the attorney?" a man asked

"Yes, speaking, how can I help you?"

"You ought to fry with the Baby Killer!" and then nothing.

* * *

"This is Cam Burton, how can I help you?"

"Cam! Matt Davenport! How are you holding up down there?"

"Been better, Matt, been better."

"I saw the news. About your client, it made papers up here. They want the death penalty for him."

"This is going to be a tough fight. All sensationalized, locals making my client a poster child for everything from the evils of homosexuality to the need for women to leave the workforce."

"Collin is homosexual?"

"No… but that doesn't mean certain local yokels won't find some way to connect this to their agenda. The irony of course is that no one has even begun to speculate about what really triggered this. Blame the schools, blame the parents, blame it on low church attendance, working mothers, banning prayer from school, but no one wants to point the finger at Monarch, the working conditions, the stuff we talked about."

"You're seeing it for yourself now?"

"As close as I can get, which isn't as close as I'd like to get. I'll tell you what. I didn't doubt you, Matt, but I thought, ok, no offense, I thought you were just one of those…. passionate people, you know? Those vegan people who cry when you mow the lawn because of the taking of innocent life and whatnot…"

Matt let out a hearty laugh.

"I believed you were on to an interesting lead, but I never," Cam wrestled for the words to describe it. He didn't like feeling so vulnerable. Especially knowing how close to home this case was beginning to hit. "I never could have possibly expected. Matt, the things these people are telling me. I just can't believe it. I'm no Pollyanna. I've seen rapists acquitted on technicalities, I've seen men go to prison for lengthy sentences and I would swear on my mother's grave they were innocent. I know the system is messed up. I'm a Black Man in the south living in a suburb, you know? I've seen people screwed out of their homes, jobs, strike breakers, union busters, you name it. But these people at Monarch, it's like this one corporation singularly embodies all of what is rotten at the core of this country."

"Do you believe what they are telling you is the truth?"

Cam paused to consider this.

"Yes. Yes, I do, these folks don't have anything to gain by talking to me, and they sure have a lot to lose. They tell me consistent accounts. I believe them."

"You say you have seen innocent men sent away. I believe you. Have you ever seen an innocent man executed?"

"I know where you're going with this, Matt. But Collin, he's not entirely innocent. Do I believe he is a monster? A villain? No! Of course not. He committed a horrible act. Does committing a murder make him a 'murderer' knowing his circumstances I would say no. But is he innocent? There is no doubt that he killed his son, but that he was mentally incapacitated at the time."

"Ahh us lawyers, let me put it to you another way. Have you ever seen a man executed who didn't deserve to be?"

"I don't believe any man deserves execution. I'm a Christian first, an attorney second," Cam answered solemnly, surprised at this uncharacteristic divulgence of his faith which while informing his views, was often kept out of his conversation, especially professional conversations.

"On this we are also in agreement," Matt replied. "I'm an atheist myself, raised in a religious household but didn't carry my family's tradition or beliefs into my own life. I believe in something. That it's more than just us, that there is more to life, but until I understand it better, I feel I am not the one to put it into my words, but I digress. I am with you Cam, I am against the death penalty. Just one of the aspects of my being one of those vegans who doesn't mow the lawn."

"I'm sorry I didn't mean to."

"You didn't offend me. Humor is good medicine and I can laugh at life, and myself. If I didn't, I would probably end up not too far from where your client finds himself. I don't believe in the death penalty, but your jurisdiction is itching for revenge. Just one more symptom of the illness plaguing America these days, find a scapegoat, grab your pitchfork, restore law and order. That is the reason I called, Cam. There are some things you should know about your adversary. You are just getting a glimpse when you talk to these grunt workers. I assure you. You are getting the tip of a very large iceberg. Have you spoken to anyone in management, corporate or any of the inspectors? Anyone in the health centers for Monarch?"

"Can't get near them," Cam replied in frustration.

"I didn't think so. Sorry to say you most likely won't and that isn't me doubting your capabilities. You know the nature of the beast. How the old boy's club can be."

"Old boy's club," Cam cut in. "I'm sorry, you just, you triggered something in my mind, it may sound crazy but it's just like that day at the PigPen, when I had the hunch to even tell you about this case. Something just flashed. That ever happen to you?"

"I think I know what you mean. For me it feels like time pausing just momentarily, like I'm watching a movie, and someone pauses it for emphasis. What was your flash?"

"Well, we got a visit from an old good ol' boy's club. A few nights back, someone left a burning cross on my lawn."

"Geez that's terrible! I'm so sorry! Are you and your family ok?"

"Between this case and the racist rhetoric coming out with an upcoming election, I don't know how much more ugly things are going to get."

Now it was Matt's turn to pause in reflection.

"Your efforts to bring justice for your client and thousands like him, require you to take on a behemoth. I have known of investigative journalists being harassed, intimidated and threatened. Your client's family, have they reported anything suspicious?"

"What would be suspicious? The entire town has condemned Collin as a baby killer!"

"Yes, but his wife? In their eyes she too would be a victim, right? I would check in with them and keep a close eye on them, prepare safety measures for any of the witnesses on board. The workers you have interviewed. They aren't just worried about their jobs, you know?"

Cam sighed heavily. He rubbed his temple as Matt went on.

"To your question specifically though, I don't know. It could be. It could be some crazy Trump supporter, but I wouldn't rule anything out. Monarch has extensive resources, great amounts of power. Influence, they have the ear of politicians, lawmakers, you name it. I wouldn't put it past them to pull out the stops. They're going to try anything they can to discredit your client and to bring you down and anyone else who comes close to exposing their dirty laundry."

"Have you seen this before?" Cam asked.

"I have colleagues who have been personally and professionally destroyed going up against corporations like this. A good friend of mine, excellent lawyer. He had a DWI in college. Straightened himself out. Went up against one of these giants spraying pesticides onto crops. This company's illegal practices contaminated the drinking water in a little town. Babies, kids with defects, health problems, cancer, bizarre diseases. When they were done with this guy, they had dredged up so much crap from his past. Some may have been true, most were lies. He lost his marriage, his license to practice law. Ended up hanging himself."

"Oh, shit," Cam replied before he could censor himself.

"They ruined him, Cam. Even after the case was dismissed. They kept at it, humiliated him in the papers. I just hope you appreciate how far Monarch's reach could go."

"At this point, Matt, nothing would surprise me."

CHAPTER 62

October 20, 2016

Collin

Collin tried to put his hands in his pocket, an old nervous habit from childhood. But his jumpsuit had no pockets. He tried to distract himself. The room offered little distraction. He began to bite his nails. He waited for his lawyer in sterile, cramped room. Still, he thought, it was still better than the cell. He sneezed and rubbed his eyes, irritated from crying and from mounds of dust circulated by a noisy ceiling fan.

He was showing signs of improvement, the lady, Dierdre, had told him. He didn't need a guard to watch him all day and night, and that was a relief. He stared at the grey table. So much grey here, he thought to himself. The CO opened the door and Cam walked in.

"How do you do it?" Collin asked abruptly. He hadn't meant to sound rude but hadn't yet regained the social skills of his previous baseline. The question had been puzzling him all morning, and when Cam came to visit, this time in the conference room, Collin couldn't help blurting it out.

"Excuse me?" the man named Cam Burton asked evenly.

"How do you... do it? How do you defend people who do bad things? Do you... don't you hate them? Don't you wish they got punished?"

The man sat down and looked at him earnestly. Collin wondered if he had offended the man. But then he finally spoke.

"I don't always get to choose who I will or will not represent. My work is important to me, Mr. Griffen, and while some lawyers will stretch the truth to justify whatever befits them economically, I do not believe in using my profession in that way."

Silence again. Collin thought about this. He deserved punishment. What could this man possibly say to convince a jury otherwise? The deep, calm voice drew his attention again, his lawyer was speaking.

"I don't advocate for clients to go free in the community if I believe they are a danger to society or to themselves. To your other question, I don't hate my clients," Cam paused again. Collin wondered about this.

Cam continued.

"I guess you could say I hate things a lot of people do. But I can't even name a person I hate right now if I wanted to."

"Do you really think I deserve to live after what I did?"

"I have a lot of beliefs about you. Ultimately, my beliefs don't matter. What the jury believes does."

* * *

Cam thought for a moment, he examined the young man. He hadn't been prepared for this kind of conversation and feared he was not winning his client's confidence. He hadn't meant to sound dismissive. He knew what Collin was looking for. He just didn't know how to answer. He took the easy way out. Stuck to what he knew.

"I need to ask you some questions. I need to insist on your complete honesty. I can't represent you to the best of my abilities if I am not given all the facts that you are, um, able to recall. I understand there may be things you do not remember, but I need you to be honest in that regard. An 'I don't remember' or 'I don't know' is much better than making something up. Do you understand?"

Collin nodded, appearing serious.

"Ok. I want to hear, in your own words, what happened that night."

* * *

Collin paused, straining as if he had been asked to give a speech in a language he didn't know. Did he even know for certain what had happened? The memories that had come to him seemed like clips from a movie. Scenes from a dream. What if it had been a dream? What if he said the wrong thing?

He looked up to see his lawyer, Cam waiting.

"I didn't remember anything for a long time. I remember some things now. I am still not sure what is a memory, or a bad dream."

Collin's voice trailed off and he looked off into the distance.

* * *

Cam wasn't sure if he had lost his client in the deep tides of psychosis once again. But before he can interject, the young man continued.

"Sometimes I don't know what is a dream and what is real."

For a moment, Cam heard his grandmother's voice and is dragged back into his own nightmare from the night before. He blinked to refocus himself. Now was not the time for his thoughts to wander.

"I have put a lot of pieces together but there are still so many foggy things. I was at work. I came home, and, in the dreams, in the nightmares I am at work and the pigs are all squealing and I am chasin' them down with a pipe the way we do, and knocking them on the head to shut em up and get them on the line."

Cam noticed his client's hands begin to tremble. He seemed to have shifted into a part of his mind that was distant, but still here. Cam noted Collin's voice had changed as well, smaller and unsure of himself. Collin continued.

"But then I wake up from the dream and I wasn't at work and I am home. I am in my house, in the living room. I'm holding a piece of the table. I broke the table and I... I see...."

The tears appeared, but Collin remained stoic, his voice like a monotone. Cam wasn't sure if he should encourage the young man to continue. He feared his client's progress may be lost just in recounting this story. He looked around, wishing Dierdre had been in the room to discern if he had gone too far. Maybe, Cam thought, Maybe it's too soon. But then Collin spoke again.

"I see Quinn there. It used to all be a nightmare. Now I know. I know the beginning is a dream, but the end is real."

Stifled emotion threatened to break through now. His voice cracked on the word 'real' and Cam observes his client has grown pale. Cam wondered if he should change the subject, walk it back. Revisit this another time. But this is the most lucid he has seen his client. Who knows, if Collin regresses, Cam thought, this may be the last chance to hear the story directly from him.

Collin saved him the trouble of intervening by continuing on his own.

"I know it now. I know it and I did it, but I didn't mean to. I didn't know."

He inhaled deep and let his breath out slowly before continuing.

"Next thing I remember I am here and this Black guy... oh excuse me, this African American guy, my age... he comes in and brings his dog and books and we talk. Over time, I figure it out but that's all I really remember and even that, it's like watching a movie, it doesn't feel real."

Cam let his breath out slowly. He hadn't realized he had been holding his breath in anticipation. He waited to see if Collin will add more, when he didn't Cam proceeded.

"How did you like your job at Monarch?"

Collin flinched at the name.

"I fuckin' hate that place... sorry, excuse my language. I hated it."

Now his voice cracked again. Cam was relieved that Collin swore. Relieved he's showing more emotion. He didn't know for sure but sensed on some level that it was a good sign. Collin started to shed tears, the façade he struggled to maintain melted away completely.

He told Cam about the changes. His voice back to what Cam assumed was his baseline. In between brief bouts of crying, Collin wiped his face with the back of his hand and spoke candidly.

About kicking Suzie, yelling at Quinn and Jolene when he never meant to. He told him how the only thing his peers did, that he refused to do was stop by the PigPen on the way home to drink. How he never wanted to follow his father's example and now look what he had done. He commented that the liquor might have been an improvement. Anything better than this.

"I'm not blaming it on my job, sir. It's just, it changed everything, and I haven't been myself. I haven't been able to sleep. I can smell it. I cared less about people, started to not really see them as real after a time. I still have nightmares. That night, I thought it was a pig, and it was Quinn, but I didn't know."

"That was my belief," Cam said. "It is my belief that you suffered Post Traumatic Stress Disorder and a psychotic break. It is also my belief that you love your family and under normal conditions would never have acted this way. It is my belief that the job exposed you to conditions far from normal for an extended period. It's my belief that you need lots of help, treatment, and rehabilitation. It's my belief that you are a fundamentally good person reacting to an acute degree of stress which had a profound impact on your sense of reality."

Cam let his words sink in before continuing.

"But... and listen carefully, young man."

Collin leaned in and faced Cam, looking him in the eyes.

"We've got to work very hard to convince a jury. A jury full of people who are no doubt out for retribution, that you are in some ways the victim here. Young man they will not be easy to convince. Do you understand me? I need to know as much as you can recall about what working conditions were like at Monarch."

CHAPTER 63

October 2016

Cam

With two days left to prepare for the trial, Cam almost let the call go to voicemail as he sorted through his reports. But on instinct, he answered it.

"Mr. Burton, Cam, It's Jolene, Collin's wife." Her voice sounded vacant, Cam thought.

"Yes, Jolene, how are you?"

"I'm not good. I've been having trouble. With pills. I'm in a rehab. I can't testify. I'm sorry."

"Well, we can send someone to pick you up from the rehab just to give testimony."

"No, I can't. I can't do it. I can't. It's not the rehab. It's me. I can't do it."

They had agreed she would provide a written statement. Not the same as the impact of seeing a person face to face, but it was something. Maybe for the best. A fragile witness kicking drugs would be easy prey for the DA. Could even potentially discredit her statements to know she was now addicted to drugs, and they would know, Cam reminded himself. That left Maggie as a potential personal character witness. Cam had his doubts about putting Collin's mother on the stand, but after a moment of weight his options, he picked up the phone again and dialed.

Opening Statement

Cam always rehearsed before a case. After all these years practicing law, he still got stage fright when it came to presenting opening statements. He rubbed a handkerchief between two sweaty hands and looked over his notes one last time. Then faced the menagerie of characters who would decide the fate of his client. The Grocery Clerk, Motorcycle-Riding-Retired-English- Teacher turned Cat-Lady among them.

"Ladies and Gentlemen of the Jury, this is not going to be an easy case. But you were chosen and are given a heavy responsibility. The responsibility of separating your feelings from the facts. The responsibility of considering the person who you'll hear about and even get to meet."

He paused for effect.

"You have the responsibility of deciding whether this young man is truly the monster the state makes him out to be. Or whether he's just like you," to drive the point home, Cam paused to make eye contact with several jurors before continuing.

"A hard-working young man with dreams to build a better life for his family. A young man who, in spite of being intelligent, was kept out of the opportunity for college because of financial status." Cam eyed the younger demographic of the jury as he said this part. He then turned to face the working-class jurors, making deliberate eye contact.

"A young man who, like many of you, fell on hard times during the recession. Who was out of work. Who was desperate for a job, and who turned to an industry that operates in the shadows of this town. A powerful, profitable, influential company. Monarch Industries. Looking for a job, like you all have at some point. A young man whose compassion and sensitivity, just like yours, a young man who loves his wife, loved his son, loved animals, but who was so traumatized by work at Monarch, a slaughterhouse, a place where he is given the task of killing animal after animal after animal, wore down his empathy. Wore down his mind. Until he became so mentally ill that he couldn't tell reality from hallucinations."

Cam let his words percolate before continuing.

"You have the responsibility to decide whether this young man deserves another chance at treatment and rehabilitation, or death. As you listen to the testimony, I implore you. Forget what you've heard in sensationalized stories about this young man. Listen to the words of those who know him. And those who worked at Monarch. And experts who have seen this kind of trauma again and again. And ask yourself, if you were in my client's shoes, could you guarantee that your best mental defenses would protect you from a similar traumatic reaction?"

* * *

During the break, Cam walked over to check in on Collin's mother, who sat silently watching the proceedings.

"How are you holding up, Mrs. Griffen? Are you ready to take the stand?"

"I don't know if ready is the word, but you said I'm up next, so I have been thinking over what we talked about."

"Ok good. Just remember, breathe, be calm, don't let them intimidate you, you know your son, they don't. You just have to be honest and tell them what you know. If you don't understand, ask for clarification. If you need a break, you can ask for a break. I will be right here. Ok?" He gave her hand a light squeeze.

"Yes sir. Ok," she sighed heavily. Her hands were shaking.

"Breathe," he reminded her.

* * *

When the court was back in session, Maggie was called to take the stand. Cam smiled at her and nodded in encouragement. He thought she looked like a scared child giving a report in front of the class. He tried to emulate calm as he spoke, hoping it would rub off on her.

"Please state your name for the record."

"Maggie- Margaret Griffen."

"And tell us your relationship to the defendant."

Her voice cracked, and she rasped a barely audible reply.

"I'm sorry, ma'am can you please say again so we make sure the jury hears you?" Cam was trying to be as unintimidating as possible, but he could tell his witness was struggling to hold back tears. She tried again.

"I'm his mother."

"Thank you," Cam went on. "Mrs. Griffen, I know this must be terribly hard for you. You lost your grandson at the hands of your only child. Can you tell the jury how you first heard the news?"

"I got a call. The night it happened. From Jolene, my daughter-in-law. She said police are here. She said Collin lost his mind," as she spoke these words, Maggie's voice grew shrill as she fought back tears. She cleared her throat and continued.

"Said he just snapped. And he hurt the baby," Maggie began crying and covered her face in her hands.

Cam gave her a moment, then he began questioning her. "What was your first reaction? Do you recall? When you heard the news?"

"I had no idea what to think. It was impossible. I was shocked. I didn't know by 'hurt' she meant 'killed' I don't know if she knew Quinn was dead. Yet. But even to have hurt the boy, I thought that just can't be. This couldn't be happening."

"You didn't think it was possible that Collin could have hurt your grandson? Not just kill, but not even hurt?" Cam asked.

"That's right. Never. Never in a million years."

"Why not? I mean, surely, he gave his son a spanking once in a while, as discipline? Or maybe one occasion where he may have handled the boy a little too rough, even by accident?" Cam deliberately prodded.

"Oh, no, no not at all. Not ever. He was against spankings. Both he and Jolene were. They got parenting books from the library, believed in talking to children and being lenient and all. Collin never lifted a hand to his son, ever. Not until that night."

"So, this was completely out of character for your son, is that what you would say?"

"Absolutely out of character," She agreed. She appeared to be regaining her composure and Cam saw this as a good sign.

He continued. "Were there any other changes, any earlier signs that Collin wasn't himself?"

Maggie took a deep breath and recounted the timeline, a month or so leading up to the murder, Collin growing more distant, then his lashing out at the dog and immediate remorse.

"Even with these changes in behavior, did you ever suspect your grandson was in danger?"

"I wish I had any inkling, but no. I was startled by his reaction to the dog. He loves that dog. But I never in a million years thought he would hurt Quinn or that he would even hurt the dog again. I thought he was having a really stressful time and lost control. He showed regret immediately, and I thought that was that."

"What had changed as far as you know that brought on the stress that led him to act that way?"

"Well, at the time I didn't think too much of it, but the only thing that really changed was his job."

"What was his job?"

"He worked at Monarch. In the slaughterhouse."

Cam let this hang in the air. He turned to the jury. Cat Lady was scowling. Grocery Clerk seemed to be digesting this, his face somber. An older man with a salt and pepper beard rubbed at his neck. Cam turned back to Maggie.

"Did Collin say how he liked his new job?"

"He didn't say specifically. But I could tell he didn't like it. He needed it to get back on track. He was out of work for a few months, what with the recession. So, he stuck it out. But I could tell he wasn't suited for it. He mostly shut down. Even his wife was starting to worry about him. He was acting depressed."

"Did you visit your son after he was incarcerated?"

"I tried. Several, maybe five or six times."

"What happened?"

"That man in the cell, that was my son's body, but not his mind. I would get too upset, and it would stress him out, so usually we would have to cut the visit short."

"Did your son ever have mental health problems, drug use, depression, anxiety, symptoms of anything, as a child, or growing up?"

"No. Not at all. He was shy, kinda kept to himself, but nothing that was a disorder. Nothing that kept him from having a few friends, going to school. No trouble, no violence, nothing."

Cam thanked her and asked her to remain seated for cross-examination.

"Mrs. Griffen, you're the defendant's mother. Are you also a trained mental health professional?"

"No, sir, I am not."

"Have you studied psychology as a hobby, even?"

"Not, no, no I haven't," she was getting nervous, Cam could tell. The DA was being a dirtbag, he thought. Then reminded himself that he was doing the job the state expected him to do.

"So, you actually have no qualifications to assess whether your son may have suffered from longstanding, undiagnosed mental illness.?"

"Objection!" Cam interjected.

"Sustained," Judge responded. Cam thought he actually sounded bored.

"I'll repeat my question. You have no grounds to evaluate your son's mental health, your only qualification is being his mother, correct?"

"I don't have a professional degree, sir, but anyone who knew Collin would see something had changed. This was not him. He would never hurt his son."

"Just answer the question, are you a mental health professional?"

"No," Maggie looked down at her hands.

* * *

At least there would be a professional witness next, Cam told himself. He was starting to get annoyed with the DA. Cam called Dr. Holland, the Mosier County Jail staff Psychiatrist who had initially examined Collin. He gave testimony about PTSD, psychosis.

"So, Dr. Holland, help us understand, when someone is in a psychotic state, if I, for instance, went into a psychotic state right now, would I have control over my actions and thoughts?"

"It depends on the severity of the psychosis. Some people hear voices while maintaining insight that they are not accurate, but it takes a lot of self-reflection and self-discipline to keep that awareness in most cases."

"Ok, so if I had the type of psychosis Collin exhibited when he was first arrested, how much awareness of this courtroom would I have?"

"Likely none at all. You may be operating more like in a dream. When dreaming, you're in your bed but in your dream, you're somewhere else. It's closer to that. Your reality would not be based on actual reality."

"So, what could that look like?"

"Depends. The bottom line is, you Mr. Burton, the professional, would not be in charge. Some other parts of your brain would be feeding you misinformation. You might think I'm a walrus, you may not even see me at all. You might think the Jury is your high school chess club, you may not even see yourself in a courtroom."

"So, what you're describing is a temporary inability to tell what's real."

"That is correct. In some people it can become a long-term or even permanent state. Luckily for Collin, it was a temporary state. But even then, it took some time for him to become lucid, in touch with reality, again."

"What other symptoms did you note when you examined Collin?"

"Hypervigilance, or a higher than normal startle response."

"Like someone who jumps at the sound of a loud noise?" Cam asked for clarification.

"Yes. Also, he appeared to be highly anxious."

"What diagnosis did you give Collin Griffen?"

"Psychotic Disorder, not otherwise specified, and PTSD. Post-Traumatic Stress Disorder."

"What trauma did you base this diagnosis on?"

"On information Collin seemed to ruminate, obsess, about. He repeatedly saw himself inside his work at the slaughterhouse. He would repeatedly yell about the tasks involved in his day, what he would see, he would break into tears talking about people and pigs being injured or running loose or both."

"So, is it fair to say his work at Monarch led to his PTSD?"

"That is the connection I drew, yes." Dr. Holland replied, remaining calm and professional.

"Based on the family history and assessment you've taken and based on your experience, is it possible Collin had long standing mental illness, and no one knew it until now?" Cam asked.

"Anything is possible, but it is highly unlikely that an illness like this, if it existed earlier in Collin's life, would have gone unnoticed. In other words, it is much more likely that this was recent onset, not chronic."

"Thank you, no further questions."

As Cam returned to his seat, the DA declined cross examination. Cam thought Steuben looked annoyed. The Judge called for a break and Cam turned to survey the jury. Some looked thought-ful. Some looked bored. Some, he thought, still looked skeptical or doubtful. Usually he could read the body language and take the pulse of the Jurors, but this was a tougher call. Cat lady seemed to be pondering the latest information, thoughtfully.

His thoughts were broken by a shaky voice.

"I'm sorry, I screwed up the cross-examination," it was Maggie.

"No, not at all. You did fine. It's the DA's job to come down hard on people. But you did great," Cam hoped he sounded more reassuring than he felt.

* * *

For the next round, Cam called witnesses who worked for Monarch. Ricardo took the stand first. After the initial formalities were cov-ered, Cam asked him to paint a picture for the jury about what life at Monarch was like.

"It's hell," he began shaking his head. "I was warned. Before I started there, I was warned about a guy I knew who worked there and ended up shooting himself."

"Really?" Cam hadn't recalled this from his initial interview, but he decided to go with it.

"Yeah, my friends tried to talk me out of taking the job, but I thought, that guy must have just been a pussy, excuse my French."

"It's alright, but just to clarify, you thought the person who killed himself was just too weak? To handle the job? You thought you would be different, is that correct?"

"Yes sir. That's it. I thought for what they pay, and I can't get that rate somewhere else, I can do it. I thought it would be just like making barbecue in the yard."

"But isn't it? I mean, you cut meat at home? What was the difference?" Cam knew the answer to this well from his many interviews, but he led Ricardo to help the Jury understand as he now did.

"A world of difference. For one, you aren't cutting meat. You're cutting a live animal. A pig who is showing you every day he's as smart as you and wants to live like you do. And not just one, thousands."

"Thousands per day?" Cam asked to clarify.

"Thousands per hour."

"You slaughter a thousand pigs per hour?" Cam heard it right the first time, but wanted the Jury to digest this information.

"That's right. Per hour. So that's the second difference. Its crazy fast and stressful. People all around you getting hurt. No breaks. Some people, sorry to sound gross, some people end up peeing their pants right there in the line because they can't get a break."

"Why can't they get a break?"

"Because it slows productivity."

"So, let me make sure I understand," Cam turned to the jury. Not a single face was bored now. Some were squirming in their seats. Some covering their mouths with their hands. Cam continued, "Let me just understand, for a profit, Monarch has you cutting up a thousand or more live pigs per hour? So fast that it isn't safe, and people get hurt? Some people urinate on themselves in line?"

"Yes, sir."

"Well, they have to stop when someone gets hurt, right?"

Ricardo chuckled, then covered his mouth with a hand. "I'm sorry sir, it's not funny, what's funny is the idea that you would think that. No. When someone gets hurt, they stand there and bleed. They bleed on the meat if that's where they are in line. Now if they cut something off, like a whole finger, then they go get stitched up."

"Then what?"

"Well, if they want a job, then they go back to work."

Cam allowed a pause for the Jury to bear the weight of the scene his witness was describing, and the burden workers like Ricardo and Collin faced every day. He then continued.

"Is this unique to Monarch?"

"I only ever worked there, but some of the other guys worked other places. They said its pretty much the same. Except Monarch is maybe a little worse, that's how Monarch gets to be the top."

"So, Monarch is the top in the industry because their employees, employees like you used to be, are forced to work in unsafe conditions?"

"Yes, sir."

"What about the mental health of people who worked with you? You heard Dr. Holland's testimony. Is it safe to say that you saw PTSD or some kinds of mental health changes in people who worked with you?"

"I saw it in myself. I got more violent working there. I'm not proud of it. Not at all. But it brought out a lot of anger and I guess fear, and it makes you aggressive. Not just at work, not just to pigs. It's like, once I got used to killing pigs, used to making myself not care about their lives, it actually got harder to care about anyone's life. Killing becomes normal, so all the normal consideration for politeness and anything, it all goes out the window. I would leave work and if someone parked in my parking spot at home, I would see myself cutting them up, in my mind, just like they were a pig. Because why not? It became normal."

"Did you ever act on that fantasy and act violently toward another person?"

"Not exactly in those terms," Ricardo appeared to become anxious for the first time.

"In what terms, then, remember you're not on trial, you're just sharing your experience."

"Yeah, I, there's a culture, at Monarch. It's almost everybody. I was part of it. I became part of it."

"What kind of culture?" Cam asked.

"It's a violent job, and it brings out the worst in people. So, there's a lot of bullying and bullshit, excuse me, nonsense. Like if someone's new, they'll take a pig's eye and stick it in his lunch box just to mess with him. Like those kinds of things. Sometimes worse."

"Sometimes worse?" Cam asked for emphasis.

"Yes. A lot of racism, sexism, In the meat industry, everyone is a piece of meat and that's how they act, the bosses, and that becomes normal, for all of us."

"Thank you, no further questions."

* * *

The DA came in for the kill.

"So, the culture, you speak of, was Collin part of that culture? Was he bullying others?"

"No. He was one of the easy targets."

"So, you harassed the defendant and now, what you feel guilty?"

"We all did it. Most of us. And I know I can't undo what I did. But I can tell people the truth about what it's like there."

"But you're not psychotic, you didn't develop PTSD, why not? If it's so bad?"

"I don't know. I'm not the doctor. Make no mistake, we all are traumatized from being there, maybe mine just comes out differently. Maybe because I became one of the bullies, I had an outlet, while Collin didn't until he snapped, I don't know."

Steuben looked down at his file, then continued. Cam was impressed that Ricardo hadn't lost his temper, but he clenched his fists around his pen and pad, wondering how much more his witness would take from this line of questioning.

"Do you still work at Monarch?"

"I think you know already that I don't," Ricardo was getting irritated.

"Why not?"

"They fired me."

"Says here in your file, you were accused of sexual assault. Was that also just you being one of the guys?"

Ricardo took a deep breath. Cam interjected. "Objection your Honor, the witness is not on trial."

"Sustained, but Steuben get to the point."

"My point is that you have a bone to pick with your former employer. You had a good job, and it paid well, and you just couldn't keep your hands to yourself. So, they fired you. And then you decided to be part of a smear campaign against them.

"That's not true. I never put my hands on anyone. The person who did was my supervisor. I saw it happen. He got mad at me for talking to Collin's lawyer and threw me under the bus for it. The woman, she quit, she didn't press charges. She just didn't show back up."

"Then why is your name on this report?" Steuben asked.

"Because my name is Ricardo, and the guy who did it is named Mitch, not too hard to figure out, is it?"

* * *

Cam had expected Steuben to dig around and get dirt on his witnesses. But the DA had a trick up their sleeve he hadn't expected. The next day when court was called to order, the prosecutor's first witness was called to the stand. A man Cam had heard plenty about but had not yet met.

Steuben took the floor. Cam thought he looked more smug than usual. He addressed the jury. "You've heard from the defendant's mother, a sob story about her boy being a perfect angel who just got into a bad job and then fell apart. Well, today you're going to meet Collin's father and I assure you, you'll hear a very different side of the story."

He then turned to the witness.

"Please state your name."

"Ronald Griffen."

"And your relationship to the defendant?"

"I'm his father."

Cam blinked. The man seated on the stand was clean shaven but weathered. He had the voice of a drinker or smoker or both. Cam recalled the stories of Collin's father being the living cliché of the alcoholic Vietnam Veteran.

"You heard your wife's testimony the other day, correct?"

"Yes sir, I did."

"And now that you have your chance to tell your side of the story, please tell the jury the truth of the matter, and remember, you are under oath."

Cam thought he saw the DA wink at Mr. Griffen.

"The truth, yes. Well, the truth is everything that my wife said, earlier in the proceedings…" Ronnie seemed to hesitate to go on. "Everything you heard my wife say is the truth."

Steuben's face abruptly changed. Cam wondered what he thought he had up his sleeve. Whatever bomb he had hoped to launch had just imploded on itself.

"Excuse me?" Steuben asked.

"You've heard the truth about my son from my wife, from the doctor. You've heard it. I got another truth to tell you. I am a veteran, son. I had my share of problems. There are a thousand things I should have done different to be a better father. And it's too late to do all of them. Except one. And that is to tell the truth."

Ronnie looked past the DA and faced the jury directly. He pointed a finger as if accusing them as he went on. "I was visited but a couple of men from Monarch Industries. They came to my house. They told me that if I didn't take the stand today and make all kinds of lies to discredit my son, that they'd ruin me. They offered me a bribe to lie about my son. To call my son a liar. They offered me a bribe."

The Jury broke into collective murmurs of surprise. Some, Cam could hear, questioning if Mr. Griffen was making this up. If he himself were hallucinating.

The Judge pounded the gavel and called for silence.

"That is the truth!" Ronnie exclaimed. "Those sombitches ruined my son, and they tried to bribe me, but if there is one thing I can do right by my son before I die, it will be to tell the truth."

There were no further questions.

Maybe, Cam thought, returning to court, maybe they had a shot after all. The jury had heard from medical professionals, Matt Davenport had testified as an expert witness, they heard from former Monarch employees. They heard from Collin's family.

Soon the decision would be made.

Cam debated the risks, or benefits of letting Collin take the stand. On the one hand, Dierdre and the medical staff were concerned that Collin was still too mentally fragile. On the other hand, a demonstration of his symptoms in real life could drive home the point that he is mentally ill. Or the jury could interpret him as a monster, unpredictable, a time bomb posing a threat to the community.

He had tried to explain this to Collin in the days before the trial.

"I want to testify." Collin had insisted.

"You realize the DA is going to come at you with everything he's got. He's going to push your buttons, Collin. Are you sure you can handle that?"

"No. I won't know for sure. But it's my life. I want to speak for myself. I don't want it to just be what other people say about me. I want to tell my own story."

Court was called to order. The preliminary proceedings were underway. The air conditioning had been fixed, or the setting had been adjusted, Cam reflected. It was comfortable in the crowded courthouse, though some in the jury still fanned themselves with makeshift fans. Cam could see outside the window, the sky was overcast. It matched the mood in here, he thought to himself.

He stood and addressed the jury. His last shot. "Ladies and Gentlemen of the jury, I had extreme hesitation about allowing my client to take the stand and testify directly. I didn't want to do it. I know, from my early and continued work on this case, that public opinion has been unfavorable toward my client. I also have seen my client struggle to regain his sense of reality. His mental stability has been fragile since the night in question. I've seen it. I've seen it documented. I had extreme concerns about my client's mental health and the pressure of testifying. It's a stressful experience for anyone. Heck, until today, sitting in this hot courtroom was a stressful experience for all of you."

Cam was reassured by the spread of chuckling in the jury.

"But my client, Collin Griffen, he asked for this opportunity. Even if it triggers an exacerbation in his mental health symptoms. He wanted to address you personally. So, I call my client, Collin Griffen, as my final witness."

Collin stood, hands and feet shackled, and shuffled slowly. Cam eyed the jury as discreetly as he could. There were murmurs, some gasps. He couldn't make out what anyone was saying. He read disgust on a number of faces, sympathy on others, and some appeared surprised. The sheepish, gaunt young man was clearly not who they were expecting.

"Please state your name for the record, young man."

"Collin Griffen."

"Thank you. And Mr. Griffen, please tell the jury why you are here."

Collin cleared his throat and leaned as much as he could to speak into the small microphone on the stand.

"I'm here because I did something horrible. I killed my son," His voice broke. Tears began to stream down his face. He took a breath and closed his eyes for a moment. "Every day I wake up from dreams, and into a nightmare. Every day I wake up and open my eyes and any peace, any escape is gone. Any dreams where I see my son again, where I see him smile and hold him, gone. I wake up every day and the nightmare begins. Because I have to remember, all over again, that it really happened. That I really did it. For months I was in what felt like a dream. I would feel like I was waking from one dream to another. But I wasn't awake. I was hallucinating. I didn't know it at the time. Just like the night I came home from work for the last time."

Cam left a pause. He glanced at the jury before proceeding, they were on the edge of their seats. He thought that was a good thing. Then he intervened.

"Collin, what happened that night? The last thing you remember before your hallucinations set in."

"I was getting more and more stressed out for a few weeks. Stressed out, didn't want to talk to anyone, kind of staying in my own shell. I just wanted to get out of there."

"By there, what do you mean?" Cam asked.

"I wanted to quit my job. But we were so close. We were so close to paying off the debt from when I was out of work. So close to just being able to breathe again. So, I stuck with it."

"I see, and so what do you remember from the night you killed your son?"

"My head hurt for over a day. It was getting worse. A few times, driving home, I felt lost, like I had to remember where I was. I pulled into my driveway. The car was making a noise. It needed a repair, I guess. It made the noise and for a minute I was back at work, hearing the pigs scream. Then I was back in the driveway. The last thing I remember is closing the car door."

"So, the last thing you recall is getting out of the car, closing the door, and then?"

"I was at work, I was walking through the kill floor at work. It was like it always looked, blood and noise. It stinks in there and I could smell it. Like bleach and blood. My head hurt. I felt one of the pigs and looked down, I saw pigs around me, and I was at work. I was reacting to something, maybe it was my dog, maybe it was Quinn? I only know from what I was told long after. I didn't know where I was."

"When did you learn about what happened to Quinn?"

"Months later. I was in a psychosis I guess, I didn't know it at the time, it just felt like nightmare after nightmare. I was in the nightmares and then would see myself in jail, but it didn't make sense then I would get confused again."

"So, for a long period of time you didn't know where you were? You didn't know what happened?"

"It was all confused. I felt like something bad happened, I knew something bad had happened when I was seeing jail cells and seeing dead pigs and seeing blood everywhere but that was hallucinations. I didn't know where I was for a long time. When I finally started to come out of it, there was a guy visiting me."

"Visiting you?" Cam asked.

"Yeah, Bobby Ray. A volunteer at the jail with his dog. It took a few days, and I started to come out of it, and then they had to tell me why I was in jail."

"Who do you mean when you say 'they'?"

"The doctor. The social worker. They met with me and told me."

"What was that like?"

"For the first time, I wanted to go back into the psychosis, into the bad scenes I kept seeing. Because it was better than facing the reality. I couldn't believe it."

"So, it didn't bring back any memories?"

"No sir. It's all a blur. I didn't remember it, but I have to believe them. My wife was there. She saw it."

"How did you feel?"

"I wanted to die. I feel horrible. I can't stand the guilt most every day. I can't even imagine a life without my son, let alone knowing I hurt him. I would never hurt my son. I wish I could go back in time, quit my job sooner, do something different, keep it from going this far. But I can't and every day I have to live with this."

"Why was it so important for you to testify?"

"Because I wanted to speak for myself. I can't bring Quinn back, but I need to let people know. Quinn, my son, didn't die because I'm a monster. He didn't die because I was a bad father. He died because I was out of my mind. And I was out of my mind because of my job. A job people are still doing right now," Collin's voice got louder. "Right now! People are being desensitized, dehumanized, because they don't have any other options. They don't have other qualifications or jobs available. So, they're going to a place that is worse than any horror movie you can imagine. They're being trained to kill without feeling. Without remorse. They're doing it because every day normal people, just like you and me and all of us, pay them to do it. But it's killing them. It's killing their souls. And then they're going to leave that job, dead inside, and hurt other people. Whatever the jury decides, there is still going to be another Quinn, another Collin, another family somewhere out there, destroyed. Because of Monarch Industries. Because of slaughter work. And I wanted.... I needed to say that. To let the Jury know. Because maybe it will save someone else. If people just know."

THE VERDICT

It had taken two days of deliberation before the Verdict was reached. As Cam entered the courtroom, he saw Collin's parents seated side by side. They were whispering to each other. Collin's father had an arm around his mother, and Cam thought it seemed counter to how their relationship had been described. But crisis had a way of bringing people closer. Dierdre was talking to Dr. Holland. She looked worried, Cam thought. Collin was seated with his hands in shackles. Cam knew it was for appearance, Collin wasn't a flight risk. He looked strangely at peace.

Cam nodded at Maggie and Ron, who had seen him take a seat. He turned to Collin. "How are you holding up today?"

"I couldn't sleep well last night, but then I figured, no matter what, it's out of my hands. And I've gotten used to being unable to control things lately."

"You did well, no matter what, you were very brave, and you did a great job keeping your composure."

"Thank you, I guess, but I don't deserve recognition. No matter what I ever do right again in my life, it will never outweigh what I've done wrong."

The judge called the court to order. Shuffling movement came to a halt. In the silence that followed, Cam could hear only the whirring of the ceiling fan. Time seemed to drag.

"Has the jury reached a verdict?"

"It has," the Bailiff replied, handing an envelope to Judge LeClair.

Cam's heart froze. He couldn't recall the last time he'd felt so emotionally entangled in a case. He tried to keep his anxiety at bay. If anyone should be on edge, it was Collin. Cam looked to his client and observed the young man sitting still. Unreadable. He thought to himself the one who has reason to panic looks like he had just completed a crash course in Zen meditation.

Judge LeClair glared at the paper over his glasses and read the final verdict.

"The people of Mosier county find the defendant, Collin Griffen, guilty of first-degree homicide in the murder of Quinn Griffen."

Cam heard nothing beyond the word guilty. Without thinking, he put an arm around Collin's shoulder and squeezed. His ears were ringing, but he still heard sounds throughout the court. Cheers, groans, and a woman's voice crying "No!" before the reverberation of a thud brought him back to the present. Looking over his shoulder, he saw that Maggie Griffen had passed out, hitting her head on the chair in front of her before collapsing on the floor.

CHAPTER 64

November 2016

Jolene

Jolene couldn't stand the torment anymore. This morning was the closest to committing suicide that she had come. Even if the pills weren't lethal, she had tested herself, she had taken them. Even the false expectation of lethality had not brought the relief she longed for, and another thought, a new sound bite from the crazy making machine inside her head, had thrown a new angle into the mix.

"Collin is going to die," the voice inside taunted her. "If you die now, you will have to deal with him soon! Real soon! Maybe as punishment you will have to be his tour guide through Hell?" She couldn't stand it anymore. She couldn't possibly talk to her mother; it would freak her out too much.

She couldn't talk to Pastor Bradley. He had always been generous with his time and support, but you can't talk to a pastor about suicide. That alone must be some kind of sin! Besides, what would a Pastor understand about realizing that God doesn't exist, and neither does the rest of the fucking road you had been cruising on.

She didn't want to do it but figured this was an emergency and as her supervising RN used to say it's easier to ask forgiveness than permission.

She pulled her mother's credit card from her wallet and dialed the number from the TV screen.

"Psychic Line, this is Tasha."

"Tasha, you probably won't remember me. I called once before, about my... uh, husband"

Had she really? Had she really thought Collin had been having an affair? She would give anything now for him to have only been cheating!

Tasha spoke up. "Well, today is a new day. What would you like guidance on today?"

Jolene could feel tears battling to break through and she held them back.

"I'm.... my life has gotten really fucked up," she was stammering now. "I don't want to kill myself, but I don't know what I am supposed to do next. So much has happened, I don't know where to begin."

"Well," Tasha said in a soothing voice, "the good thing about calling a psychic hotline dearie, is I don't need to know the story. All I need to know is what Spirit tells me to tell you ok dolly?"

"Ok," Jolene managed as her voice began to crack.

Her heart pounded. Would this stranger be able to see all the fucked-up shit in her head? Would she judge her as a loser? Weak? Selfish? A failure?

"Ok, there is someone coming through for you. He tells me he is your family. He is showing me a little toy farmhouse, and he is telling me that his transition into the Spirit world was very unexpected and very recent, and that it has been the source of much suffering for you and his father, he tells me you suffer his loss in a way that is different from his father, that while you are both extremely heartbroken, his father carries guilt and shame. He is saying, 'I love you mommy and daddy,' so this is your son. He is saying 'I love you mommy and daddy' and he wants you to know he is not suffering, he is standing by a door and he says that he is helping daddy to heal and get ready... do you understand?"

Jolene began to tremble. She could no longer contain herself. The tears came in a steady stream that seemed to have released a pressure valve somewhere inside her. She felt at ease hearing this woman's words. She had no idea how this woman could know these things, but hearing it gave her more relief than anything else, even the pills.

"Pills," the psychic went on. "He is telling me there are pills that are making things worse for you. He wants you to heal and feel better and to face what happened to him and he is helping you to do this but he is very concerned about what has happened to you with these pills… do you understand?"

"Yes."

"He is telling me you had to move, you are very sad about that as well because you left the house behind where your family lived."

"Yes."

"He is telling me he wants to still be a part of your life and he will do that no matter where your house is. He says Grandma is with you, correct?"

"Yes."

"He says grandma will take care of you and that within six months you will have a new job and a new apartment, and he will still be with you. He is telling me he understands you are hurt and that you are very sad. He wants you to know he loves you and he keeps saying 'and I love daddy and I forgive daddy' he also tells me that his father was sick, or is still sick? His father was sick, and it wasn't his fault. Do you understand what he is referring to?"

"Yes!" Jolene sobbed.

"He tells me that your job is to get better now. He is showing me a scene, I am not sure what he is saying with this, but I will describe it to you ok? He is showing me he is taking your hand, and you are walking down the road, like a paved road and he points to a sign that says 'Under construction' and he is showing me that he is mixing cement and paving a bridge. He says even when it's under construction there is still a bridge and he is helping you build it, do you understand?"

"Yes!" Jolene said through tears, which were now both tears of sadness and joy.

November 11, 2016

Dear Collin,

I feel like I should be strong enough to be strong for you, but I can't. I'm not. I'm sorry. I love you and I forgive you.

Love,

Jolene

Jolene set the letter on her bed and stared out the window at the rain. Her roommate was in Gratitude Group. She was supposed to be in group, too, but instead was waiting to speak with her case manager. Day five in rehab following a brief detox and she received the news.

Her husband, like her son, would be dead soon.

Put to sleep.

Put out of his misery.

Justice.

That was a lie. She knew there was no justice. If there was, it would not be Quinn who was dead. It would not be her husband who would be killed. If there was justice, she thought, a man who had never done anything wrong would have been given a chance to succeed. Not a one-way ticket to the bottom of the career pile where he would slowly lose his mind.

She knew the lawyer was right, though she hadn't connected the dots until the day Cam Burton had visited her and asked about Collin's behavior. He had listened patiently and then laid out his plan.

It was like a bomb dropped right there in the kitchen.

Monarch Industries, the long hours, the treacherous conditions. The work itself.

Slaughter.

In an instant, Jolene was cured of any desire she ever had for pork or bacon.

Unfortunately, her addiction had not been stymied by the visit. She couldn't wait for the attorney to leave. She had gone directly to her room, and that was where her mother found her, overdosed, several hours later.

And now, this.

Jolene thought, mimicking the newscasters in her mind.

She suddenly couldn't wait any longer. For a day she had felt hopeful. After talking to that psychic. She had felt some peace. Had decided to get help. But that feeling was gone. She was sure it would never return. Not now. Not ever.

Peaceful Acres was a voluntary program. She decided to end her stint at volunteering to recover. Jolene put on her shoes, grabbed her purse, and left everything behind. Even the letter to her soon to be late husband. Less than a quarter mile from the rehab, she broke down and called her dealer. Less than an hour later, she shot up for the last time.

CHAPTER 65

November 2016

Ronnie

His hands shook as he held the phone.

"What're you going to save? Your ass or your face?" the old man from the meeting had told him.

Today he decided to save his ass. He typed in the rest of the numbers and within moments his sponsor's voice came through.

"I was waiting for you to call," The voice said patiently.

"Did you see the news?" Ronnie asked after a moment of silence.

"I did. How are you holding up, Ron?"

"I don't know. I don't know what to do."

"You know what we talked about," His sponsor continued.

"Guess the clock is ticking isn't it."

Ronnie thought he could just wait it out. Delay. The time would pass and then... it would be too late. Maybe for the better. For them both.

"Let me come by and pick you up," His sponsor replied and hung up the phone.

* * *

Collin expected Bobby Ray and Dodger to walk through the door and was surprised instead to see his father and some strange man.

The stranger said politely, "I'll just be outside here." And stood outside the door, with the guards.

Collin felt uneasy, as he always did when his father was around, but this time it was worse. The expression on his father's face was unusual, pained. He wished his dad was scowling like normal. Grumbling, swearing, even if it was at him. Anything but this solemn face he didn't know.

Collin finally spoke.

"I'm sorry, Dad."

"No," Ron cut in. "No, you have no reason to be sorry."

Collin sat silently as his father seemed to wrestle with his next words.

"I got," he began, "I got apologizing to do enough for every day since you were young. I owe you apologies for things I can't even remember yet. And by the time I remember... it will be," he sighed deeply, fighting off tears.

Ronnie tried to start over.

"I did wrong as a father. I thought I was preparing you. I was wrong. I thought my best option was to make you tough. Mean enough to stand up to an ugly world. That is what my daddy used to say. 'ugly world, son, you got to be twice as ugly to get by.' I was wrong. I used to think I failed you because I couldn't make you a fighting man, but I failed you because I tried to make into someone you're not."

Collin was silent for several moments that seemed to drag on forever.

"I used to think I hated you, did you know that?" he finally said. "I used to think I hated you, wished you would go away and never wanted to be anything like you. I think though, maybe I know, a little bit, now maybe I know what got inside of you. Same as how that darkness got into me. Maybe if I had been tougher, maybe I would have been able to deal with a job like Monarch."

Ronnie shook his head violently and tears escaped as he did.

"Bullshit," He spurted. Ronnie started to reflexively bang his fist on the table but caught himself. He squinted his eyes shut and grit his teeth, speaking through tears. "No reason you, or anyone else, should have to. No reason a company gets to destroy a man or his baby, to take away his life even while he's still alive! No reason a government gets to destroy a man or his family."

He fought to regain composure, then continued.

"What the fuck is wrong with the world if the only way a man can survive is to drink himself stupid every day after work?" Ronnie used the heel of his hands to rub his eyes. Collin averted his gaze, not sure how to handle this version of his father. He remained quiet. Ronnie continued.

"I got clean. When you got into here. When all this happened, I went to rehab. I been clean now for a few months…" He reached into his pocket and took out his AA coin. Collin smiled.

"What I am feeling and seeing and learning now, I should have never forgotten. I should never have been robbed of all that's coming back. No job, no world, should take from a man what was taken from me, or you."

CHAPTER 66

December 13, 2016

Finch

"You hooked that one, didn't you?" Michael Finch remarked, hoisting himself into the golf cart. Donald took the seat beside him. Profits at Monarch had never been higher. He took a golf vacation to celebrate this, and his other victory.

Finch drove the cart up the path.

"We can't all pull off a birdie putt like you just did, Finch."

"Dodged more than that, thanks to you. I appreciate you representing Monarch with the uh, Griffen issue."

"Don't mention it, there's my ball," His lawyer replied.

CHAPTER 67

December 15, 2016

Cam

You win some; you lose some. Cam's mentor's words came back to him. He had been around long enough to know justice was a farce. Yet this was unbearable. He stared at the newspaper, the photo of Collin in handcuffs. To anyone who didn't know the man, it would look as if he was a monster. The photographer had caught him as his facial expression was breaking down into tears, yet the pained grimace came across as a sneer on the page.

No one cared. They had their villain. They had come with the pitchforks and torches blazing and gotten their monster. In a week they would be focused on something else and it would be over. For Collin, it would be over permanently. No justice.

The phone rang.

"Hello."

"Cam, its Matt. I saw the news."

"Hey Matt. Thank you for calling."

"How are you holding up?"

"I wish I could say I am keeping a professional level of detachment but...."

"I'm so sorry. Look, for what it's worth, and it may not be worth much right now, but this story is making quite a bit of buzz."

"Oh, I know, it's Collin the baby killer, signs posted all over the place down here."

"Don't you watch Facebook?" Matt asked.

"No, got no use for social media, it's a time waster for me."

"Right I forgot you are a member of the International Brotherhood of Luddites," Matt joked. He gave Cam a moment to chuckle, relieved he had taken the joke, then continued.

"Well, here in the twenty-first century, your client's story has been picked up by several prominent labor rights and animal rights groups and a very different side of the story is going viral. The case you tried to make for him in court didn't convince the jury, but it's catching on with the public on social media."

"What does that mean?"

"Sadly, for Collin it probably won't mean much because he lost the appeal, but for the long range, for progress, for people who still go into hellholes like the one Collin worked in, it could lead to change, eventually. Could be enough to put pressure on places like Monarch. It means that the case may be over, but there may still be hope. This case tore the door open on the realities most people are unaware of. Collin's legacy may mean a real change in the future."

"Well, I will be sure to let him know," Cam said, more sarcastically than he intended.

"I know it sucks. It doesn't change things for a man who was placed in terrible circumstances and who will lose everything."

There was a moment of silence, and Matt spoke again.

"Cam, is there anything I can do for you?"

"Yes," Cam replied after pausing for a moment.

"Keep telling Collin's story."

Maggie had tried several times to visit Collin in jail but her inability to remain calm had led the guards to end visitation often before it started. Today was her last chance. The car pulled up in the parking lot and she began to breathe faster.

Ronnie noticed from the driver's seat and placed a hand on her arm.

"You sure you ok to do this?" he asked.

"I need to," she replied.

"One day at a time," he replied on instinct. He had taken to the AA slogans, and it seemed to help him, but Maggie wondered where all this wisdom was over the past thirty years.

She had hoped and prayed Ron would stop drinking, and now that he had, she was grateful mostly. It didn't seem fair. Why couldn't the real Ron be there sooner? With her son, daughter-in-law and grandson? Why couldn't her husband have been sober for the birthdays, the picnics, the baptism, the graduations?

He was sober now, and everything else was destroyed. Why did she have to lose her grandson and son in order to get her husband back?

She took his arm as they walked toward the jail.

"My boy will be in Heaven," she kept telling herself. "With Jesus and Quinn and…." She couldn't bear the thought of it. It took another half hour to get through the parking lot and into the jail. She managed to get through her first, and last, visit with her son. She somehow kept from crying once they had entered the room. She was back in mommy mode. The same survival mode allowed her to focus on playing games with him on the floor when Ron was drunk and angry in the other room. The same detached fog that helped her reassure Collin that everything was ok after Ronnie had kicked in the screen door in another drunken rage. After he had left the house in a tirade again. She found the mask that had served her so well in the past decades and put it on again. The happy "I can do this" mask and it seemed to reassure Collin, as it always did.

The visit was over, but the mask was still on. It would be for years to come.

CHAPTER 68

Almost One Year Later

November 2017

Bobby Ray

It had been a long time since he had gotten angry. He joked that if the brain injury had done anything beneficial; it had dulled his temper. Some folks got more aggressive with concussions, some more impulsive. Bobby Ray, however, had been slowed down just enough that he could hesitate before reacting.

He had also given up on anger after spending time inside the military machine. To say you can't fight city hall was nothing compared to what he saw from the higher ranks of the US government. The crazy shit that you don't read in the papers or see on the evening news. Some of his more privileged fellow soldiers had really gotten their minds fucked when the war showed them that the only difference between a hero and a terrorist was which side the reporter was on.

He didn't though. He had known from the time he was a child in Georgia. The righteousness so many had paraded around as patriotism was a thin veneer hiding something much more sinister underneath. Imperialism, colonialism, slavery. He saw that the way his working-class family traded hours of the day, years of their lives, to still be at the mercy of the landlord, the banks, the credit holders. In 7th grade he had challenged Mr. Fitzgibbons, the social studies teacher, on the definition of indentured servitude.

He had been sent to the principal's office for "disrupting class" and by then had been old enough to know that a white student raising the same question would have made the Honor Roll, but was also wise enough to know to keep his mouth shut so he wouldn't be punished worse, both in or outside, of school.

Although deeply saddened on 9/11 he was not surprised the way his classmates were. They had held their cotton candy visions of America's post WWII glory in the eyes of the world, but he knew better. When he enlisted, he had done so for purely economic reasons and felt bad about it at first. His justification, however, was in the realization that the war was not just abroad but at home. He could, he had reasoned, worked for a fast-food chain and declare war on the cardiovascular systems of children in the town, or he could enlist, get himself a good foundation, and then start a real career.

It had been a long time since Bobby Ray had been fired up. He hadn't been on a rampage against the Arab world, nor was he a vigilante against his own government. He hadn't been angry at the IED that staged the coup-countercoup, as he liked to think of the coup d'état that had scrambled his brain. He wasn't angry when his girl Justine had left him because it was too hard to deal with the new Bobby Ray who came home from war all fucked up.

And even today he had not gotten angry, furious the way he wanted to. He wanted a good surge of rage. He tried to find it, to conjure it, to tap into its primal existence and dredge it up. In its place he had felt only a hollowness with a rattling of despair. He had decided to be strong for Collin, who had come to be his friend and for whom he felt a special understanding.

He had sat and stared at the screen on his android phone, where his Facebook had taunted him with the local news.

Not the stories of Antifa protesting the inauguration of Donald Trump, or the many national headlines with one controversial story after another about the portends marking the changing of the guard. The headline that no doubt appeared because of some algorithm that determined his interest in local events.

Trending: Mosier Baby Killer Convicted: Faces Execution.

He had to go. To bid a final farewell to his friend Collin Griffen. It wasn't for the spectacle; he had seen so much death and violence the last thing he had wanted was to volunteer for front row seats at this horror show. But he had had to go. And be brave and let Collin know he wasn't alone in his final moments.

Prisoner 16-2763 was walked into the visiting room in shackles, a guard holding each elbow. Bobby Ray had thought this was more a show of power than necessity. The last thing Collin appeared ready to do was to bolt for the door.

The two men faced each other on either side of a beat-up wooden table.

"I don't even know what to say, man. I'm sorry," Bobby Ray began.

"You don't need to be. I don't want you to be. It's like I told the jury. I accept their decision. Maybe it's for the better. What would I possibly do with my life? My son, gone, my wife, gone, where could I go in the world where I would ever have a chance to be something more than a baby killer? At least this way," tears started to roll down Collin's cheek and his voice cracked. "At least this way I can see my son again. And if God forgives me and Quinn forgives me, I can make it up to him every day for eternity in Heaven. Or if I go to Hell, I can spend every day for eternity burning and make it up to him that way. Either way, I am already in Hell. At least if I end up there, it will be real... do you know how hard it is to think you're in Hell and then wake up, and then not know what is real and what isn't?"

Bobby Ray tried to think of the right comeback, and before he could speak, he felt a rustling at his leg. He looked down to see that Dodger had found his way to Collin and sat firmly on his feet, his full weight leaning into the man. His big, wide doggy face smiled up at Collin. He placed a front paw on Collin's knee and gave the man a knowing look.

"I guess," Collin continued, "I guess maybe I don't have to think I'm going to Hell. Dodger here seems to forgive me, and if Dodger can see something good in me, maybe God will, too."

"God gave us all the heart to love each other. Maybe we tune it out but the dogs, the animals, they never did. Maybe that makes them closer to God. Maybe we have it backwards. But it sure looks like he loves you. He is friendly and all that, but he doesn't just do that to anyone."

Bobby Ray gestured to the dog now trying to establish residency on Collin's lap. The sight of the 90-pound pit bull trying to lift himself onto Collin's lap took the men by surprise. Even the guards cracked a smile, and Collin laughed out loud.

"Here boy, easy boy, good boy…" Collin leaned down to let the dog lick his face, clearing away the marking of tears.

"I want you to know," Bobby Ray said finally, "I have been blessed to know you. I will never forget you and I will never think of you as a monster. You are a good man. I will tell anyone, everyone, anyone who will listen. I will tell them the truth. And I will pray for you. I already asked my grandma, she's in Heaven, and I already asked her to look out for you and take you by the hand and I know she will."

"Thank you, Bobby Ray. You are a good man, too. My dad, he's also a veteran. Did I ever tell you that? You, you're nothing like him. You didn't let the war ruin you. I don't know. I don't know what I'm trying to say. You'll make a good father someday, I guess. And a good teacher. All them books you read. Thank you for the books. They helped me a lot, you know. Thank you. And maybe someday you'll even write a book."

"Maybe I will. Maybe I will write a book about you and tell your story."

"Just write the truth, ok?"

"I will."

PART IV

Slaughter

2018

CHAPTER 69

June 2018

Dodger

The air suddenly turned cold, though no one had opened the doors, and there were no windows. Dodger knew this chill. It came not from the wind but from a changing in the hearts of men. Like a door closing. He knew the feeling of doors closing often came before fighting or shouting. But there was no shouting. Not even a word spoken. The quiet alerted Dodger.

The Man, not *his* man but the man he had come to regard as a distant member of his pack, the man now sitting in a harness and leashes, leashes held by two big men, this man with the blond hair was guided up out of the chair, and Dodger didn't want to move. He sensed something bad coming for this man.

Dodger went completely limp, setting all of his weight on the man's legs to stop him. He couldn't follow those men with the chains and keys. He couldn't. That is where the cold was coming from.

Dodger's efforts were to no avail. *His* Man, the young man, the man with the crooked eye, HIS Man called his name. He disobeyed. He didn't want to disobey *His* Man, but he felt the danger.

At times like this he wished men had the intelligence to understand. *Danger*. But men had inferior senses to dogs and had to be humored and treated with patience.

"Come Dodger, Come!" His Man persisted, finally pulling him by his own harness so that the young man in chains could also be pulled away.

Dodger knew not to bark, but he whimpered to his man, eyeing the man in chains.

His Man led him, and they followed into a room with bright lights, people huddled around behind a wall, and a large window into a smaller room with a bed. Not a bed like *His* Man with blankets and pillows.

A steel bed. Cold. Sterile.

Dodger began to tremble with fear, for the danger was in the room with the bed. He wouldn't let His Man go in there and was relieved when he saw that his man stopped behind the wall.

It was the Man in being led with the chain leashes who was being brought to that room.

His man pulled hard, walking him in the opposite direction, down the hall they'd come from. Out to the front of the building. The afternoon sun brought no warmth. Dodger was still shivering and shaking. He tried to pull back. He had to go get that Man. But His Man wouldn't. Why was he leaving? Why was he leaving that Man behind? Where it was cold? Where a bad thing was about to happen? Dodger couldn't convince him to turn back, so he stayed close to his Man. They walked through a crowd. People were everywhere, with signs. They were yelling. Angry. Dodger didn't like them. In front of the pack of angry people stood a few Men in uniforms, Dodger had seen these kinds of men before. They weren't angry. They were empty. They were Cold Men. At their heels sat members of his tribe.

He smelled their ancestors, the Alsatians, their hair longer than his, these dogs were chained to the men, exuding a sense of purpose that barely covered a deeper uneasiness.

They could feel the cold too.

The Alsatian pack saw Dodger and regarded him with respect, a slight nod of the head, and then returned to their military stance.

* * *

Dodger felt the sadness from His Man and tried to comfort him, men, he had learned, needed so much soothing, they knew so little of how to manage themselves and needed dogs to look after them. Left to their own devices, men would become destructive and violent. They needed dogs to help train them to behave, to help them stay out of trouble. But how to push past his own trembling? His own fear?

Dodger stood with Bobby Ray outside of the building, a crowd of protesters chanting, some in opposition to the death penalty, some calling for the blood of the Baby Killer. The pit bull wasn't there to see the tourniquet around Collin's arm. He didn't smell the alcohol that cleared the spot where the needle would be inserted. He wasn't there to see the stony look in the eyes of the person whose job it was to take a life.

Dodger was standing outside, waiting as His man stood in silent vigil, tears rolling down his cheeks. Dodger didn't see Collin close his eyes forever, his last words, "God forgive me," and "please let me be with Quinn soon."

Dodger couldn't see this, but he knew the moment Collin's heart stopped.

No longer trembling, Dodger began to howl. And the German Shepherds standing by the officers gave way to their primal urge and howled in grief along with him.

CHAPTER 70

Today

From the time he had been born, it was one box to the next and the next.

He now had lived four months of days and nights, but having never seen the sun, he only had a vague sense of the passing of time, like the excruciating rhythm of a slowly dripping faucet.

What he wouldn't give in this moment to slow the time down, to pause the drip drop drip, the timepiece.

What he wouldn't give to not know that his time was almost up.

And what had it all been for?

Looking back, it all seemed a cruel joke. Here he had been born with drives, desires.

A universe inside him. He inside a tiny box.

Even while he had grown, the boxes never seemed to fit his spirit.

He couldn't remember a time when he didn't feel alone, even in a crowd.

He stayed inside the lines. He had no choice.

Feeling the cold, steel edges of the world, one big machine passing him from one box to another.

He longed for the softness of his mother, the touch of a mate, the touch of anyone would have been just fine. But he had only the edges in this box.

He recalled the day he lost his mother and time had stood still since. The water faucet of seconds dripping away as he had lived his life in fear, confusion and.....

Waiting.

Waiting for the chance to breathe, to give in to his nature. To stand in the sun and stretch his legs. To savor fresh food. To have a family. To feel one moment of joy that, regardless of any past suffering, would have given him the ability to say "yes! This is what it was all for."

As if he had spent his entire life on the edge of his seat waiting for the punch line to be delivered. But it had been no joke.

No lover.

No companion.

No children

No sunshine

He had been born into a world of work.

A cog in the machine.

At four months old, he was now of age to serve the Monarch.

Unlike Collin Griffen, he had no hope of redemption. No man with a dog would bring mercy to his final days.

Unlike Ricardo, he couldn't hide himself in the machine, turning his fear to ferocity.

He couldn't wrestle free a final act of will in the taking of his own life as Jose had done.

When he was finally freed from the tiny box, it was only to be corralled, with the others, into darkness. Chaos, fear, some of them defecated on the spot, terrified. Lured with shouts and shoves, electric shocks.

Then the darkness began to move.

All he could feel were bodies, surrounding him on all sides and fear in the many voices. They squealed and shrieked until their parched mouths were completely dry.

No one had been given water since.... how long had it been?

He hadn't learned to mark time in the passing of a sun he had only now just glimpsed. Yet he knew hunger and thirst, and both plagued him. They had not been fed. They had not been given water, since long before the moving began.

He tried to hide his snout, to avoid the rancid odor, knowing it came as much from him as it did from all the others.

He could smell the collective terror amidst the ripe scent of bodies. As the truck lurched to the left or right, he was thrown into the bodies beside him.

Time went on in the darkness, the motion and sounds drowned out only by his own heartbeat.

When the movement stopped, he heard a door creak open. Fresh air returned. Space opened around him only for a moment, yet he didn't feel relief.

If he had known Cam Burton's Nana, he would have recognized that what he felt in his spine was the Chill... but he didn't know Cam or his grandmother. He did not even know his own grandmother.

And as the Man approached, again, he shrank as far as he could in the dark corner. He tried to hide from the bright lights to make himself small. He tried to bury himself in the corner, cringing away from the electric prod.

This, he thought at last, was what it had all been for.

He buried his face from the stench of electrified skin, hunched low, forcing his face into the mass of huddled pigs around him, as if in search of sanctuary. Yet he was forced away, even from the others, suddenly more alone than he had ever been.

He collapsed to the floor in fear and denial. Willing himself to be somewhere else, as Jose had once done. But he had no memory of music or books or fantasies to retreat into. His escape consisted only of the sudden longing for the metal crate which had previously been his home. Anything. Anything but this.

Another shock, the smell of burning skin, a burning he couldn't escape.

Trembling in fear he squealed his last plea for mercy, unheard and unheeded like all the others.

AFTERWARD

Bobby Ray didn't write the story of his friend Collin Griffen's life and death. That is because, like Collin, Bobby Ray is a fictitious character.

The story line for *Quiet Man* is a work of fiction. All characters referenced in this book are the product of imagination mixed with the undercurrent of decay and unrest in 2016 America. Historical characters, incidents, and even books are mentioned by name and may be recognizable.

Matt Davenport is a fictional character, but his field, animal rights law, is very real. In real life, there is an animal rights lawyer named Mark Devries whose work has been an inspiration to me. Yes, he does take drone footage of factory farms. He is also the director of the 2013 film *Speciesism: The Movie.* Any similarities in appearance or personality between the real and imaginary animal rights lawyer and activist are coincidental. For more information on Mark Devries' work, visit https://speciesismthemovie.com/mark-devries/.

Monarch Industries does not exist, but practices similar to those portrayed have been documented by animal rights activists in America and abroad.

Bernie Sanders didn't visit Mosier North Carolina in April 2016 because Mosier is a fictitious location. He did visit my hometown of Albany, NY, and seeing him that day was a highlight in an otherwise increasingly dismal year.

Greenfield aka Shitstorm is also a fictitious place and any resemblance to actual locations is coincidental. The practices of irrigating fields with animal manure and ensuing health problems for local residents (and animals subjected to farming) is well documented. Mercy for Animals has produced information on this phenomenon, which can be found here. https://mercyforanimals.org/this-man-uses-drones-to-expose-factory-farms

While Collin Griffen's death didn't make news against the backdrop of the inauguration of Donald Trump in 2017, for some this shift in American leadership felt like a death of sorts. Not knowing the full extent of future attempts to rewrite history and instill alternative facts on the consciousness of the public. Though I would assume the definition of the Ku Klux Klan would not need elaboration, we may reach a day when the intentions of this white supremacist terrorist organization have been obscured or sanitized. In fact, in the four years since I began writing *Quiet Man*, I have already seen evidence of this occurring. While the Klan didn't set fire to a cross on the lawn of an attorney named Cam Burton in the summer of 2016, they have terrorized many and continue to do so.

Finally, if you are reassured by the knowledge that this is a work of fiction, it is worth noting that the events described are based on actual accounts of the realities of work in slaughterhouses, and documentation provided by undercover animal rights activists. Descriptions of the abuse of animals and employees, including exploitation, threats, physical and sexual abuse of both animals and humans, are real. It has been documented for decades in various works, some of them mentioned by name in this book. *Slaughterhouse*, by Gail Eisnitz, for example, is a real book and is the inspiration for this work. Following is a list of resources for further reading.

Details about the meat industry, including the history of animal agriculture, unsafe line speeds and worker conditions and basically all the boring detail included in between the exciting parts of the story, are based on facts.

Resources

Slaughterhouse; The Shocking Story of Greed, Neglect, and Inhumane Treatment Inside the U.S. Meat Industry, Gail Eisnitz, Prometheus Books, 2006.

The Meat Racket: The Secret Takeover of America's Food Business, Christopher Leonard, Simon & Schuster 2014.

Nickel and Dimed: On Not Getting by in America, Barbara Ehrenreich, Picador, 2011.

Gig: Americans Talking About Their Jobs, John Bowe, Broadway Books, 2001

Some We Love, Some We Hate, Some We Eat: Why It's So Hard to Think Straight About Animals, Hal Herzog, Harper Perennial, 2011.

Project Animal Farm: An Accidental Journey into the World of Farming and the Truth About Our Food, Sonya Faruqi, Penguin, 2016.

Chickenizing of Farms and Food: How Industrial Meat Production Endangers Workers, Animals and Consumers, Ellen K. Silbergeld, Johns Hopkins University Press, 2016.

The Chain: Farm, Factory and the Fate of Our Food, Ted Genoways, Harper, 2015.

About the Author

Angela Kaufman is an author and writer. She has been an outspoken agitator for change since childhood. As an adult, she has taken an interest in the intersection of human and nonhuman animal rights. Her debut novel, *Quiet Man* was a Finalist for the Siskiyou Prize for Environmental Literature. She has written a number of short stories and is the author of *Queen Up! Reclaim Your Crown When Life Knocks You Down- Unleash the Power of Your Inner Tarot Queen* (Conari Press, 2018). She has co-authored several books including *The Esoteric Dream Book* (Schiffer, 2013). In addition to her work as a writer, Angela is also an Intuitive Tarot Reader and Astrologer. For more information, visit angelakaufmanauthor.com.

Made in the USA
Middletown, DE
18 December 2020

28708736R00179